**Praise for the Novels
of Vicki Lewis Thompson**

The Wild About You Novels

Werewolf in Denver

"A clever lighthearted tale.... The story line is fast-paced as the lead couple fights each other and their respective hearts." —*Midwest Book Review*

Werewolf in Seattle

"A fun frolic starring two likable protagonists ... witty." —*Midwest Book Review*

"I really love this book. Vicki Lewis Thompson did it again. She can't write fast enough for me! This is another keeper for my very full bookshelf. It will have you reading long past bedtime and still wanting more." —Night Owl Reviews

"A fun, lighthearted romance, as are the previous books in this series. It's a feel-good read that will brighten any bad mood or reading slump. If you're not sure what to read next, try this one. It's time for some fun!" —The Good, the Bad and the Unread

"A sweet romance which has humor and love throughout the entire book.... I love werewolves, love, and humor mixed together, and this series seems to have it all." —TwoLips Reviews

Werewolf in the North Woods

"Perfect for when you need to add some romantic comedy to the daily grind. Thompson does her werewolves justice.... Sparks and fur do indeed fly." —*USA Today*

continued ...

"A great read." —Bitten by Books

"Sizzling as well as howlingly funny." —Fresh Fiction

Werewolf in Manhattan

"A humorous and romantic comedy." —*USA Today*

"Enough heated sex scenes to satisfy any werewolf romance fan." —*Publishers Weekly*

"Readers will enjoy Vicki Lewis Thompson taking a bite . . . out of the Big Apple." —Genre Go Round Reviews

"I loved this book and I can't wait for the next one. . . . A definite keeper and will be on my shelf for a lifetime." —Night Owl Reviews (top pick)

The Babes on Brooms Novels

Chick with a Charm

"Thompson again gives readers a charming, warm, humorous, sexually charged romance with likable characters, a magical dog, and a feel-good ending." —*Booklist*

Blonde with a Wand

"Extremely readable . . . terrific writing and great character development. . . . Readers will fully enjoy this confection." —*Romantic Times* (4 stars)

Werewolf in Alaska

A WILD ABOUT YOU NOVEL

Vicki Lewis Thompson

A SIGNET ECLIPSE BOOK

SIGNET ECLIPSE
Published by the Penguin Group
Penguin Group (USA) Inc., 375 Hudson Street,
New York, New York 10014, USA

USA / Canada / UK / Ireland / Australia / New Zealand / India / South Africa / China

Penguin Books Ltd., Registered Offices: 80 Strand, London WC2R 0RL, England
For more information about the Penguin Group visit penguin.com.

First published by Signet Eclipse, an imprint of New American Library,
a division of Penguin Group (USA) Inc.

First Printing, July 2013

ISBN 978-0-451-41567-7

Printed in the United States of America
10 9 8 7 6 5 4 3 2

PUBLISHER'S NOTE
This is a work of fiction. Names, characters, places, and incidents either are the
product of the author's imagination or are used fictitiously, and any resemblance
to actual persons, living or dead, business establishments, events, or locales is
entirely coincidental.
   The publisher does not have any control over and does not assume any responsibility for author or third-party Web sites or their content.

To the cheerful residents of Skagway,
who helped me fall in love with Alaska

ACKNOWLEDGMENTS

As always, I treasure Claire Zion's perceptive editing, which never fails to improve the book. I'm also grateful for support and career guidance from my agent, Robert Gottlieb. My assistant, Audrey Sharpe, traveled with me to Alaska, so her photographs and personal recollections were invaluable. And finally, I'm thankful for the talents of cover artist Lucy Truman, who perfectly captures the spirit of this series.

Prologue

July 14, 2010
Polecat, Alaska

Lurking in the grocery aisle of the Polecat General Store, Rachel Miller pretended to shop while she eavesdropped on the conversation between the store's owner, Ted Haggerty, and the broad-shouldered customer he'd called Jake. She'd recognized the guy the minute he'd walked in, despite the fact that he was fully clothed.

Although they'd never met, she knew three things about Jake. He lived across the lake from her grandfather's cabin, he liked to skinny-dip, and he was built for pleasure. Among other items, Grandpa Ike had left her his high-powered binoculars.

She'd accidentally caught her hot neighbor's skinny-dipping routine one warm summer night while watching an eagle dive for a fish. After that, she'd planned her evenings around it.

After opening the screen door of the general store, Jake had glanced in her direction but hadn't seemed to recognize her. Apparently he hadn't been keeping tabs on her the way she had on him. That was disappointing.

Then again, she spent only a couple of weeks in Polecat every summer, and she wasn't the type to plunge naked into an alpine lake. Still, she would have taken this opportunity to introduce herself if he hadn't paused in front of the small display of her wood carvings.

She'd immediately turned away, grabbed a can of salmon, and studied the label with fierce intensity. If she ever intended to move from hobbyist to professional, she'd have to get over being self-conscious about displaying her work for sale, but she was brand-new at it. Asking Ted last week if he'd like to carry her art in his store had required tremendous courage.

Today when she'd come in and noticed that nothing had sold, she'd been tempted to cart it all back to the cabin. Ted had talked her out of giving up, and now her gorgeous neighbor was discussing the carvings with Ted. She hoped to hell Ted wouldn't mention that the artist was right here in the grocery aisle. Then the guy might feel obligated to buy something, and how embarrassing would that be?

"So who's this Rachel Miller?" Jake had a deep voice that matched his lumberjack physique. His name fit him, too.

Rachel held her breath. Now would be the logical time for Ted to call her over and introduce her. She prayed that he wouldn't.

Ted hesitated, as if debating whether to reveal her presence. "She's local."

Rachel exhaled slowly. She might not be a skinny-dipper, but there were many ways to be naked, and this, she discovered, was one of them. She could leave and spare herself the agony of listening to whatever Jake might say about her work, but then she'd be tormented with curiosity for days.

Besides, she'd already put several food items in the basket she carried over one arm. Leaving the basket and bolting from the store would make her more conspicuous, not less.

"I like her stuff."

Clapping a hand to her mouth, Rachel closed her eyes and savored the words. He liked it!

"Especially the wolf."

"That's my personal favorite," Ted said.

Validation sent a rush of adrenaline through her system. It was her favorite, too. The other carvings were forest animal figurines, none any bigger than eight inches tall. Her friends back in Fairbanks raved about them, but friends were biased. She cherished their praise but didn't always believe it.

She'd broken new ground with the wolf, though. After finding a ragged chunk of driftwood about two feet long, she'd left the basic shape intact while carving the wolf in bas-relief on the smoothest side. Powerful and majestic, the wolf appeared to be emerging from the piece of wood.

Ted had praised the carving, but Ted had a natural tendency to encourage people. His comments didn't pack the same punch as those from someone who didn't know her and had no reason to protect her feelings. Excitement made her giddy.

A moment of silence followed. She wondered if Jake had wandered away from the display to begin his grocery shopping, but she didn't dare look to make sure. If he'd finished admiring her work, that was fine. He'd given her a gift simply by commenting favorably.

"I want to buy it."

Her chest tightened. *A sale.*

"All righty, then!" Ted sounded pleased.

Rachel was in shock. A complete stranger was willing to pay money for something she'd created! She stifled the urge to rush over and shower him with thanks. On the heels of that urge came another—to snatch the piece and announce it wasn't for sale after all.

Once Jake bought that carving, she'd never see it again. She hadn't expected to be upset by that. Apparently the wolf meant far more to her than she'd realized.

Jake might like what she'd done, but he couldn't fully appreciate it unless he'd also caught a glimpse of the magnificent black wolf that had inspired her. She'd seen it only once, poised in a clearing. Grandpa Ike had taught her how to get good pictures of wild creatures—stay downwind and seek cover. She'd been in luck that day, perfectly positioned for an awesome shot.

The photo was still tacked to a bulletin board in the cabin, so she could use it to carve another likeness. Yet she couldn't guarantee the next attempt would capture the wolf's essence in quite the same way. She'd known this piece was special the moment it was completed.

Finishing it had given her the confidence to approach Ted in the first place. She shouldn't be surprised it was about to become her first sale. If people bought her work, maybe she could give up her veterinarian internship and carve full-time.

She'd thought she'd love being a vet, but the surgery and death that were an inevitable part of the job drained her. Wood carving gave her nothing but joy. Still, it might not bring in enough to support her. One sale was hardly a guarantee that she could make a living as an artist.

It was a positive sign, though, and thanks to what

she'd inherited from Grandpa Ike, she had a place to live and a little money to tide her over if she decided to switch gears. The prospect was scary but exciting, too. She had Jake the skinny-dipper to thank for jump-starting her dreams.

From the corner of her eye she could see him rounding the aisle where she stood, a basket over his arm. Walking in the opposite direction, she ducked down a parallel aisle and carried her basket to the counter, where Ted was wrapping her carving.

He glanced up and smiled. "Do you want to tell—"

"No." She kept her voice down. "Thanks for not saying anything."

Ted spoke softly, obviously sensing her nervousness. "Decided that was up to you." He finished taping the end of the parcel and set it aside. "Congratulations, though. He lives across the lake from you."

"Thought I recognized him. What's his name, again?"

"Jake Hunter. He's a wilderness guide. Earns good money doing it. Quite well-off."

"I see." Judging people's financial status was tough in a place like Polecat, where everyone kept a low profile, dressed casually, and drove dusty trucks and SUVs. She was flattered that a successful wilderness guide found value in her work.

Ted rang up her groceries and bagged them in the canvas tote she'd given him. She hadn't bought much because she'd been so distracted, so Ted finished quickly. Fine with her. She'd prefer to be out the door before Jake returned to the counter.

She almost made it. She was tucking her change back into her purse when he walked up, his basket stuffed with everything from canned goods to paper products. He must be a fast shopper.

Not wanting to appear antisocial, she met his gaze while keeping her expression friendly but neutral. "Hi."

"Hello." He glanced at her with the same carefully neutral expression. But then a spark of interest lit his green eyes.

Her breath caught. She'd never looked into those eyes before. Grandpa Ike's binoculars were good, but not that good. Yet she felt as if she'd met his gaze before, and seeing it—again?—brought back a half-remembered thrill. Crazy.

Even crazier, she flashed on the image of the black wolf in the clearing—a green-eyed wolf with dark, luxurious fur the same color as Jake's collar-length hair. Clearly his purchase of the carving was messing with her mind.

The interest reflected in Jake's eyes slowly changed to speculation. Maybe something in her expression had given her away, or maybe he'd picked up enough of her quiet conversation with Ted to figure out who she was. In any case, she needed to vamoose before he started asking questions.

Quickly breaking eye contact, she grabbed her canvas bag from the counter. Her smile probably looked more like a grimace, but it was the best she could do. "You two have a nice day!" She headed for the screen door.

As exits go, it wasn't her best. Heart pounding, she climbed into the old truck Grandpa Ike had willed to her, started the ancient engine, and pulled out onto the two-lane road that skirted the lake. She'd escaped, but the adrenaline rush of making her first sale stayed with her.

Logic, the tool that her lawyer father embraced, told her that Jake buying the wolf carving wasn't reason enough to change her life. Intuition, the tool that her photographer mother preferred, whispered that she'd reached a major turning point and shouldn't ignore it. Grandpa Ike, who had been more intuitive than anyone else on her mother's side of the family, would have told her to listen to her instincts.

Rachel wondered what Jake Hunter would have said if she'd had the courage to admit she'd carved that wolf. Or maybe, judging from the quiet assessment in those green eyes, he already knew.

Chapter 1

Jake finished answering e-mail from members of the group he'd founded the previous year, Werewolves Against Random Mating (WARM). Shutting down the laptop, he headed for the kitchen and snagged a cold bottle of Spruce Tip ale from the refrigerator. Then he twisted off the cap and walked into the living room. As usual, his gaze drifted to the Rachel Miller carving displayed on his mantel.

The soot from the hearth fires of three consecutive winters had darkened the wood. Maybe he should clean and oil it, now that summer had arrived once again. Or not. The soot that had settled into the grooves added character, in his estimation. Reaching out, he traced the distinctive and familiar slant of the wolf's wide-set eyes.

When he'd bought the piece, he'd had no clue that Rachel would become internationally famous. But he'd suspected that his impulse buy might come back to haunt him, especially after he'd walked up to the counter and she'd turned to look into his eyes.

Leaning against the mantel, he gazed across Polecat Lake toward her property. It was nearly nine in the evening, but it might as well have been midday. Sunlight continued to play on the water, and the metallic whine of her power saw drifted in through his open window. She must be starting another large project, one that required the saw and the extra space provided by the workshop she'd had built about ten yards from her cabin.

Now that she was bringing in the big bucks, he kept expecting her to tear down that cabin and build a McMansion in its place. So far she hadn't, and he respected her for keeping her operation low-key. Understatement was a Polecat tradition, one of the reasons he loved it here.

She'd bought a new truck, but he couldn't blame her for replacing the unreliable bucket of bolts she'd inherited from her grandfather. She'd also hired a local kid named Lionel, who was part Native American, to clean her workshop and wrestle the bigger pieces onto her truck. A new truck, a roomy workshop, and a part-time assistant seemed to be the only concessions she'd made to her success, and Ted Haggerty claimed that she was the same down-to-earth person she'd always been.

If so, then props to her, because she'd created quite a stir, the kind that could turn a person's head. No telling what this hunk of driftwood was worth now that she had commissions coming in from wealthy collectors all over the world. He should probably have it insured and protected in a climate-controlled safe.

Rachel Miller's first wolf carving, if it surfaced, would bring a pretty penny on the auction block. To her credit, she'd never identified him as the buyer of her initial effort, and neither had Ted. Apparently no one except the three of them knew this work existed.

She'd sent him a note a couple months after he'd made his purchase, though. He knew that note by heart.

Dear Mr. Hunter,
   You bought my wolf carving from the Polecat General Store on July 14. You were my first sale. There have been others since then, but yours was the most significant. It inspired me to leave my veterinarian internship and try my luck as a full-time carver. I was in the store that day and we met, but I didn't have the nerve to identify myself and thank you for making the purchase. I want to thank you now. You literally changed my life.

With gratitude,
Rachel Miller

He hadn't needed the note to tell him that he'd met her that day. His acute hearing had picked up snatches of her conversation with Ted, and he'd pegged her as the granddaughter who'd inherited Ike's cabin. Ike had been a carver, although not nearly as talented as Rachel.

Then Jake had met her gaze, and her nervous excitement had given her away. Although he wasn't an artist, he could imagine that putting your stuff in front of the public would be scary, and having someone buy it might take some getting used to.

He'd debated for days whether to respond to that note, which was still tucked under the carving on his mantel. In the end he'd decided not to. If he'd replied, she might have thought they could be friends. But he'd known from the moment they'd met that friendship wasn't going to cut it. He wanted her, and he couldn't have her.

That made living across the lake from her cabin a difficult proposition. Closing his eyes, he pictured how she'd looked three years ago, her hair falling to her shoulders in shades ranging from dark walnut to warm cherry. Her gaze had locked with his for one electric moment, making him think of summer storms and silvery rain.

She'd worn jeans and a faded T-shirt, an unremarkable outfit intended simply to cover her tall, lithe body. She hadn't tried to entice anyone with those clothes. Yet she'd enticed him without trying. He couldn't explain why that was, except that it was somehow linked to the carving on his mantel.

Her ability to capture the wolf's spirit in her work had spoken to him on an unsettlingly deep level. Something wordless and intense had passed between them that day at the general store. He feared that she saw things about him that she shouldn't see.

He'd also sensed she was attracted to him, and if he was right about that, any further contact would be unfair to her and irresponsible of him. Thinking about her still brought a surge of lust that should have weakened by now. Instead it grew stronger by the day. And that was damned inconvenient for a werewolf who despised the concept of Weres having sex with humans.

He'd dedicated himself to that cause for personal and family reasons, and he wasn't about to stray because of his tempting neighbor. He had a duty to uphold Were tradition, partly because his mother, Daphne, had been a Wallace, a direct descendent of what had once been werewolf royalty in Alaska.

Under the leadership of the Wallaces, the Alaskan Were community had amassed a fortune following the gold rush in the late 1890s. As the pack had prospered, splinter groups had migrated throughout North America. No Wallace pack members lived in Alaska anymore.

His mother had mated with Benjamin Hunter, whose pack was based in Idaho, and that's where Jake had grown up.

Werewolves, including the Hunter pack, had created financial dynasties in all major North American cities, a fact unknown to the human population. The pack based in New York was the only one to continue the Wallace name.

Jake's mother had settled in Idaho with her mate, but she remained proud of her Wallace heritage. Before Jake had reached puberty and developed the ability to shift, his mother had taken him to visit the historic Wallace lodge set deep in the forest near Sitka. It was now a private museum known only to Weres.

That trip had convinced Jake that he wanted to live in Alaska and dedicate himself to protecting the Were legacy. Because he believed that Were-human mating threatened that legacy, he had been opposed to it ever since.

Unfortunately, prominent werewolves had already mated with humans. Worse yet, two of them were from the historic Wallace pack. So far those humans had not revealed the existence of werewolves, but some Weres believed the time had come to end the secrecy. Jake viewed that as a recipe for disaster.

During last fall's WereCon2012 in Denver, a newly formed governing body called the Worldwide Organization of Werewolves, or WOW, had tackled the issue. To Jake's disappointment, they'd left it open to interpretation by individual Weres. Although Jake had been an elected WOW board member, the group's liberal stance had forced him to resign. He'd founded WARM and had cut back on his wilderness guiding while he rallied support for his cause.

Meanwhile, Rachel Miller's career had skyrocketed, and her trademark was the wolf. Not just any wolf, either. Her name had become synonymous with carvings of a particular wolf—one that looked just like his carving. One that looked almost exactly like Jake when he shifted.

Any Were who'd seen him in wolf form and also knew Rachel's work had remarked on the similarities. She'd captured the shape of the eyes and the faint diamond pattern on his forehead created by a soft mixture of gray and black. Humans might think that all wolves looked alike, but Weres recognized even subtle distinctions. Rachel's wolves all resembled Jake.

He'd seen the speculation in the eyes of his fellow Weres. No doubt they wondered if he'd been careless enough to accidentally let Rachel photograph him in wolf form, or, even more damning, if she knew him this well because he'd had a relationship with her. No one had accused him of anything . . . yet.

If and when they did, he could honestly say Rachel's wolf wasn't him. At first he'd thought it was, too. But after the initial shock, he'd examined the carving more closely. True, it looked very much like him, but it looked even more like his father.

No doubt Rachel had worked from a picture of Benjamin Hunter in wolf form. She wouldn't have had to try very hard to get the photo, either. During his parents' summer trips to Alaska from Idaho, his father had chafed against the midnight sun, which robbed him of concealing darkness. He'd taken his nightly runs in defiance of Jake's warnings, gallivanting through the forest surrounding Polecat Lake as if discovery didn't matter.

It mattered a lot. Alaska's native wolves weren't nearly as large and magnificent as those found in a Were pack. Sightings of unusually large wolves might arouse the interest of wildlife experts, and if they ever managed to capture and tag a werewolf . . . Jake didn't even want to think about that. But Benjamin Hunter had been a headstrong Were determined to get his exercise.

On the day Jake had bought the carving, he hadn't been able to lecture his father about his carelessness because Benjamin and Daphne had been killed in an avalanche during a skiing trip the previous winter. As their only offspring, Jake had inherited all their considerable wealth. He was prepared to spend most of it in support of WARM.

He'd hoped his dedication to that cause would sidetrack his interest in Rachel, and to some extent it had. Traveling to gather support kept him away from Polecat Lake for long stretches of time. It also brought him into contact with eligible Were females, and theoretically that should have helped, too. Instead he still yearned for Rachel.

Fortunately she was gone a lot, as well. Ted had mentioned that she preferred to meet with clients on their turf rather than bringing them to Polecat. Jake admired her desire to preserve her privacy and that of her neighbors. There wasn't much he didn't like about Rachel.

Summer nights like this, when they both happened to be home, severely tested his resolve to avoid her. The everlasting twilight meant he could easily see her place from any back window, and he could hear her working into the night, especially when she used the bench saw.

To keep himself from going crazy, he'd developed a routine. If the urge to be near her became overpowering, he'd shift into wolf form. Carefully navigating the perimeter of the lake, he'd creep close enough to breathe her intoxicating scent, a mix of almond lotion and human female. He'd count the visit a success if he caught a glimpse of her walking down the path connecting her cabin with her workshop.

When that happened, he'd melt into the shadows, mindful of how observant she was. Often she'd sing as she worked, and the happy sound only added to his desire and frustration. Then he'd vow to stop the visits once and for all. But after several nights, he'd find himself circling the lake again.

Standing by the mantel, he ran his hand over the driftwood, well aware that having it close by was part of the problem. In lovingly carving this wolf, she'd revealed a part of herself that wholly captivated him. He really should get rid of the thing, but he had to find a way that wouldn't draw attention to him. Maybe he should give it to Ted and let him sell it to the highest bidder.

But not right now. Draining the last of his ale, he walked out on his deck, unbuttoning his shirt as he went. Tonight, as he often did, he'd immerse himself in the cold water of the lake and swim until he was exhausted. Maybe this time he'd be too tired to pay her another late-hour visit. That would be a blessing.

Rachel cruised past the Polecat General Store at midmorning to check for vehicles. The parking lot was empty except for Ted's battered truck, so she flipped a U-turn and pulled in. She needed a few things, but she no longer shopped when strangers were there.

If the store was busy and she was desperate for groceries, she sometimes sent Lionel, or occasionally she called Ted, who'd deliver what she needed after locking up for the day. Although she refused to be a hypocrite and complain about the price of fame, she missed the days when she'd been able to pop into the general store whenever she'd felt like it.

As Polecat's most high-profile resident, she had to be more cautious now. Fortunately the town was off the beaten path, so only the most rabid collectors showed up looking for her. The residents of Polecat were extremely protective and pretended they'd never heard of her. She'd set up a simple alarm system in her cabin and workshop but usually forgot to activate it. She hadn't felt the need for a privacy fence or locked gates. With luck she could keep from turning her cozy home into a fortress.

Ted beamed at her when she pushed open the screen door. He had a great smile, a fringe of gray hair that he kept threatening to shave off, and thick glasses. He was going soft in the middle and didn't seem to care, especially after his wife ran off with a life insurance salesman from Spokane. Ted seemed fine living alone and tending the store, but he'd canceled the life policy he'd bought from the guy.

Rachel returned his smile. "I noticed the parking lot was empty, so I thought I'd chance it."

"I figured you must be running low on coffee and eggs."

"And candy bars." She'd discovered that nothing solved a creative problem like dark chocolate. "Lionel refuses to buy them for me."

Ted laughed. "I noticed. You could threaten to fire him for that."

"I couldn't, either." The thought of firing Lionel, the most earnest nineteen-year-old she'd ever met, made her stomach hurt. "He honestly believes sugar is evil and I should give it up for my own good. But I don't intend to."

"Just got a shipment yesterday."

"Great." Picking up a basket, she started toward the grocery aisle.

"Jake Hunter came in this morning."

"Oh?" As she paused and turned back toward the counter, she hoped she wasn't blushing.

Hearing Jake's name conjured up a potent image of his extremely ripped and completely naked body right before he'd plunged into the lake the previous night, and the night before that, and every night since he'd come home. He had a predictable routine that included skinny-dipping around nine p.m. Once she'd identified the pattern, she'd organized her work schedule around it.

She justified her ogling as harmless entertainment for a thirty-two-year-old woman who wasn't getting any. Jake's was the only ogle-worthy male body in her world these days. Lionel was too young and Ted was a sweetie but not exactly hot stuff. A girl had to have some fun, even if it was only of the voyeuristic kind.

She'd been trying to remedy her lack of a love life, but the logistics were tricky. She didn't want a guy who was attracted to her money and fame, and she was protective of her privacy. Her girlfriends in Fairbanks had talked her into signing up with an online dating site so she could preview potential dates without giving her true identity or exact location.

Unfortunately she hadn't found anyone on those sites who merited a coffee date, let alone a lifetime commitment. She was on the verge of giving up that effort but hadn't devised an alternative plan. Oh, well. She loved her work, and finding time for a relationship would be difficult, anyway.

Of course, if Jake Hunter came calling, she might sing a different tune. But he obviously didn't want to interact with her at all. He hadn't even responded to the note she'd sent three years ago. It seemed for now she'd have to be content with her binoculars and her fantasies.

Ted rubbed the top of his bald head, which he did whenever he was uncomfortable with the conversation. "I thought I should tell you . . . he wants to give me the carving he bought."

"Give it to you?" She was thoroughly insulted. And hurt. All this time she'd felt some satisfaction that Jake at least liked her work even if he didn't much like her. "Does he realize that it's worth a lot?"

"Guess so. He told me I could sell it and take a cruise."

"A very long cruise." The more Rachel thought about it, the more irritated she became. Jake had the distinction of owning her first-ever wolf carving. Knowing that he was trying to dump it and wasn't even interested in making money on the deal galled her. "Why doesn't he sell it himself?"

"I don't know."

"If he's worried about the notoriety of owning that first piece, he could sell it through a third party."

"I offered to handle that for him, or find someone else who would. He told me to do whatever I wanted with it because he didn't need any money out of the deal. I suppose he doesn't, but still, it's strange."

More like a stab to the heart, but Rachel didn't want to let on how much it bothered her. He'd rejected her gesture of friendship three years ago, and now he was rejecting her work. He might be gorgeous, but she would have to stop ogling him every night, because he was turning out to be a cold bastard.

Unless there was more to the story. She gazed at Ted. "Is there something you're not telling me? Did you save his life years ago and you became blood brothers? Does he owe you his life and giving you the carving is his way of settling the score?"

Ted laughed. "That's a creative thought, Rachel, but

I'm afraid that's not the answer. We've had a friendly relationship, but I wouldn't say we're close. I pick up his mail for him whenever he leaves town, but Jake's a hard guy to get to know. He's lived in Polecat for around ten years, but I couldn't tell you much about him except he gets a lot of outdoor magazines."

"And now he's ready to give away a valuable piece of art rather than risk selling it himself . . ." Rachel brightened. "I'll bet he's in the witness protection program!"

"I seriously doubt that."

"Okay, he could be an international spy, or a drug runner, or a hit man for the mob, or—"

"Whoa, there, Nellie. Don't go letting your imagination get completely out of control. Jake's your average Alaskan backcountry character, maybe somewhat quirky, maybe somewhat antisocial, but with a good heart. Little towns like Polecat draw people who don't care for country clubs and cocktail parties. You know that."

"I do." Rachel smiled a little sheepishly. "It's why I'm here, after all. When I'm working, I can be as antisocial as anybody."

"And God help the person who comes between you and your chocolate."

"Exactly. Lionel's lucky he's so adorable, or he'd be toast." She sighed. "Okay, you've convinced me that Jake is no more weird than the rest of us, but it's damned irritating that he wants to dump my carving. I have to admit it feels like a slap in the face."

"I knew it would, but I had to tell you. If he shows up with the carving this afternoon like he promised, I didn't want it to come as a surprise to you that I have it."

"I appreciate that."

"In fact, I'll call you if he brings it over, because I want you to sell it instead of me."

She nodded. "I can do that for you, Ted. I have more contacts and can get you a really good price." She might even decide to buy it herself and keep it as a reminder of her first sale. No, that wouldn't work, because it would also remind her of her first customer, Jake the Jerk.

"I don't want the money, either."

"What the hell? Why doesn't anybody want the money? Is this carving cursed in some way I don't know about?"

"No, of course not. But it doesn't seem fair that I should profit from something I didn't make in the first place. You should have the money."

"But he's giving it to you, not me."

"Well, he could hardly give it back to you, now, could he? That would be rude."

And it would require him to actually talk to her, unless he left it on her doorstep like a piece of unwanted trash. "Ted, he's already being rude. Surely he realizes that I'll find out what he did with it. Obviously he doesn't care."

"Would you rather he'd pitched it into the fireplace and hadn't bothered to contact either of us?"

Her heart gave a quick thump of alarm. "Oh, God, do you think he would do that? Is he so eager to get rid of it?"

Ted's gaze gentled behind his glasses. "Apparently he doesn't want it anymore, Rachel. People change. Their tastes change. Maybe he's dating someone who doesn't care for it."

Rachel made a face. She'd rather have this be Jake's decision than one dictated by some woman who planned to redecorate his cabin. "Is he dating someone?"

"Not that I know of. I'm just looking for reasons like you are. Listen, you have the world at your feet. Forget about Jake's opinion. It doesn't matter."

"You're absolutely right. I just . . . no, it really doesn't matter. And if Jake wants to ditch that carving, we need to find someone who would be thrilled to have it." She had another thought. "Do you want to keep it?"

"Knowing what it's worth . . . I don't. Thanks, anyway, but it would make me a nervous wreck. I couldn't tell anybody, and you know how talkative I get after a couple of beers. I'd end up blabbing about it to somebody, and then I'd have to install a sophisticated alarm system, and then—"

"Chaos. Jake Hunter has created chaos."

"Just remember that he didn't throw it in the fire. He could have done that and we'd never know."

"You're right, and I'm grateful he didn't. Call me if and when he brings it over. I'll come and pick it up. Then we'll decide what to do next." With another sigh she resumed her grocery shopping.

When she came to the candy display, she loaded up. Now that Jake was discarding her work, watching him skinny-dip would bring more pain than pleasure, so that nightly pleasure would go the way of the dodo bird. In order to compensate, she'd need a lot more chocolate.

Chapter 2

Delivering the wolf carving to Ted had been tougher than Jake had expected, almost like giving up a family member. In a way, he had been. But as much as the carving resembled his father, he didn't think of Benjamin Hunter when he looked at it. He thought about Rachel.

The mantel looked a little empty now, but he'd get used to that. Her note from three summers ago still lay there, and he walked over and picked it up, intending to throw it away. Unfolding it, he read it one last time.

Maybe he wouldn't throw it away just yet. He glanced at his bookcase on the far side of his living room. The books were a hodgepodge of paperback mysteries, sci-fi, and his collection of Alaskan trail guides. None were expensive except for the glossy full-color hardback titled *Alaskan Artisans of Today*.

Crossing to the bookcase, he pulled out the book and opened it to the section devoted to Rachel Miller, woodcarver. He tucked the note there, closed the book, and returned it to the shelf. Someday he'd get rid of the book, too, but it had a really nice picture of Rachel next to illustrations of her work. You didn't just chuck a book like that. Anyway, he didn't look at it much.

At least the carving was out of here, and in three days he'd be on a plane bound for San Francisco to meet with Giselle Landry, a prominent Were who supported his cause but continued to serve on the Worldwide Organization of Werewolves board. He hoped to talk her into resigning and joining WARM. Plus she was an attractive female Were, and he needed to spend more time with his own kind instead of pining for a human he couldn't have.

Whether his meeting with Giselle worked out well or not, it would be a welcome relief to come home from that trip and not be greeted by the carving on the mantel. Or so he tried to convince himself. At the moment he missed seeing it there.

Ted had acted reluctant to take the piece. After it was too late, Jake figured out that Ted probably would tell Rachel. She'd likely be insulted that her first customer had given away her valuable work, but he couldn't put her hurt feelings ahead of banishing his obsession with her. Ditching her carving was a necessary first step.

Knowing Ted, he'd turn around and give the piece to Rachel if she asked, and maybe that was what should happen. It was her first wolf, so she ought to have it for sentimental reasons. One thing was for sure—he couldn't keep it any longer.

If ridding himself of the carving didn't work, then he'd put his place up for sale. He didn't want to do that. Polecat suited him, although getting out of here to travel for WARM was a challenge, especially in the winter.

Ironically, Rachel had solved that problem for him. She'd lobbied for better Internet service in the area, and last fall she'd succeeded. Jake's remote location combined with his new political cause meant he needed to become adept at navigating the Web, and he had. Face-to-face contact was important during this first year of the campaign, but soon he'd be able to manage WARM almost exclusively online.

That meant more time for his business and more time to enjoy his cabin and its proximity to the lake. He liked that idea, assuming he could get over his fixation on Rachel. If he couldn't . . . well, then, he'd put permanent distance between them by moving to some other small Alaskan town.

In the meantime, he'd continue with his nightly swims, which helped dampen his lust. Walking out on his deck, he began stripping off his clothes. Then he paused when a movement off to the far right of Rachel's cabin caught his eye. Leaving his shirt unbuttoned, he walked back inside and grabbed his binoculars.

He swore softly when he got a good look at what had caught his attention. A good-sized grizzly meandered along, headed toward Rachel's place. Uh-oh. A cub trailed behind. Mama and baby bear. Not good. He knew from close observation that Rachel liked to roam back and forth between her cabin and her shop while she worked. A mother bear with a cub could be extremely touchy.

He cursed himself for not having Rachel's phone number, although with her power saw running, she probably wouldn't hear the ring. He could drive around to her place, but navigating that winding road would take too long.

He knew the fastest route very well. Running full out, he could make it to Rachel's cabin in less than ten minutes. In wolf form he could communicate telepathically with the bear and assure her that Rachel was no threat to her cub. It might help avert a potential disaster.

Ripping off his clothes, he stretched out on the wooden floor of his cabin and willed himself into his shift. Contrary to what most humans believed, he didn't need a full moon to do it. He could shift on demand. Also contrary to human belief, a Were's bite couldn't turn a human into a werewolf. A werewolf was born, not made.

But Jake couldn't imagine humans giving up their cherished ideas about menacing werewolves, even when confronted by shape-shifters who were members of the Fortune 500 and wore Armani to the office. Revealing their presence in society would cause panic at the very least. Personally he thought bloody battles would follow as fear replaced reason on both sides.

His transformation complete, he rose from the floor and shook himself from head to tail. Jake Hunter, wilderness guide, had been replaced by a midnight black wolf with green eyes, a Were that many claimed was the spitting image of his father. But Jake's nose was squared off, a trait he'd inherited from the Wallace side. He was proud of that nose.

Before opening the slider and walking onto the deck, he checked the surrounding area. Deserted. He nudged the door open with his nose. His parents had urged him to install a werewolf-friendly door with paw-sensitive commands on a keypad, but he'd resisted.

Unlike the mansion his folks had owned in Idaho, this was a simple cabin by the lake, one he might sell someday. So instead of an elaborate electronic keypad, he'd put in a top-of-the-line sliding door that moved effortlessly with a simple nose bump.

Locking it wasn't necessary. Polecat had a zero crime rate, and no wild animal would push its way into a cabin that smelled like a dangerous predator. Besides, his door solution wouldn't arouse curiosity in any human who might buy the place eventually. He was out in a flash and slid the door closed. One quick bound took him to the path leading around the lake.

He kept to the shadows and stayed alert to any noise or movement that would betray the presence of humans, either on foot or riding trail bikes. With luck he could handle the bear without attracting any attention. If the grizzly had moved off in a different direction, he'd hang around a while to make sure Rachel was safe. Then tomorrow he'd notify Ted that he'd spotted a bear and cub near her place. Ted would let her know to be careful.

As he neared her workshop, he picked up the tang of fresh-cut wood wafting from the open window, along with the almond scent he associated with Rachel. Unfortunately, the musky odor of bear grew stronger by the second, too. Mama and baby had continued on the same trajectory, bringing them closer to Rachel's cabin with each lumbering step.

Maybe he could head them off before . . . nope. Too late. The cub rounded the corner of the cabin and ambled across the well-worn path that ran along the lake between Rachel's back door and her workshop. Its mother was about to follow when Rachel came out of her shop carrying a cardboard cylinder in the crook of her arm.

Chances were it contained plans for an installation of her work, but Jake thought it looked way too much like a rifle. He hoped the bear wouldn't think so, too. Rachel was talking on her cell phone. Ordinarily she was very observant, but for whatever reason, she was too engrossed in the conversation to notice her surroundings.

Jake held his breath. Maybe, just maybe, she'd keep walking, oblivious, and the mother bear would let her pass by. She was halfway between her workshop and her cabin when that hope died.

A warning growl from the mother bear caused Rachel to glance up. The cub shuffled its feet, and Rachel's gaze slowly swung to the other side of the path. The color drained from her face. Anyone who'd lived in the backwoods of Alaska understood the danger of standing between a mother and her cub.

Hidden in the trees bordering Rachel's property, Jake sent a telepathic message to the bear. *Don't harm the woman. She won't hurt your baby.*

The reply was filled with panic. *She has a gun! She's going to shoot him!*

Jake kept his eyes on the bear as he edged out into the open, closer to the bear. *It's not a gun. It's a cardboard tube.*

It is a gun! She's too close!

The bear's hysteria worried him. He moved a few more steps toward her. *Just walk past her and take your baby out of this area. Nothing will happen to him. I promise the woman's not a threat.*

She's going to kill him!

No, she isn't. Don't attack!

Must save my baby.

Rachel looked back toward the mother bear, but then she broke eye contact immediately. She remembered Grandpa Ike telling her that staring at a predator could be interpreted as a challenge. Some challenge. Terror sent cold sweat trickling down her sides.

On the other end of the phone connection, Otis Wilberforce, a Chicago attorney, kept asking what was wrong.

She whispered her response. "Bear."

"A bear? Well, stay inside, okay? And lock the door!"

How she longed to be behind a locked door. Her heart pumped frantically as all her instincts told her to run. She resisted. Her grandfather had also told her that running was the worst thing a person could do.

Besides, the bear was too close and she was too far from either door to make it safely inside. Maybe, if she stayed very still, the bear would go away. Or maybe not, with the little one on the other side of the path.

Stupid, stupid, stupid! Why hadn't she looked before she'd walked out the workshop door? But in all the time she'd spent here, she'd never come face-to-face with a bear, let alone two of them.

She struggled to think clearly. What would be the smartest response? Drop and roll into a ball? Lift her arms and look bigger and more difficult to manage? Her paralyzed brain refused to guide her.

"Rachel? Are you okay?" Otis sounded worried. "You're not outside, are you?"

"Yes. 'Bye." Locating the disconnect button with her thumb, she ended the call. From the corner of her eye she could see the animal's powerful muscles bunch. Oh, God. The mother bear was going to charge. Rachel sensed the intent before the low growl came, a growl filled with menace.

She was about to be mauled by a bear with claws the length of carving knives and teeth that could sever an arm in one bite. She might survive and she might not. But either way, she was in for a world of pain.

Gulping with fear, she faced the animal. Maybe if she threw the phone right at its head . . . no, not good. She was shaking so much her aim would be lousy, and besides, the phone was too light. It would just bounce off.

Shoving the phone in her pocket, she lifted the cardboard tube, brandishing it as if prepared to do some damage. The tube might look scary enough to fool the bear. In any case, she'd be damned if she'd go down without a fight, short and pitiful though it might be.

As the bear charged, something black streaked in front of it, blocking its path. Rachel stumbled back, eyes wide. A wolf! Surely not *the* wolf, and yet . . . no, it couldn't be. Launching itself at the bear, the wolf closed its jaws over the bear's throat and hung on.

The bear roared and stood on its hind legs, becoming a seven-foot nightmare of animal rage. It wrapped both front paws around the wolf and raked its claws down one side of the wolf's body. The wolf didn't let go. Dropping to all fours, the bear swung its massive head from side to side, flinging the wolf around like a rag doll. The wolf held on.

After what seemed like hours, the mother bear stopped trying to shake the wolf loose. She bowed her head, trembling. Slowly the wolf released its grip and backed away. It was bleeding profusely from deep gashes in its side. Neither creature seemed to have won the battle, but miraculously, it was over.

With one more glance at the wolf, the grizzly walked past Rachel and over to her cub. Both of them padded away as the wolf gazed after them. It was as if they'd agreed to disagree and end the fight.

But the wolf had paid a high price for interfering. Blood soaked its black coat. Its flanks heaved as it watched the bear and cub move out of the area. Rachel couldn't get her mind around what had just happened. Why had one wild creature rushed in to protect her from another?

Perhaps the wolf wasn't wild, after all. Although keeping a wolf was illegal, not everyone in Polecat followed the rules. This animal had instinctively tried to save her from the bear, and she needed to make sure it would be okay.

Her cell phone chimed. Probably Otis, worried sick. Keeping her attention on the wolf, she pulled the phone out, turned it off, and returned it to her pocket. Then she spoke to the wolf as she might to a faithful dog. "You're hurt." She stretched out her hand. "Come. Let me help."

The wolf swung its broad head in her direction and stared at her with green eyes that looked disturbingly familiar. Those eyes were filled with pain, but there was intelligence lurking there, too. The wolf seemed to be considering whether to come closer. Seconds passed. Then it turned and walked away on unsteady legs.

"Wait! Don't leave! Please!" Hurrying after the wolf, she managed to get in front of it. The poor thing couldn't move very fast, and it paused, panting from the effort of walking. It had no collar, of course. Anyone who was daring enough to keep a wolf around wouldn't want to be identified as the owner.

She couldn't even be sure the wolf belonged to someone. It might have been domesticated and then abandoned. Whatever its story, her life had been spared because this animal had come to her rescue. She wasn't about to let it wander off into the forest, where anything might happen.

Those wounds could get infected. The brave creature could die in agony after throwing itself into harm's way for her sake. "You're coming with me." Reaching out, she grabbed hold of the wolf's ruff. "You need help, and I can provide it."

The animal stiffened.

For one heart-stopping moment, she wondered if it would turn on her. That made no sense considering its former protective behavior, but the moment she closed her fingers around that silky black fur, she knew this was no docile house pet.

The wolf controlled its own destiny, although that ability had been compromised by lethal claws that had dug deep. When the wolf staggered, Rachel exerted gentle pressure on its ruff and managed to change its direction.

"This way," she said softly. "Come with me. I'll tend your wounds, and when you're better, I'll let you go. I'm not going to hold you prisoner. That would be a poor payback for what you did. But I won't let you die from these wounds, either."

She kept her grip on the wolf's ruff all the way back to her cabin. Twice the creature faltered, which told her just how injured it was. And this *was* her wolf. She'd carved the image so often that she knew it by heart. Here was an animal built for grace and coordination, but it was not moving gracefully now.

"You gave me a career," she murmured as they navigated the three steps to her back deck. "And you saved my life. I would be an ungrateful person if I didn't take care of you now." Crossing the deck, she opened the wrought-iron screen door.

She'd left the reinforced storm door open to catch a breeze off the lake. She hadn't thought of a bear coming in, but she should have. The screen door wouldn't stop a bear. She'd allowed herself to get complacent and careless, and the wolf had paid the price.

Once inside, she led him straight into her bedroom. "Stay right there. I'll make you a spot to lie down." Pulling the quilt from her bed, she folded it into a large square and placed it in a corner of the room. The wolf might get blood on it, but she didn't care.

After creating a bed for the wolf, she guided the animal over to rest. Its resistance to her commands was fading as its stamina ebbed. Sinking down to the makeshift bed and lying on the side that hadn't been injured, it closed its green eyes, which had become dull and lifeless.

"I'll make you well." Crouching down, she caressed the large head and once more was amazed at the silky texture of its fur. Then again, she'd never touched a wolf before. Maybe they all felt like that.

Leaving the bedroom, she made sure the doors and windows were closed and locked to keep the wolf in and the bears out. Then she collected the supplies she'd need—towels, washcloths, a basin of warm water, antiseptic, and gauze. She also grabbed a prescription liquid antibiotic. It was the first time in a long while she was grateful for her internship with the vet.

Polecat was so far from the nearest medical facility that she'd talked a doctor friend into letting her keep an antibiotic on hand for times when she needed it and the roads were closed. If she could get some of that down the wolf's throat, so much the better.

When she returned, the wolf lay motionless except for its heaving flanks. Correction, *his* flanks. She confirmed what she'd assumed was true, that she was dealing with a male wolf.

She used towels and gentle pressure on his wounds until the bleeding stopped. Now to see if she could get some of the antibiotic into him. Filling the eyedropper with the liquid, she sank to her knees and wondered if this was the craziest thing she'd ever done. If she tried to give him the medicine and he mangled her hand, he could ruin her career.

But without this wolf, her career wouldn't have started in the first place. She leaned down and touched his muzzle. "I want you to swallow this. It will fight any potential infection from those claws."

The green eyes opened. She had the oddest sensation that he understood exactly what she'd said. Silly, of course. He was a wolf, and he might understand intonations, but he wouldn't know the meaning of the words.

"I'm going to ease open your jaws and squirt this in. I want you to swallow it." She talked to him as if he had a full command of the language, which helped her deal with the surreal nature of this moment. A wild wolf was about to spend the night in her bedroom.

Whether the wolf understood her intentions or not, he didn't object when she pried his powerful jaws apart and squirted the antibiotic into the back of his throat. He gagged a little, but he didn't bite or snarl. He just swallowed as instructed, like a good dog.

Rachel sat back on her heels and took a deep breath. "Okay. That was a start. Now I need to clean your wounds, and that's going to hurt. But if I don't, you'll run the risk of infection. The antibiotic will help, but I want to cover all the bases."

The wolf sighed and closed his eyes. Once again, she suspected he had lived in someone's home because he was so comfortable inside a house. Maybe he was a wolf hybrid. In any case, she'd be careful about broadcasting his presence until she had a better idea of where he might belong.

Lionel was scheduled to come over in the morning, and he might know something about this wolf. If not, he'd keep quiet if she asked him to. He might refuse to buy her chocolate candy, but he wouldn't betray a confidence.

If Lionel knew nothing, she might ask Ted if he'd heard of anyone domesticating a wolf or keeping a hybrid. No, maybe not Ted. He could get gabby. She'd be careful what she said to him. In any case, this wasn't the time to nail fliers to telephone poles or post an update on Facebook.

No telling what sort of wildlife regulations she was flaunting by having this creature in her house. But he'd protected her and she'd return the favor. If it weren't for all her traveling, she would consider keeping him if he seemed willing to stay. It might mean breaking a law, perhaps, but having a constant source of inspiration for her carving would be very cool.

Impractical, though. She was away so much that keeping an animal would be unfair. Besides, this one was far too magnificent to be at some human's beck and call. He might have been tame once, but if he'd returned to the wild, she wouldn't dream of taking away his freedom. Come to think of it, he probably wouldn't let her.

Chapter 3

If Jake could have dragged himself away from Rachel after the fight with the bear, he would have done it. But tangling with the grizzly had taken its toll, and he'd been dazed by the encounter and in shock from loss of blood. Shifting into human form would have helped because a shift always aided the healing process. It was one of the benefits of being Were.

But he hadn't been able to retreat into the forest to accomplish that before Rachel had grabbed a fistful of fur. In his weakened state, he'd allowed her to guide him into her house. Now, in the confines of her bedroom, he *really* couldn't shift.

If he were with anyone besides Rachel, he'd be freaked-out right now. He'd never interacted with a human while in wolf form. But he thought that he could trust Rachel. Her empathy for wild creatures, especially wolves, should keep her from putting him at risk.

She wasn't likely to spread the word about him, because she didn't want to attract attention any more than he did. At the most she might tell her assistant, Lionel, and maybe Ted. Lionel wouldn't blab and neither would Ted, unless he drank beer with his poker buddies.

Jake could play the role of faithful wolf-dog for a day or so, until he felt strong enough to slip out the door when Rachel wasn't looking. In the meantime, he'd been handed an excuse to be near her, and maybe he should relax and enjoy it. He'd never have trusted himself to spend hours alone with her in human form, but as a wolf, he'd be fine.

As she dipped a washcloth in the basin, he realized he'd never experienced first aid, human-style. Whenever he'd hurt himself as a wolf or human, which hadn't been often, he'd simply shifted to accelerate the healing process and let it go at that. Two shifts helped twice as much.

This time he'd find out how nonshifters dealt with injuries. When she touched him with the wet cloth, he nearly went through the ceiling. The stab of pain made him jerk violently, and he began to pant.

"Sorry." She spoke to him in a low, crooning voice. "I'm sure that hurts."

No shit. He began to question whether hanging out with Rachel was worth it after all. If he'd made a greater effort to get away from her, he could be deep in the forest healing his wounds by himself. He wouldn't need her primitive warm-water-and-washcloth routine.

Apparently he'd overestimated the joy of being nursed by her and underestimated the amount of suffering he'd have to endure. She was obviously trying to be gentle, but damn, it *hurt.* He hadn't appreciated how good he had it being able to shift his way through an injury. How did humans stand the pain? Narcotics, probably, and he wasn't getting any of those.

Pride kept him from groaning every time she laid that

warm cloth over his wounds, but he sure as hell felt like bellowing. He considered his options. Leaving now might be impossible, especially if she'd closed her front and back doors.

Besides, she wouldn't let him leave if she could help it. She firmly believed he'd get sick and die without her medical intervention. Instead she was putting him through unnecessary torture, but her heart was in the right place. He was stuck here, so he might as well lie quietly and count his blessings.

And he did have blessings. As she leaned over him, he was surrounded by the sweet smell of almonds. After all the nights he'd traveled around the lake just so he could catch a whiff of her favorite scent, he was in almond heaven, so he'd better enjoy it while he could.

He'd often dreamed of having her touch him, too, and although her touch brought nothing but pain at the moment, that wasn't her fault. She was only trying to help. In fact, without the aid of shifting, his wounds actually might become infected if she didn't clean them.

She had courage to even attempt such a thing on an animal she didn't know. He'd always thought she had guts and spirit, and she'd demonstrated that strength of character tonight. He'd never forget the sight of her bracing for the attack armed with a cardboard tube of sketches.

Good thing he'd been there to stop the mother bear from tearing Rachel to pieces. He'd been lucky to get a good hold on the bear's throat. As she'd swung him around, he'd telepathically threatened to puncture her jugular if she didn't stop.

The bear had finally listened to reason and the fight had ended. He'd hoped that Rachel would run inside when the fight started, which would have allowed him to disappear into the woods after it was over. Instead she'd stayed, from either bravery or fear—he couldn't be sure.

But most people faced with a wounded semiwild wolf would have punched 911 on their cell phone at the end of the fight. Not Rachel. She'd chosen to tend him on her own, as if she understood the need for secrecy. She was truly remarkable, and although every swipe of the damp cloth brought agony, he was still honored to be under her care.

It crossed his mind that if any human could be trusted with the knowledge that werewolves existed, Rachel probably could. For the first time he understood how a Were might talk himself or herself into mating with a human, especially if that human had the sterling qualities Rachel displayed.

That still made human-Were mating a reckless decision. No matter how trustworthy the human might be, he or she could unintentionally leak information to other humans. Security would become impossible to maintain.

He discovered that thinking about the problems of mixed mating helped him forget the pain in his side, so he decided to focus on the topic as a distraction. Another major issue bothering him was the question of offspring. The ability to shift might be passed on to the next generation or it might not. Both of the Wallace brothers from New York faced this uncertainty about any children they might have, because they'd taken human mates.

As a result, they wouldn't know until their offspring reached puberty whether they'd have the ability to shift or not. The ability to shift, along with an identifiable Were scent, didn't show up for at least eleven or twelve years. Siblings could end up a mixed bag, with some human and some Were. How could that be a good thing?

He imagined having a discussion with Rachel about

it. That wouldn't ever happen, but if he could debate the issue with her, she'd probably agree with him. Weres and humans weren't suited as mates. They were from different species and they—

"I should really shave off some of this fur," she murmured, partly to him but mostly to herself.

He raised his head and glared at her. No way was he submitting to *that*.

"You keep acting as if you understand every word I'm saying." She met his glare with a soft smile. "You don't, of course, but it's uncanny how you seem to."

He'd have to watch his reactions so she wouldn't edge any closer to the truth. But he wouldn't let her take a razor to his coat, and that was final. One shift to human form and another back to wolf form, and he'd be on the road to recovery. If she started hacking up his coat while he was in wolf form, it wouldn't grow out for weeks.

"I'm sure you don't want me to shave you, but it would make dressing your wounds about five hundred percent easier. I'm going to try it and see what happens."

The hell she was. After she walked away, he staggered to his feet and headed unsteadily toward the bedroom door. He'd leap through a glass window if he had to. His fur had never been shaved, and he wasn't about to let her do it now.

"Hey." She blocked his path, scissors in one hand and a girlie-looking pink razor in the other. "Where do you think you're going?"

With one glance at the razor, he shouldered his way past her. Bad enough that she planned to shave him, but with a *pink* razor? Hell, no. Adrenaline gave him strength, and he nearly knocked her down. As he'd suspected, both the front door and the back one leading out to the deck were closed tight.

So were the windows. The bear had scared her into battening down the hatches. He didn't blame her, and he'd hate to repay her kindness by breaking through her window.

Truthfully, he wasn't sure if he could work up enough momentum to do that. The windows on the lake side of the cabin looked fairly new, which could mean they were double paned. Besides, if he succeeded in breaking through, he'd leave her vulnerable if the bear returned.

He'd told the mother grizzly to keep away, but her cub was young and unruly. He could scamper back. Curiosity might cause him to climb through a shattered window, and his mother would be obliged to follow. Jake cursed a bad situation that left him no good options.

"What's gotten into you?" Rachel approached him, still holding the scissors and pink razor. "You seemed so docile until I mentioned shaving your fur." She frowned. "Surely that isn't the reason?"

Growling, he backed away from her.

"I can't believe it's that." She tucked both hands behind her back. "You can't possibly know what I plan to do with these."

Yes, I do, toots. He growled again, louder this time. He would never hurt her, but if she thought she could trick him into getting shaved, she had another think coming. He'd find a way to escape that fate, one way or another.

"All right, I'll give up on it for now. Come on back to your bed and lie down. You shouldn't be walking around. You're shaking like a leaf and you're bleeding again."

He *was* shaking, and he hated that. He'd lost a lot of blood, and without the ability to shift, he was pathetically weak.

"Go on. Get back in there and lie down before you fall down."

He saw the wisdom in that suggestion. If he collapsed in the middle of her living room, he might not have the strength to get up again, let alone stop her from shaving him. The folded quilt she'd fixed for him was far more comfortable than this wide-plank wood flooring. He made his way back to the bedroom.

"The thing is, I want to put some salve on your wounds, and it will make a mess of your fur, which is incredibly thick. If I could just trim around the gashes, the process would be way easier. Then I could bandage you better, too."

She wasn't going to let the idea go. He imagined himself getting shaved and then heading to San Francisco in three days. Giselle had scheduled a late-night run with some of WARM's supporters in the hills outside the city, and if Rachel had her way, he'd be the mangiest looking animal on that run.

Besides, some Were was bound to ask about it, and what was he supposed to say? That he'd allowed a human female to shave off his fur, like Delilah snipping on Sampson? This time in Rachel's cabin had to remain their little secret, and that meant keeping all his fur intact. As much as he longed to curl up on the fluffy quilt, he followed his instincts and crawled under her king-sized bed.

He was too big to be doing that, but by flattening himself to the floor, he managed to wiggle his way to the very middle. Every movement hurt like crazy, but at least he'd be safe under there.

"Oh, for pity's sake. Come out of there. How am I supposed to put salve on you when you're under the bed?"

He figured he could do without the salve. She'd given him a dose of the antibiotic and cleaned his wounds. That should be good enough. It would be more than enough if only he could shift, but he didn't dare try, even hidden under the bed after she was asleep.

The space was cramped, and assuming she slept in that bed tonight, she might feel him bumping around underneath her during a shift. Just his luck she'd hang her head over the edge and spy a naked man where a wolf used to be. He'd wait out the night and escape in the morning.

She didn't appear ready to give up so easily, however. Dropping to her hands and knees, she peered under the bed. "I see you under there, wolf."

He could see her, too, and she looked adorably pissed at him. Too bad. At this moment their goals weren't aligned and she'd have to get over it.

"I wish I knew what has freaked you out. I still can't believe it was the scissors and razor."

He stared back at her and sent her a telepathic message. *It was mostly the very* pink *razor.* He didn't expect her to get the message. Humans couldn't communicate with Weres in wolf form. But he felt better after sending it, even if she couldn't hear him.

She frowned as if trying to make sense of something. He wondered if her empathy allowed her to pick up part of the transmission, even if she couldn't understand all of it. She was the most intuitive human he'd ever met, so she might hear a muddled version of his telepathic thoughts.

Testing her innate ability would be fascinating. But he'd have to reveal himself as a werewolf to do that, and he had no intention of betraying himself or his kind. He might believe she wouldn't sound the alarm, but could he be absolutely sure?

His heart answered *yes*, but his logical brain insisted

that she was human, and humans represented too great a risk to security. She could never be allowed to know who he was.

As that truth fully penetrated, he was filled with sadness. How cruel that he could be so close to her and yet so far. He chafed at the barriers, even while knowing they had to stay firmly in place. His belief system had never seemed like a straitjacket before, but it did tonight.

"All right, wolf, I surrender."

If only she knew how often he'd fantasized having her saying that in a different context.

"I get the feeling that once you dig in your heels, there's no budging you, so I'm going to leave you alone and get ready for bed. And I'll call Otis. I'm sure he's frantic." Rising to her feet, she sat on the bed and the mattress shifted above him.

Jake wondered how she'd handle the phone call. If he was right about her, she wouldn't mention that she'd been saved by a big black wolf. He wanted to be right about her.

"Hey, Otis. Sorry about that, but I couldn't talk until I'd made it safely inside." One of her running shoes dropped to the floor. Then she tossed a sock on top of it. "Yeah, I'm fine." The other shoe landed with a soft plop. "The bear decided to leave. Guess it changed its mind about eating me."

Jake exhaled in relief. He *had* been right. She wasn't going to tell the whole story, at least not to her client.

"Actually, it was my fault for not looking before I walked out of my workshop. Trust me, I'll be a lot more careful in the future."

As she stood barefoot next to the bed, he heard her unzip her jeans and then saw her shove them down to her ankles before stepping out of them. His nose twitched as he drew in the sweet fragrance she stirred up by shucking off those jeans.

"Absolutely, Otis. I should have that triptych finished by sometime next month. Once I'm closer to the end of the project, we'll figure out the best time for me to install it in the lobby." She paused. "Right. I'll need a couple of days to do that."

She was silent for a moment, and then she laughed. "All my doors and windows are locked tight. Don't worry. Okay? I'm safe now. Good night." She sighed. The click of the phone being placed on the nightstand was followed by her T-shirt joining the rest of her clothes on the floor. "And that's that, wolf."

Last of all, her underwear landed on the pile. Plain white cotton with only a smidgen of lace. She didn't dress seductively, not even when it came to underwear. Once again he asked himself why he found her so wildly sexy.

Part of it was her scent. He'd reacted to it from that first day, and not only because he liked almonds. Her natural aroma drew him, too.

Had she been Were, the reason would have been obvious. An attraction this strong usually meant a werewolf had found his soul mate. But he refused to consider the possibility that his soul mate would turn out to be a human.

The Wallace brothers had each justified their choice that way, but Jake thought they were rationalizing. They'd lusted after those women just as he lusted after Rachel, and they'd justified their actions by claiming a soul-mate connection. It had made the decision so much easier for them.

Jake thought they should have been stronger than that. They could have resisted, just as he'd resisted Rachel all this time. He didn't pretend it was easy, but with the fate of werewolves hanging in the balance, tough choices had to be made.

Rachel gathered her clothes and shoes and walked into the bathroom that adjoined the bedroom. By turning his head, Jake could see that she'd left the door ajar. And why not? No need for modesty if your guest is a wolf. A rush of water indicated she'd turned on the shower.

Moments later, the shower-curtain rings scraped across the rod as she stepped in. The aroma of almonds became more prominent, and he imagined her using scented soap on her lithe body. Then she began to sing some popular song about rainbows.

Sharp longing overshadowed the ache in his side. Being here with her in such an intimate way was far more tortuous than he'd anticipated. He should have known, though. Hiding in the shadows night after night had been a small taste of what he was experiencing now.

What a ridiculous situation he'd created for himself. Had he managed to save her while in human form, they at least could have spent the evening together and shared a conversation, maybe even a glass of wine. He wouldn't have allowed himself to get carried away, because that would violate his code, but they could have talked.

But as he listened to the water run and imagined her standing naked in the shower, he wondered if his code would have been strong enough to stop him from seducing her. Maybe not. In wolf form, he had no opportunity to go against his beliefs. So this situation, maddening as it was, saved him from making a huge mistake.

Sometime later, Rachel shut off the light in the bathroom and walked over to the bedroom window. From his truncated view he could see that her ankles and calves were bare, but he couldn't tell whether she slept in pajamas or in the nude.

"Wow, it's warm tonight. I sure won't need the quilt I gave you, wolf. The one you're not using, as it turns out. But it's downright hot in here, don't you think?"

Yes, he did. Speculating that she might sleep nude made the room seem even hotter. He was overheated and squished under her bed, but he wasn't going to come out and take a chance she'd try wielding that pink razor again.

"I should probably keep the window closed, but it's stifling. I say we open it a crack. The security latch might not stop a bear, but it'll slow one down, and at least we'll have a breeze." The window creaked and cool air slipped through the small opening. "Ah, that's better."

She walked back to the bed. "Alert me if you hear a bear at the window, okay?" Then she climbed in.

To preserve his sanity, Jake pictured her wearing pajamas. Baggy, opaque ones with no style whatsoever.

The sheets rustled, and she switched off the bedside lamp. "Good night, wolf."

Good night, Rachel. He closed his eyes and hoped to hell he'd be able to sleep.

Time lost all meaning as he lay in his cramped position thinking of her stretched out only inches above him, maybe naked, maybe not. Perhaps he'd been there three minutes, perhaps three hours. In the end, he concluded he'd been stuffed under the bed too long and he was too damned close to Rachel. He might start howling if he didn't get out of there.

He listened to her breathe. Slow and steady. No movement of sheets or innerspring. She must be asleep. He hoped so, because he was vacating his hidey-hole. The space was not designed for a full-grown male werewolf.

Moving carefully, he eased to the foot of the bed and stuck his nose out. Then he listened again. The rhythm of her breathing hadn't changed. So far, so good.

He worked his shoulders free, wincing at the pain in his side. Rachel slept on. Another few seconds, and he was out and standing on wobbly legs. Ahh.

Moving slowly across the wooden floor, he walked into her living room. The endless twilight of an Alaskan summer night allowed him to see the room clearly, and he took a look around.

Typical cabin furniture filled the space. If he had to guess, he'd say she'd kept most of Ike's stuff — a sofa and two chairs made of sturdy wood and green plaid cushions that had faded over the years. They were gathered in front of a rock fireplace positioned between the windows that looked out on the back deck. An oval rag rug and a scarred coffee table completed the arrangement.

Jake's cabin didn't look all that different from this, except his cushions were plain green instead of plaid, and slightly newer. Instead of a storm door leading to his deck, he had a slider so he could manipulate it as a wolf. His fireplace was quite similar to hers, even down to the slate hearth.

Glancing at the mantel, he noticed the driftwood wolf. It was a shade lighter than it had been while he owned it, which meant she'd cleaned and oiled the wood. As he gazed at it, he had the oddest feeling of shared custody. A link had been forged between them the day he'd bought the carving, almost as if he'd adopted her child.

But he'd given up all rights to it, and that was for the best. Turning away from the driftwood wolf, he continued his survey of Rachel's cabin. Like many floor plans in this part of the country, no division existed between the living room and the dining area. The round oak table and four chairs at the other end of the space seemed to be the same vintage as the sofa and chairs. The entire area was tidy and unassuming.

Jake liked knowing that despite her newfound wealth, Rachel hadn't changed the character of her grandfather's cabin. He'd made the same decision about his, which was of a similar age. Although he could afford every luxury imaginable, he'd kept his place simple, the way it had been when he'd bought it.

Well, maybe not quite. He'd added a couple of things, like a towel warmer in the bathroom and the finest king-sized mattress money could buy. He was a big guy and he appreciated a firm bed. Rachel's bed also looked new, come to think of it. He doubted Ike would have splurged on a king.

As he'd suspected all along, he and Rachel were very much alike, except for one significant detail—he was a werewolf and she was not. Thinking of that made him wonder if he could risk shifting while she was asleep. He could really speed the healing process that way.

Casting a glance toward the bedroom, he decided to move into the kitchen. It had a pocket door, and he nudged it closed. Shifting was risky, but his wounds hurt like hell and he needed relief.

With the door closed, the kitchen became darker than the rest of the house. Its only window was shaded by a large pine, and the lack of light made Jake feel relatively safe. Shifting was noiseless. With luck she'd sleep right through it.

Once he shifted, he'd be able to open either the front or back door and leave, but he'd rather not have her speculate about how he'd been able to do such a thing. No point in making her any more curious than she already was. Besides, he'd be naked. Not the best way to travel through the woods. So he'd shift to human form, shift back, and return to her bedroom as a wolf.

Lying on the linoleum floor on his uninjured side, he focused all his energy on his transformation. The glow from his shift began to flicker in the dim light. He was seconds into the process, caught halfway between man and wolf, when his concentration was shattered by the sound of Rachel's voice.

"Whoever's in my kitchen, be warned. I have a killer wolf on the premises and he'll rip your throat out without a second thought."

Jake couldn't afford the luxury of panic, or even time to appreciate the irony of being threatened by his own bad self. Refocusing quickly, he poured all his energy into shifting into wolf form before she opened that kitchen door.

Chapter 4

Baseball bat raised and heart pounding, Rachel walked slowly through the dining area toward the kitchen. The soft rumble of the pocket door had roused her, but she'd had to lie there for a moment before she'd identified the sound.

She'd tried to dismiss it as distant thunder. But the sound had come from inside the house, not outside. Taking her baseball bat, which she kept leaning against the back wall of her closet, she'd left her bedroom. Sure enough, the pocket door was closed. And she hadn't closed it.

Mr. Wolf, she assumed, was still under her bed, and he should probably stay there. Hurling himself at an intruder might cause his wounds to start bleeding again. Yet she was surprised he hadn't challenged whoever had closed that door.

If he'd been willing to risk his life to save her from a charging bear, why would he allow a stranger in the house? Maybe he didn't think people presented the same kind of threat as a grizzly. She begged to differ.

As she approached, light flickered under the door. It

was an odd sort of sparkly light, as if someone had installed a disco ball in her kitchen. As she tried to make sense of that, a chill slid up her spine.

She had excellent locks on her windows and doors, locks she'd secured after the bear incident. Whoever, or *whatever*, was in that kitchen had managed to get past those locks without making any noise or arousing the attention of the ferocious wolf under her bed. That was completely illogical, unless . . . Her brain stalled.

She didn't exactly believe in sparkly vampires or ghosts who could walk through walls, but she didn't exactly not believe in them, either. She'd thought discovering that such a thing was real after all would be exciting. A cool experience.

Not. She was rigid with terror. Her ears buzzed and her chest hurt from holding her breath too long. Her grip on the bat grew slippery.

"Look, whoever you are." Her voice quavered, and she cleared her throat and tried for a more commanding tone. "I won't hurt you if you'll just leave the way you came." Yeah, right. A baseball bat would be as useless against a vampire or a ghost as a cardboard tube had been against a grizzly.

Something dark, a snout of some kind, maybe belonging to a demon, poked through a small opening in the door. She needed to get the upper hand. Without pausing to consider, Rachel whacked it hard with the baseball bat.

The demon, or whatever it was, yelped. A scrabbling noise like nails scraping on linoleum came from behind the door. The nails made sense, but the yelp? What kind of demon sounded like a dog?

No matter. She'd scared it. "There's more where that came from!" Feeling braver, she wondered if she could order it to leave. In the movies, otherworldly things seemed to respond better if people talked like Shakespeare. Or Monty Python.

She took a deep breath. "Return from whence thou cometh, foul spirit, or I shall smite thee again!"

The demon whined in response. Exactly like a dog. Or . . .

"Wolf? Is that you?"

Another whine.

It could be a demonic trick, but if not, she'd just smacked an injured wolf on the nose with a baseball bat. She couldn't imagine why he'd be in her kitchen, but ouch.

Stepping forward cautiously, she slid her fingers along the edge of the door and began to push. "It had better be you, wolf." She gripped the bat in her other hand, just in case a demon shot through the opening and she had to defend herself.

When she saw the wolf standing on the other side of the door, her breath came out in a whoosh. "Holy shit! You scared the life out of me!"

The wolf gazed up at her in silent reproach.

"I'm really sorry I hit you on the nose. I thought you were some creature from another dimension. But what lights were flickering in here?"

The wolf looked away and sighed heavily.

"Yeah, I know. You have no idea. You can't control lights. I'm sure there's a logical explanation, but damned if I know what it could be."

The wolf brought his gaze back to hers.

"Maybe the northern lights were shining through the kitchen window. I suppose it could happen, although usually you can't see them because of the tree." Finally she shrugged. "That was probably it. My imagination ran away with me again. But I'd like to know why you came in here and closed the door after yourself."

Once again the wolf looked away.

"None of my business, huh? All right, I can accept that. I've heard that wild animals like to retreat to a cave when they're hurt, and I can't imagine you were comfy under my bed. Maybe I should put the quilt in here instead of in a corner of my bedroom."

To her surprise, the wolf started forward, as if ready to leave the kitchen if she'd only move out of his way.

She stepped aside, and the wolf walked unsteadily toward her bedroom. "Look, don't go under the bed again, okay? I won't mess with you if you want to be left alone."

Then something else occurred to her, which would have given the wolf more reason to go into the kitchen. "I'm such an idiot. I'll bet you're thirsty. You probably went in the kitchen looking for water. Maybe that's where they kept your water dish wherever you lived before."

As she thought about that, she wondered if the kitchen had been the wolf's sanctuary when he lived with people. Lots of kitchens had pocket doors. He might have taught himself to close it to signal his need for solitude.

If so, she'd screwed that up for him. She hoped he wouldn't go back under the bed, but at the very least she'd get him some water. Poor thing, he must be parched after his ordeal.

Hurrying into the kitchen, she chose a ceramic brownie pan and ran water into it. Then she carried it into her bedroom.

The wolf stood poised, as if ready to crawl under the bed again if she approached him.

"It's only water. I'll put it in the bathroom. I'd rather

you didn't drip water on the hardwood floor." Turning, she walked into the bathroom and found a spot in the corner. When she came out, the wolf hadn't moved.

"I would love to get a look at your wounds. Will you let me do that?"

He backed up.

"Okay, okay." She held out both hands, palms forward. "I said I wouldn't mess with you, and I won't. Ever since I got out the scissors and the razor, you've acted different. I wonder if your former owners hurt you with a pair of scissors. Maybe they tried to trim your fur and nicked you. Is that what happened?"

The wolf, of course, said nothing.

Rachel blew out a breath. "I have to stop asking you questions as if I expect you to answer. I wish you could talk, though, because you're a fascinating puzzle." She looked into the wolf's solemn eyes. "You're not going to move until I get back into bed, are you?"

She could almost hear the answer just by looking at him. "Right. I'll get into bed so you can have a drink of water." Climbing in, she pulled the sheet over her and lay back on the pillows. "There, I'm settled. Get your drink."

The wolf's nails clicked slowly across the wooden floor as he walked into the bathroom. The sound of lapping told her he was drinking. Good. He needed to stay hydrated. She should have thought of it earlier, but she'd been so intent on his wounds, and then he'd hidden under the bed.

After drinking the water, he came back into the bedroom. She lay very still and hoped he would choose the quilt instead of squeezing under her bed. Or maybe he'd go back into the kitchen and close himself in again.

Following the sound of his toenails on the floor and

mentally calculating where he was going, she relaxed when he walked over to the corner of her room and flopped down on the bed she'd made for him there. She'd rest easier knowing he had a comfortable place to sleep for what remained of the night. The luminous hands of the clock on her bedside table told her it was two in the morning.

Lying in the semidarkness, she longed for the eye mask that was tucked in her bedside table drawer. But she dared not get it out. The wolf might think she had secret plans to ambush him in his sleep.

On the contrary, she didn't plan to disturb him until dawn. But in the morning, he'd need to go out to relieve himself. Once he was outside, nothing would prevent him from leaving. But he was still too sick, even if he didn't realize that.

She couldn't imagine tying him up to a deck support, though. A rope would never hold him. She'd need a chain and a large eyebolt, and even then, what sort of collar, if she even had one, would keep a wolf his size from getting loose? He'd hurt himself all over again lunging against any restraint she used.

Yet somehow she had to keep him here at least another day. That would require a creative maneuver on her part. She thought of the large cut of round steak she'd bought at the general store today. Maybe the wolf could be bribed.

The water helped, but Jake was starving. Shifts always made him hungry, but he'd never had to engineer a midshift reversal before, and he'd discovered that revved up his appetite even more. To make matters worse, he'd achieved only some of the healing he'd been angling for.

He was far from healed, but he planned to blow this

taco stand first thing in the morning. She'd have to let him out for obvious reasons, and once she did, he was gone.

The evening had been a fascinating experience, but he'd come way too close to accidentally revealing himself. He wasn't about to take that chance again, which meant he had to get out of this cabin so he could heal properly. A plane ticket to San Francisco sat in a desk drawer in his cabin, and he would be on that plane, come hell or high water.

He couldn't allow himself to be distracted by Rachel, even if he was currently stretched out on a quilt that smelled like her and made him want to stay. And he couldn't let himself think about how she'd looked standing in the kitchen doorway wearing a nearly transparent tank top and running shorts, both in apple green.

And holding a baseball bat. His nose ached from that whack she'd given him. Unless he could shift soon, he was liable to end up with a bruise. But he could explain a bruise a lot easier than he could explain shaved fur.

He couldn't blame Rachel for hitting him, either. She'd sensed something major was happening in her kitchen and she'd been right to react that way. If she'd had the tiniest inkling what those flickering lights actually meant, she would have hit him even harder.

He hated deceiving her, hated it worse than he'd expected to. She'd been so earnest and sweet about his injuries and his need for privacy. She'd jumped to all the wrong conclusions, but she was trying so hard to take care of him, even as he plotted his escape.

A woman like Rachel didn't deserve to be jerked around like this, but he had no choice. That bothered him. It bothered him even more than the gnawing hunger that kept him awake until the sky grew lighter, signaling another Alaskan summer day.

Rachel woke early, sat up in bed, and immediately looked over at the corner where he lay. "Good morning, wolf. I hope you slept well."

Not a wink. But he'd taken comfort in knowing that she had slept. He'd listened to her soft breathing and been content. The bears hadn't come back, but he'd been ready to fight them off if necessary.

She looked adorable all tousled from sleep, her tank top slightly askew. He regretted that this would be the one and only time he'd see her waking up in her bed, because soon he'd be headed through the woods toward home.

Combing her hair back from her face, she swung her long legs out of bed and stood. "I'm sure you need a bathroom break."

This was it. She'd open the back door, and he'd be out of her life. He'd never be this close to her again, and that was best . . . for him, for her, for the future security of Weres. If leaving her made him sad, he'd just have to let it go.

"When you come back in I'll have a wonderful treat for you."

Surely she didn't expect him to waltz back into the cabin like a trained dog. He wondered what that imaginative brain of hers had come up with.

"I'll go get it."

Watching her walk around barefoot in that skimpy outfit was enough of a treat for him. It helped him forget the pain in his side and the empty feeling in his gut. Rising slowly to his feet, he followed her out of the bedroom.

She went into the kitchen and opened the refrigerator. His stomach clenched. Good thing she didn't know how hungry he was. When she pulled out a package of meat, he resisted the urge to rip it from her hands. A real wolf would have.

"You can have this after you take care of business." She pulled the cellophane off a heavenly-smelling slab of beef, opened a cupboard, and took down a platter.

One quick lunge and he'd have that meat. But then what? Could he imagine himself carrying it to some other part of the cabin and eating it off the floor? No, he could not. He was Were. He had his standards.

"Time to let you out the back door." Opening a kitchen drawer, she took something out and tucked it in the waistband of her shorts.

She'd done it so quickly he hadn't been able to see what it was. But it was too small to be of any consequence to him, so he forgot about it.

Then she hoisted the platter, walked through the living room, and unlocked the door to the deck. "I'll leave the storm door and the screen open, and when you're finished, you can come back and get your steak."

Oh, she was clever, all right. She'd obviously figured out that he planned to run off the minute she opened that door. She was also smart enough to realize that tying him up was not a solution.

She'd hit upon the one thing he would find nearly impossible to resist. He couldn't remember ever being this hungry with no immediate way to fix the problem. He longed for that meat.

Standing with one hand on the doorknob and one hand holding the platter at shoulder height like a waitress in a restaurant, she glanced down at him. He licked his chops, unable to help himself. The smell of that steak drove him crazy.

After she opened the door, he could knock her down, take the meat, and be off. But thinking such a thing filled him with shame. She'd been nothing but kind to him. If he shoved her to the floor, she could hit her head or twist an ankle, maybe even break a bone.

He, of course, wouldn't be around to find out what had happened to her. By talking with Ted, he'd find out eventually what sort of damage he'd caused, but what if he knocked her unconscious and the bears came back?

The knob clicked softly as she turned it. "I know you don't understand what I'm saying, but if only you did, I'd want you to think about the wisdom of resting here for another day. I'd want you to think about eating this steak and then lying on the quilt in my bedroom while you regain your strength. If you run away, you'll have to fend for yourself, and you're not well yet. It could be risky for you."

She had a point. He'd have to make it around the lake and into his cabin before he could shift again. Shifting outdoors in broad daylight was asking for trouble. So he'd have to go home as he was, slowed by his injuries.

A black wolf moving through the woods during the day could be spotted, chased, possibly even shot by a rogue trophy hunter. When he was fit, he had a decent chance of escaping that fate, but he wasn't at the top of his game. Then, if he even made it to his cabin, sneaking in undetected would be tricky.

And he was so hungry. He wouldn't be able to eat until he got home, either. Lack of food was making him dizzy. That would also hamper him on the journey back.

Yet every moment he spent with her in this cabin was filled with danger, too. He was essentially trapped here, and all his Were instincts screamed that he couldn't let that continue. He had to leave and take his chances getting home.

Maybe he could grab the meat before he left, though.

He wouldn't knock her down to get it, but two could play the game she had in mind. While she tried to coax him in, he'd try to lure her out.

"Okay, wolf. Make the right choice." She opened the storm door and then the screen.

Freedom! He bolted out the door but stumbled on the steps and almost fell.

"Careful!"

Embarrassed, he straightened and kept going. He really was weak, damn it. He needed that steak to boost his energy level. After ducking around the corner of the cabin to find privacy for the task at hand, he returned to the steps.

Climbing them winded him, which was alarming. If he couldn't navigate three steps without panting, what chance did he have of making it home safely? He'd always counted on stealth and speed, and he had neither.

The steak might revive him, though. He'd carry it into a secluded part of the woods, eat it, and then maybe rest a little. If he found a good enough hiding place, he'd wait until dusk to finish the trip.

Both the screen door and the storm door were still open, as promised. Rachel stood five or six feet back from the door, and she lowered the platter so he could see the meat. "Come and get your reward, wolf."

He edged toward the door and stopped short of the threshold. *Come toward me, Rachel. Tempt me with that steak.*

As he'd hoped, she came closer. "You can smell it, can't you? I see your nose twitching. Lucky I didn't hurt your nose last night. I feel guilty about that."

He had far more reasons to feel guilty about last night than she did. He put one paw into the room. As long as the door stayed open behind him, he could get away. She couldn't close it from where she stood holding the platter.

Once he realized that, he grew bolder. He might not have his old speed for long, but he could manage it for a few seconds. Stepping cautiously toward the platter, he gathered himself. Grab the steak and run. That's all he had to do. She couldn't get to the door fast enough.

Seizing the meat in his jaws, he whirled at the same moment the screen door slammed shut. What the hell? The steak dangling from his jaws, he turned toward her in confusion. *How did you do that?*

"Sorry, wolf." She held up a narrow spool of fishing line. A nearly invisible filament stretched from the cardboard spool in her hand to the handle on the screen door. "It's for your own good."

She'd outsmarted him. *Damn it.* Humiliating though that was, he couldn't help admiring her ingenuity. Apparently he wouldn't be escaping today.

As that truth settled over him, he waited for anger and frustration to heat his blood. Instead he felt a far more dangerous emotion. *Relief.*

It seemed that he wasn't all that eager to leave after all.

Chapter 5

When Lionel drove up around ten that morning, Rachel heard his truck and closed her bedroom door before going out to meet him. She'd debated whether to tell him about the wolf at all, but she trusted him completely, and discussing the odd situation with someone else would help ease her mind.

Lionel climbed out of his old blue Dodge with a smile on his broad face, as always. He was built like a linebacker, which made him very handy to have around when she had to wrestle large pieces of wood into submission. She didn't have a little brother, but she would have wanted him to be sweet and funny like Lionel.

He wore his dark hair down past his collar, and he shoved it away from his forehead as he walked toward her. She smiled at the unconscious gesture. When she'd hired him two years ago, he'd been less sure of his place in the world. Today he carried himself with the loose-hipped, casual stride of a nineteen-year-old who had decided he was someone of value after all.

Part of that confidence might come from the totem on a silk cord around his neck. She'd carved the small wolf for him last year, and it had become his badge of honor. It signaled to everyone in Polecat that she thought enough of him to give him a job *and* one of her carvings. She was grateful for the impulse that had prompted her to do both of those things.

"How's it going, Miss M?" He'd come up with that nickname on his own. His grandmother was a Bette Midler fan and he'd grown up hearing about *The Divine Miss M*. Because he hadn't felt right calling her Rachel, he'd decided on Miss M, and Rachel was honored to share a nickname with Bette Midler.

"I'm fine."

"Just wondered, because you don't usually come out to meet me. Is there a problem?"

"Sort of. Well, I hope not." She'd discovered early in their relationship that Lionel picked up on her moods very quickly.

He had an artist's soul, and she'd encouraged him to try carving as a way to express his creativity. So far she'd seen no evidence he was doing it, but he could be working in secret. That would be like him, to want to surprise her.

"So what's going on?"

She took a deep breath. "I have a wolf in my bedroom."

His face turned a dull red. "I don't think you should be telling me that, Miss M. I know you've been going online looking for guys to date, but—"

"Not a guy-type wolf, Lionel. An actual wolf. A big black wolf."

His embarrassment was replaced with alarm. "Wow. Did you kill it?"

"No! Would I do something like that?"

"I didn't think so, but I can't see how you'd get a real wolf into your bedroom unless he was dead, and I thought maybe you needed help getting rid of the evidence, which I would totally do for you, even if it meant we'd get in trouble."

"I could still get in big trouble for not notifying Fish and Game that I have him. I took him in the house because he's hurt."

"Bad?"

"I think he'll make it."

Lionel exhaled noisily. "Good. That's very good. But listen, you should call Fish and Game right now and make up some story about why you didn't contact them earlier. I'll back you up."

"I'm not calling them, Lionel. Last night this wolf came swooping in and attacked a grizzly that was about to chew me to bits."

"No way!"

"That's how he got hurt. He might be a hybrid, but I'll bet he once belonged to someone, because he's used to people and obviously thought he should protect me. But I think he's on his own now. I plan to turn him loose once I'm sure he'll be okay. That's only fair."

Lionel gazed at her, his dark eyes filled with concern. "What if he has rabies?"

"I've seen no evidence of that. Remember, I worked with a vet."

"Okay, maybe he doesn't have rabies. I suppose you'd recognize the signs. But he's still a wild animal. Wild animals can seem like they're friendly until bam! They turn on you. There was this guy in India whose pet hippopotamus ate him."

"This wolf saved me from a bear. He's not going to turn around and eat me."

"You can't know that for sure. Has he ever growled at you?"

"No." She realized that wasn't exactly true. "Well, once, but I think that was because I tried to shave his fur so I could dress his wounds. He's afraid of either the scissors or the razor, or both."

"But he *did* growl. You say he's in your bedroom?"

"Yes."

Lionel's eyebrows rose. "Did you sleep in there last night?"

"I did. So what?"

"So *what*? He could have attacked while you were sleeping, that's what!"

"Well, he didn't, and I don't expect him to."

"Meaning that you're going to sleep in the same room with him again tonight?"

"I was planning on it."

Lionel shook his head. "Bad idea, Miss M. Maybe he was too weak to attack last night, but with another day's rest, he might be a whole different wolf."

"I'm not worried."

"Well, I am. Can I see him?"

"All right, but you have to promise me you won't tell *anybody* about this."

Lionel looked genuinely offended. "Like I would."

"I'm sorry. I know you wouldn't. But . . . I feel protective of this wolf. I'm sure it's the same one I saw years ago."

"You mean the one you took a picture of? You're absolutely sure? Because wolves can look alike, you know."

"This one's very distinctive. His black coat's the same, and his green eyes are exactly like the one in the picture. Plus the hair on his forehead grows so there's a faint diamond pattern to it. It's the wolf I saw, no question. Every wolf I carve is basically him."

Lionel gazed at the ground as if pondering something.

Finally he looked up again. "This is starting to sound like what my grandmother studies, that tribal stuff about kindred animal spirits."

"I remember you telling me about that."

"She'd probably say you have some kind of special connection with this wolf."

"I think I do. So you see why I can't bring Fish and Game into it. I want to handle this my way."

"I'd still like to see him."

"I want you to. I'm curious as to how he'll react to another person, especially a guy." She glanced at him. "I'm making you an accomplice, though."

"Like I care about that. I was ready to help you bury the body."

She grinned. "You're a good friend, Lionel."

"So are you, Miss M. The best."

"Ready to see my big bad wolf?"

"Lead the way."

As they walked toward her front door, she looked over at him. "Just so you know, if I did happen to have an actual guy-type wolf in my bedroom someday, I wouldn't tell you about it."

He laughed. "Good. 'Cause that would be way too much information."

Jake both heard and smelled them coming and decided to crawl under the bed. He could understand why Rachel wanted some support in her wolf-saving venture, but he'd rather not have Lionel get a close look at him. The fewer humans who could ID him, the better.

Rachel had the good grace to call out to him before she opened the door. "Wolf? I'm bringing Lionel in to see you. He's a good guy. He won't cause you any problems, I promise."

Lionel's voice penetrated the barrier of the door. "Miss M, you do realize the wolf doesn't understand a word you're saying, right?"

"I'm not so sure."

"Oh, boy."

"What?"

"I learned about that in school. It's called anthropo-morphizing, and it means—"

"I know what it means." Rachel sounded irritated. "I don't think this wolf is like a human. But if he lived with people, and he's really smart, he could understand some basic words."

"Yeah, like *sit* and *stay*. But you just gave him a de-tailed explanation of what's going on. He's not going to get all that."

"Then he'll understand my tone of voice and know you're not a threat. Ready?"

"Guess so."

The door opened, and from his position under the bed, Jake saw Rachel's running shoes and a pair of work boots coming in behind her. Rachel's scent was already familiar to him—too damned familiar, in fact. Lionel's was not, but Jake didn't find it unpleasant—a little hu-man sweat, a little Ivory soap, a little mint aftershave.

"Oh, dear, he's gone under the bed again."

"What do you mean, *again*?" Lionel didn't sound happy with the situation. "Are you saying he did that before?"

"Last night, after I got out the scissors and razor."

Exactly, sweetheart. If you'd kept those things out of the mix, I wouldn't have had to hide. Jake still shuddered when he thought of what might have happened if he'd been more out of it.

"You slept with this wolf under your bed all night?"

"Part of the night. Lionel, he's not dangerous."

"How do I know that?" Lionel got to his hands and knees and peered cautiously under the bed. "Jesus. He looks *enormous*."

"He's pretty big."

Lionel got to his feet. "I don't like the idea of you staying alone in the cabin with a wild animal."

Jake's laughter came out as a snort, which made his side ache. *Wild animal, indeed.*

"Did you hear that?" Lionel became more agitated. "Like a sneeze or a snort or something?"

"Probably from the dust bunnies under my bed."

"But there could be something wrong with him. I mean, he could have fleas, or ticks. . . . What if he brought ticks into your house and you get Lyme disease? Did you think of that?"

With great effort, Jake kept himself from laughing again. It hurt his side, and strange noises coming from under the bed scared the shit out of Lionel. A self-respecting Were wouldn't tolerate the presence of a tick, but if Lionel knew Rachel had a werewolf in her house, he'd go ballistic.

"I'll watch out for ticks," Rachel said. "But he saved my life. I owe him—"

"What? He chose to attack the bear, but it might not have had anything to do with you. They might hate each other for other reasons, and you happened to be around for the smack-down."

"I suppose that's always possible, but I don't think so. I think he was saving me."

"Miss M, don't be a hero. Call Fish and Game."

Jake tensed. That was all he needed.

"I'm not doing that, Lionel."

"Seriously, let them come out. They can tranquilize

the wolf, check him for ticks and other parasites, and figure out where he came from and where he belongs. Don't you want to know that?"

"Not really. I want him to return to whatever routine he had before he rushed in to save me. I don't need to know all the details about his life."

Lionel blew out a breath. "I think you're asking for trouble keeping him here, but it's your decision."

"It is, and I'll deal with any consequences."

"But you have to promise me, if this turns into a big problem, you'll call me."

"You'd still help? Even if I'm ignoring your advice about notifying the authorities?"

"You bet I would, Miss M. If you don't want anybody to know about this wolf, then that's the way it'll be. If he turns rabid and you need me to come and shoot him for you, I'll do that."

Rachel gasped. "Nobody is shooting this wolf!"

"If he becomes a danger to you, or if he harms a single hair on your head, I'll shoot him without a second thought."

Jake didn't relish being shot, but he was glad to hear that Lionel was so protective. That meant Jake could leave for San Francisco without worrying so much about Rachel's safety. Before he could catch that plane, though, he had to get out of this cabin.

"The wolf's no danger to me," Rachel said. "But I appreciate your support."

"Anytime."

"I guess he's not going to come out from under the bed, so we may as well leave. We both have work to do."

"Yeah, how's the triptych coming along?" Lionel moved toward the door.

"I'm making progress." Rachel followed him. "I'd like

your opinion. Oh, and I've created an unholy mess in the shop. Sawdust everywhere."

"I'm sure." Lionel chuckled. "Hey, that carving on your mantel wasn't there last time I was in here. Where'd it come from?"

"I sold that to Jake Hunter three years ago. He didn't want it anymore, so I have it back."

"What is he, dumb or something?"

"Yes, I think he is." She closed the bedroom door.

Jake felt about as dumb as Lionel thought he was. What a situation he'd created for himself. He waited several minutes before he crawled out from under the bed. If he could be sure they'd leave him alone for a while, he could shift to human form and back to wolf form to speed the healing. In fact, in human form he could crack the front door a couple of inches so that he could leave as a wolf.

He'd have to be very sure she wouldn't come in, though, because if she found him naked in her cabin, that would be extremely difficult to explain. But if he could pull off the maneuver, he'd be able to leave today. Rachel might think she'd left the door open by mistake.

Just as his plan began to seem possible, the bedroom door creaked and Rachel walked in. "I knew you'd come out once Lionel was gone, wolf."

He stood still and watched her.

"I still think you understand a lot of what we say, and that conversation I had with Lionel might have spooked you. But don't worry. I'm not going to call in the troops. This is between you and me. And you can trust Lionel not to squeal on us."

Thank you. He hoped she could sense his gratitude.

"You're welcome."

Wow, that was strange. She'd responded as if she'd picked up on his thoughts.

"I'm going out to the workshop now, but I'll come back from time to time and check on you. I'm not leaving you alone for the day, so don't worry about that, either."

Please do leave me alone.

She smiled. "I swear it's like I can see the wheels turning in there. You're too clever. I'm not giving you hours of solitude so you can figure out some way to get out of here."

Damn.

"Boy, do you look disappointed! I swear you got the gist of what I just said. Well, just forget about escaping. You need more time to heal, and this is the best place to do that."

Says you.

"Don't look at me like that, as if you don't believe me. I'm a doctor, or I was *almost* a doctor. I can tell that you're supersmart, but I know more about this process than you do, so why not relax and let me do my thing?"

Her logic was impeccable. But she was working with the wrong information. If he were a true wolf, she'd be absolutely doing the right thing for him.

She couldn't know that she was impeding the healing process. Because he'd been unable to shift fully soon after his injury, he would likely have scarring, something that didn't happen when Weres took care of their wounds themselves.

He'd been hurt several times in his life, and he bore no marks as a result. But he felt certain he'd end up with red welts from the bear's claws once he became human again. In time they'd fade, but his skin would never be perfect again.

In some ways that seemed fitting. It was as if Rachel herself had left her mark on him. He might as well accept the inevitability of that and realize that he would never completely erase her memory.

"See you soon, wolf." She had the audacity to wink before she turned, walked out the door, and closed it firmly behind her.

Curses, foiled again.

Chapter 6

Rachel's famous concentration took a beating the rest of the morning. Even Lionel remarked on it. She kept pausing in her work to check on the wolf, and when she returned, she spent long moments staring into space, her carving tools lying unused on her bench.

Finally she turned to Lionel. "How are you at tracking?"

"Okay, I guess." He dumped a large dustpan full of shavings into a plastic garbage can. "I learned from my best friend Willie's dad, on account of mine not being around to teach me." He said it without a trace of resentment or self-pity. His dad had left when he was a baby, and he'd been raised by his mother and grandmother, but he'd never said a word against his absent father.

"If I let the wolf go tonight, do you think you could track where he goes?"

Lionel stopped sweeping to glance at her. "I thought you didn't want to know his story."

"I don't, and if I could keep him a few more days, I wouldn't be worried. But I can't figure out how to do that. He'll need to go outside again tonight, and I won't be able to trick him again."

"Again? You already tricked him once?"

"Yeah, and it cost me a very large steak." She described her maneuver, which made Lionel chuckle. "Anyway, the fishing line won't work twice, so when I let him out to do his business, he'll be gone."

"And you want me to follow him?"

"Not so he'd know. He's very smart. That's why I thought if you could track him from a distance, then you'd have some idea of where he goes but he wouldn't know you were doing it."

"I could try. But Willie's dad could do a better job than me. Even Willie's a better tracker than I am."

Rachel shook her head. "I don't care. I don't want anyone else in on this, so you're my guy. I'll pay you for your time."

"Hell, no, you won't. You pay me to help you out. And I'm already aiding and abetting you instead of notifying Fish and Game. If I take money for it, that'll look even worse."

"Would you rather not do it at all?"

He grinned at her. "Are you kidding? I'm *dying* to do it. First of all, I'm really happy that you're getting this wolf out of your house before something bad happens. Second of all, I want to know where he heads off to as much as you, maybe more. This job has always been interesting, but today's been the most interesting so far."

"Glad I'm proving to be entertaining."

"Definitely. What time are you planning to let him go?"

"As late as possible." She glanced at the clock on the workshop wall. "I'm not sure how long he can make it without needing a trip outside."

"I can't say for wolves, but a big dog can go about ten

hours, maybe a little longer if they have to. You think this wolf is housebroken, right?"

She nodded. "He seems to be. Anyway, that still puts us at six or seven tonight. The sun's very bright then."

"So what are you going to do?"

"Don't have much choice. He'll have to do the best he can to stay hidden. At least tracking him should be easier."

"It should, but . . ." He sighed. "Seriously, I'm not a very good tracker."

"At least you know something about it, which is more than I can say. Can you also look for blood spots along the way? In case he starts bleeding again?"

"And what if he does? Does it matter?"

She thought about that. "Good point. Once he's loose, there'll be no getting him back. If I could think of some way to let him out on a temporary basis, I'd do it, but it's not as if I can take him out on a leash like a poodle."

"Nope." Lionel gazed at her. "If you're that worried about whether he'll survive on his own, there's always Fish and Game. At least then you'd know that he—"

"I'd know that he'd be miserable and I would have broken the promise I made to him last night."

"You made a wolf a promise?" Lionel shook his head. "But listen, it would be for his own good."

"Would it be? My instincts tell me that given the choice, he'd rather die on his own terms than deal with more human interference."

"Then I guess it's settled." Lionel's phone chimed, signaling the end of his workday with Rachel. He silenced the alarm. "I need to get over to the mill. Just tell me when you want me here."

"Plan on seven." Rachel wished she had reason to employ him full-time so he didn't have to work at the sawmill thirty miles away. But cleaning the shop, buying groceries once in a while, and helping her with heavy pieces of wood didn't take forty hours a week. And he'd be too proud to take more per hour than the job was worth.

"I'll be here."

"I'll call you when I'm getting ready to let him out. If you park on the road instead of driving in, then he won't know you're coming."

Lionel nodded.

"I really appreciate this. Are you sure I can't pay you extra?"

"I'm sure." He glanced at a shelving unit that held various pieces of wood waiting to become Rachel Miller originals. He pointed to a gnarled piece of cedar about two feet long. "If you'd be willing to let me have that, I'd consider us even."

She happened to love that particular piece and had looked forward to carving it. But she was desperate for Lionel's tracking skills and she was also thrilled at this first indication that he'd taken her suggestion about working on his own carvings. "It's yours."

"Really? I was sort of kidding. That's a beautiful hunk of wood. You don't have to give it to me. I'm sure you could make something amazing out of it."

Sliding off her work stool, she walked over to the shelf and picked up the cedar. "I'll bet you could, too. I only have one condition. Let me see it when you're finished." Using both hands, she held it out.

Instead of taking it, he stepped back. "Never mind. That was a dumb impulse on my part. I'm not ready for wood that beautiful."

"Lionel, you *are* ready, or you wouldn't have asked for it. Don't wimp out on me."

He eyed the wood. "I'll probably screw it up."

"That's not the best attitude for beginning a new project. Try again."

"You're really putting me on the spot, Miss M."

"I mean to." She continued to gaze at him. "Daring to be an artist takes guts. You've only been here during the glory days, but I went through a lot of self-doubt before I arrived where I am now. I still have self-doubt."

"You? That's ridiculous."

"Probably, but it's true. So man up, Lionel. Take this piece of wood, put your heart and soul into carving it, and then show me the results. Because that's what artists do. They put their heart and soul out there for everyone to see."

Lionel swallowed. "Okay." Moving toward her, he took the piece of wood. "Don't expect miracles, okay?"

"I always expect miracles." She smiled at him. "And so should you. See you tonight."

When Rachel didn't come in to check on Jake all afternoon, he wondered what was up. She'd made a pest of herself in the morning and then had left him completely alone in the afternoon. But he hadn't been able to trust her absence enough to try a double shift. It had turned out to be a very long day.

Toward the end of it he desperately needed to relieve himself. He wondered how she planned to handle that. If she tried the fishing line again, he'd be ready for it, but she probably realized that. So how could she expect to let him out and get him back in the house?

Around six he heard her come in the cabin, but she didn't open the bedroom door. He paced by his quilt while he waited to see what would happen next. She had to let him out. And then what?

He was also hungry, but not as famished as he had been in the morning. If she tried to bribe him with food again, he wouldn't be as susceptible. The ding of a microwave made him curious. Was she nuking her dinner, his dinner, or both?

The overriding concern, though, was the pressure on his bladder. She had to know he was in dire straits. Once she opened that back door, their time together would be over. Surely she knew that, too.

He scented her approach to the bedroom, both because he was attuned to her aroma and because his nose told him she carried a bowl of raw hamburger. Sadly, he was more eager to see her than to eat the hamburger. That indicated how enmeshed he'd become.

Halting his pacing, he faced the door. Considering the microwave ding he'd heard earlier, she must have used it to defrost some ground round from the freezer. Damn, he was turning into a regular Sherlock Holmes.

He appreciated the thought of the raw hamburger, but he looked forward to shifting back to human form. These days he preferred his meals cooked and well seasoned. He longed for a few side dishes and a bottle of good red wine.

She wouldn't know that, of course. She viewed him as a wild animal that caught its prey on the run. Werewolves hadn't done that for centuries. Despite his surname, Jake had never hunted anything, and the concept made him shudder.

As a carnivore, he required daily helpings of meat. As a thinking carnivore, he understood that somebody had to provide the fine cuts of sirloin that he enjoyed. But he preferred not to dwell on what he considered an unsavory process.

"I've brought your dinner." She left the bedroom

door open as she crossed the room and put the bowl in front of him.

He had to pee, but he wasn't about to turn down the possibility of food. She didn't seem to be using the hamburger as a trick to get him back inside this time, and he was grateful for that. He began gulping down the ground meat.

Halfway through, he paused. She could have buried a knockout pill in the hamburger and he'd never know. He glanced up. *Did you hide a pill in this meat?*

"It's okay, wolf. You can eat it. No tricks." She crouched down so they were eye to eye. "I'm going to let you go."

His heart thumped faster. *Freedom!*

"You understood that, didn't you? I have a feeling if scientists ever examined your brain, they'd discover you're a super-intelligent wolf."

If any scientist examined his brain and reported the findings, they'd risk ruining their reputation. Everyone knew werewolves were mythical creatures. He pitied the poor scientist who dared to claim that they weren't.

"I'm letting you out because there's no way I can keep you any longer. We both know you have to go outside and take care of some necessary business. I figured out a way to fool you this morning, but that won't work again, will it?"

He lowered his head and kept eating, but he trembled with excitement at the prospect of escaping at last. From the corner of his eye he evaluated the light coming through her bedroom window. Too much light, but he couldn't be particular. If she opened that back door, then he would take off.

"I'm still worried about you. I doubt you'd let me examine your wounds, and besides, I'd have a tough time seeing anything with all that fur in the way. They don't seem to be bleeding anymore, though, and maybe you'll be okay. I hope so."

He was touched by the genuine concern in her voice. As much as he wanted—no, *needed*—to leave, he would miss her. He'd been an intimate part of her life for nearly twenty-four hours, and she'd proven to be every bit as wonderful as he'd imagined.

Too bad. He'd have to be content with his memories. He took some satisfaction in knowing that she was likely to remember this interlude for a long time. It wasn't every day that a woman brought a wolf into her bedroom. And she didn't know the half of it.

He supposed that eventually she'd find a man to love, and she'd tell him about the brave wolf that had defended her from a mother grizzly. Jake didn't like thinking about her with someone else, but there could be no other outcome. He would end up with someone else, too, maybe even Giselle Landry.

"So I want you to be really careful after you leave here," she said. "I wish you'd stay until it's a little darker, but I know you won't. It's just that you're black, and if someone sees you . . . I worry that they'll . . . well, maybe they'll be awestruck the way I was when I saw you years ago and they'll leave you alone."

It wasn't me you saw. It was my father.

"It *was* you, so don't try to convince me it wasn't."

His head came up and he looked into her eyes. Had she just replied to his telepathic thought?

"I will say, though, that I haven't been carving your nose quite right. I thought it was a little longer and sharper than that."

Exactly. Because you saw my dad.

"But it had to be you. How many others could there

be with those distinctive green eyes, thick black coat, and a diamond pattern on your forehead? You're very unusual looking. And larger than most wolves, too."

Right, but I'm not a— He caught himself before he finished the sentence. He was only thinking, but he had an uneasy feeling she was hearing some of those thoughts. He didn't want to take a chance that he'd plant an idea in her head.

"Anyway, I'll miss you, wolf. I wouldn't mind having you drop by now and then, but I don't suppose that's wise. The more often you're spotted near a residence, the more likely someone will decide you're a danger to small children and lapdogs. You need to stay away from people. I promise I'll be more careful about bears from now on, so you can relax on that score."

He couldn't seem to stop gazing at her. She was so beautiful, with her soft hair framing her face and her gray eyes filled with affection for him. He could easily stay away from other humans, but he wasn't sure if he'd be able to stay away from her.

"Go on, now. Eat your hamburger." Reaching out, she stroked his head. "I didn't mean to distract you."

The warmth of her touch ran through him like a jolt of electricity. He quivered in reaction.

"Your coat is incredibly soft. I always imagined it would be coarse, but it's not." She looked into his eyes as she combed her fingers through his fur. "We do have a connection, don't we?"

Yes. He leaned into her caress.

"I think that's very cool, but I don't want to put you in danger." With a sigh, she lifted her hand and stood.

Please don't stop stroking me.

"Finish that hamburger. It's time you were on your way."

He swallowed a whine of longing. The urge to stay and somehow blend their two very different worlds had become powerful, almost too powerful to resist. No doubt the Wallace brothers had felt this way, and they'd succumbed. He would not, by God. He would *not*.

Summoning all his willpower, he returned his attention to the hamburger and finished it off. When he looked up, she'd moved into the living room. He walked out of her bedroom knowing he'd never see it again.

Good thing he needed a bathroom break. At this moment, it was the only thing propelling him out the door. Yet his belief in a clean separation of the two species—human and Were—was the only world order that made sense to him. He had to adhere to it, no matter how much he longed to hold on to his connection with Rachel.

"Come on, wolf. Let's get this over with." Striding toward the back door, she opened it with a dramatic flourish. "I'll bet you can hardly wait to be free again."

No. I want to stay.

She turned back to him, her expression puzzled. "You do want to leave, right?"

There was only one good answer to that. Lifting his head, he met her gaze. *Yes.*

"I thought so." She opened the screen door and held it for him as she walked out on the deck. "Then go, wolf. And don't pick any more fights with bears, okay?"

To his astonishment, she sounded emotional, as if she might be on the verge of tears.

I won't.

"Good," she murmured. "Now, take off."

He did. This time when he bounded down the steps, he didn't stumble. He was stronger now. At the bottom he looked back.

She stood with her arms wrapped protectively around her midsection, as if in pain. Her expression was bleak. "Go!" she called out.

He sprinted for the trees. Lingering would only make everything tougher on both of them. He emptied his bladder and started the journey back home. It was only later that he realized that she'd made some response to every telepathic thought he'd had.

That wasn't supposed to be possible.

Chapter 7

Rachel pulled her phone out of her pocket and pressed the buttons that connected her to Lionel. "He's taken off. He went to the right, headed around the lake."

Lionel's voice came through the phone. "I'm on it. How is he?"

"I hope he's strong enough. It was weird, though. I imagined I could hear him thinking."

"Yeah, well, you know what they say about artists. A little bit strange."

"I know. Flaky as hell. Follow him, okay? I need to know he's made it to . . . wherever he's going."

"I'll do my best."

"Text me if you get a chance, to let me know the situation."

"I will. Go pour yourself a glass of wine and relax."

"Fat chance." She disconnected and stood staring at the spot in the woods where the wolf had disappeared. *Stay safe, wolf.*

An answer popped into her head, as if from a radio transmission. *Always, Rachel.*

She told herself she'd imagined the response. She'd

wanted to believe he was okay and she'd fabricated his telepathic message to make her feel secure. But then she thought over their last few minutes together and what she'd admitted to Lionel.

While she'd talked to the wolf and stroked his fur, he'd looked into her eyes as if absorbing every word. She'd swear that he responded, somehow, because she'd felt communication flow between them.

No doubt she was letting her overactive imagination run away with her again. She couldn't really read a wolf's mind.

But what if she could? She'd heard of people who communicated mentally with dogs, cats, even horses. Why couldn't she receive the transmissions of this wolf, especially if they had a special connection?

Closing her eyes, she tried to tune in again, but all she got was static. She sent out a question. *Where are you?* No answer came back. That made sense. If he was running for his life and concentrating on protecting himself, he wouldn't have time to play telepathy games with her.

No, she couldn't expect little messages of comfort when his very existence was in jeopardy. But she couldn't leave the deck and go back inside. That would seem like deserting him.

So she'd stay right here and enjoy the view, something she didn't do often enough. Polecat Lake, despite its unlovely name, was gorgeous. Evergreens framed the waterline except for the mirror-image clearings, where her cabin sat on one side and Jake's on the other.

Off to her right, a vista both she and Jake could enjoy, mountains rose in eternally snowcapped splendor. Had she been a painter instead of a carver, she'd be moved to capture them with her brush. But she'd always been drawn to the tactile pleasure of woodworking.

The cell phone in her hand chimed. Eager for news, she opened the text from Lionel.

Picked up his trail. No blood.

She answered immediately. *Good.* Knowing that the wolf wasn't bleeding loomed large in her mind. He had to make it to safety. He had to.

Humans. Must avoid.

She drew in a quick breath. She hadn't imagined *that* communication. The words had come through clearly, and they could be from only one source.

Somehow in the time they'd spent together, she'd managed to tune in. The connection wasn't perfect or constant, but in times of intense concentration on the wolf's welfare, she was able to pick up his thoughts.

Leaning against the deck railing, she clutched the weathered wood with both hands and focused on the wolf. If he was in danger from the humans he'd sensed nearby, she'd hear his panic. She could text Lionel, who might be able to get there in time to intercede.

Made it past them.

Her shoulders sagged in relief.

Tired.

Her tummy churned. Should he stop and rest? She had no idea. She didn't know how far he had to go before he was safe.

Getting close, though.

That was good news. She wondered if he'd moved deeper into the forest. Maybe he had a cave back in there, away from the frequently traveled hiking trails. Thank heavens Lionel was young and fit, because he'd have the stamina to follow the wolf to wherever he was going.

Her cell phone chimed again. *Weird,* Lionel texted. *Moving toward Mr. Hunter's cabin.*

Jake Hunter?

Yep. Wolf stopped in trees. I'm pulling back.

Don't let him C U.

I won't.

Rachel whirled and ran back inside to get her binoculars. Suddenly things were starting to make sense. If anyone in the neighborhood would keep a pet wolf, it would be Jake. He was something of a lone wolf, himself.

She thought of his green eyes, so like the wolf's. Maybe Jake felt a kinship there. He'd also been quick to buy that carving. She couldn't figure out why he wanted to get rid of it now, though.

As she trained her binoculars on Jake's cabin, she pondered his odd behavior regarding the carving. Maybe he planned to surrender the wolf to a zoo or sanctuary. If so, he might be riddled with guilt.

Now that she'd spent time with that magnificent animal, she thought he certainly should feel guilty even considering doing such a thing. She realized that if Jake planned to surrender the wolf, he wouldn't want the carving around to remind him of his former companion.

She couldn't know any of that for sure, but she intended to find out. She owed the wolf her life, and she was going to protect it from any threat, especially if that threat came from Jake Hunter.

Her phone chimed again. Holding her binoculars with one hand, she pulled out her phone and took a quick look at Lionel's text.

Can U C him?

She put down the binoculars long enough to send a reply. *No.*

In trees near Mr. Hunter's place.

Picking up the binoculars again, she focused them on the tree line to the right of Jake's cabin. Deep shadows pooled under the trees made seeing anything difficult, but ... there. That darker shape could be him. She watched a moment longer and decided it very well could be him.

She laid the binoculars on the railing and texted Lionel. *Think I C him.*

Want me to keep watching?

No. Go on home. And thanks!

Welcome!

Rachel tucked her phone away and picked up the binoculars again. Yes, she was now almost positive that black shadow under a large pine tree was the wolf lying down. She tried tuning in to his thoughts but got nothing.

Poor injured wolf. He was probably worn out from the effort of getting around the lake without being seen. He still instinctively stayed out of sight, and Jake, if the wolf indeed belonged to him, would have reinforced that instinct.

If the cabin was the wolf's ultimate destination, he'd have to cross that treeless stretch, which was currently bathed in sunlight. Another hour and it would be shaded, though. Another hour after that, and it would be nearly time for Jake's nightly skinny-dipping session.

Had he been at all worried that his wolf had been gone for twenty-four hours? Of course, she still couldn't prove for certain that the wolf was his, but the evidence was mounting. If the wolf went up to the cabin, then she could justify driving over there.

Jake must have really kept that animal under wraps, though. She'd never seen it except for one glimpse four years ago. The wolf was news to Lionel, obviously. Ted might know. She decided to call him.

But first she dragged an Adirondack chair over to the railing and made herself comfortable. If she was right about the wolf's plan, she had an hour to wait before he made his move. Propping her elbow on the flat arm of the chair, she braced herself so she could look through the binoculars while talking on the phone.

Ted answered, but there was noise in the background. Oh, right. He hosted some guys for a poker party once a week, and this was the night. She modified the question she'd been about to ask because she didn't want Ted to discuss potential wolf ownership with his cronies.

"Sorry to bother you on poker night," she said, "but I have a quick question."

"Sure. I had a lousy hand, anyway."

"Do we have a leash law in Polecat?"

"We might. I don't have a dog, so I never paid much attention. Why?"

"I saw a dog roaming around Jake's place and I wondered if it was his."

Amusement laced Ted's reply. "So if Jake's in violation of a leash law, you want to nail him for that?"

"Darn right. A dog could get hurt wandering around loose." Or a semitame wolf could tangle with a bear and almost get himself killed.

"Sorry, Rachel, but Jake's not your culprit. He doesn't have a dog. He travels so much it wouldn't work out."

"Yeah, guess you're right."

"You should let him know about the dog, though. If it's a stray, one of you should call the shelter and have it picked up."

"Thanks. I'll do that. Have fun with your buddies."

"I will. Fortunately I'm not in it for profit."

"That's a good attitude, Ted. See you later." She disconnected.

Good old Ted wasn't motivated by profit in any sense. She suspected that with his overhead he barely broke even at the general store. But he made enough to live on and stay in the place he loved best on earth. That was nothing to sneeze at.

Meanwhile Jake Hunter apparently made a tidy profit with his wilderness guiding business. She had no quarrel with his success, but she wondered if his long absences meant he was shirking his responsibility to the wolf, the one that nobody seemed to know about.

That was assuming the wolf was his, or at least used his cabin as a home base. She still couldn't prove that for sure, but she was determined to find out. Settling back in her chair, she adjusted the focus on the binoculars and prepared to wait for shade to find that open stretch between the tree line and Jake's cabin.

She didn't mind the waiting, but she was getting hungry. Candy bars waited in her kitchen, but she didn't dare go get them and risk missing the wolf when he moved. She felt certain he wouldn't stay where he was. Gut instinct told her Jake's cabin was his final destination.

But she had to be sure before she went over there. Assuming she did that, she might want to decide what she planned to say. For starters, she'd ask if the wolf was his. Whether he admitted it or not, she'd know from his answer. She was good at reading people.

Then she'd tell him about the incident with the grizzly and how she'd tended the wolf's injuries. Last of all, she'd ask if he intended to keep the wolf or turn him over to a zoo or wildlife sanctuary. If she could get him to admit that he was planning to do something like that, she would offer to take the animal herself.

How that would fit into her life was a big unanswered question. She'd already debated the issue and had decided she couldn't commit to keeping any animal, let alone a wolf. But this was the creature that had saved her life, and she would do whatever was necessary to ensure his welfare.

Maybe she could ask Lionel to help out when she had to travel. She could cut down on the number of trips, too. Some commissions required her to be there during the installation and some didn't. She could become pickier about which jobs she accepted.

Thinking about that, she realized it was past time to stop agreeing to every offer that came her way. She had enough money invested to make her financially comfortable even if she never carved another piece. She would always carve because that was her passion, but she could be more selective about it.

If she stayed home more, she might have a better chance of finding a soul mate. She could concentrate on it, instead of trying to grab moments to find a match online. She knew in her heart that finding the right man required as much dedication as she devoted to her art, but she hadn't been willing to make that kind of commitment.

Perhaps the wolf had come partly to teach her that she needed to do so. If Jake was no longer willing to be the wolf's guardian, then she would take over and allow that to be the beginning of a new life, a new attitude. The more she considered that, the better she liked the idea.

Shifting every so often to make sure her arm didn't go numb, she continued to watch the tree line. The wolf might not want to come with her initially, but she'd win him over. Once he realized that Jake was finking out on him, he might be grateful for someone who would buy him round steak and give him a soft bed on cold nights.

Daydreaming about her new, more peaceful life with a lighter workload, a companion animal, and perhaps the love of her life made her lose track of time. With a start, she realized the shade had reached the edge of Jake's deck. And the dark outline she'd identified as the wolf was moving.

Adrenaline made her shaky, but she forced herself to hold the binoculars steady as she followed the progress of that dark shape. It was her wolf, all right. Sometime in the past hour she'd started thinking of him as hers.

Sure enough, he moved cautiously in the direction of Jake's cabin. He looked ready to bolt at the slightest threat. Jake should be there. Anger simmered at his laissez-faire attitude toward this creature.

Neither totally wild nor totally tame, the wolf was caught in between worlds and needed human protection. If Jake wouldn't provide that, then she would. Filled with righteous indignation, she watched the wolf slink up the steps to Jake's deck.

Still no Jake. Was he relaxing with a beer while an injured wolf, desperate for shelter and care, crept into his cabin? What an insensitive idiot! The creep didn't deserve the wolf's loyalty, but the animal probably gave it without question.

As she watched, the wolf reached the sliding door and nosed it open. Then he slipped quickly inside. Rachel lowered the binoculars and stood.

She probably shouldn't storm over there right now when she was furious with the arrogant bastard. But she was going to, anyway. She couldn't let that wolf spend another night under the roof of a man who cared so little.

She stopped in the kitchen for a couple of candy bars, which she began eating on the way out to her truck. So she'd confront him while she was angry and on a sugar high. So what? That might be the best way to deal with someone as obtuse as he appeared to be.

Sometime during the drive around the lake, as she

finished off the second candy bar and tossed the wrapper onto the passenger seat, she remembered that Jake was the guy who had been her first customer. That sale had jump-started her career. She was grateful for that, but bastards could do good things without realizing they were doing them. She thought Jake fit in that category.

Jake wasn't her concern, anyway. She was focused on the wolf and how she would get him away from Jake and into her truck. If Jake was tired of taking care of the wolf, then her job would be easy. Well, maybe not if she approached him in a belligerent way.

Any hope that he wouldn't be there, which would excuse his lack of concern for the wolf, vanished as she pulled up beside his truck, which was parked beside his cabin. He was there, all right, and likely had been inside his comfy home during the whole sorry drama. Meanwhile his pet wolf had feared for his life. Apparently Jake didn't give a damn.

By the time she tromped up his front steps, she was spitting nails. He had a noble animal under his care, and he wasn't paying the least attention. She hoped he was prepared to turn the wolf over to someone else, because she was ready.

She knocked on the screen door and got no response. The interior door was closed, so she opened the screen and pounded on the wooden door. Still no answer. She wasn't about to leave without having a conversation with Mr. Jake Hunter, so she banged louder.

"I know you're in there, Jake!" she called. "And I'm not leaving until you open the door! I want to talk about your wolf!" She'd raised her fist to pound again when the door swung open.

Jake stood there in a pair of sweats and nothing else. As always, he looked amazing. If she hadn't been so enraged about his behavior, she might have enjoyed the sight.

Apparently he'd had some accident recently, though, because a series of red welts marked his left side. And his nose was bruised. Maybe he'd been in a fight.

She looked into his green eyes, so like the eyes of the wolf. When she'd gazed into his eyes three years ago, they'd been warm and full of interest. Now they were like chips of green glass, cold and hard.

He said nothing. Not *hello*, or *come in*, or even *what do you want?* He just stared at her as if hoping she'd take the hint and leave.

Well, that wasn't happening. Mr. I Have a Great Body and I Know It was going to answer her questions. "A wolf let himself into your house a little while ago. Where is he?"

Jake's expression didn't change. "I don't know what you're talking about."

"Oh, yes, you do! You're keeping a wolf, either full-blooded or a hybrid, on your property."

"No, I'm not."

"Look, I'm not going to report you for it, so you don't have to lie. Reporting you is the last thing I want to do. I'm not worried about what would happen to you, but I don't want that wolf confiscated, or transported somewhere. Polecat Lake is his home, and he deserves to stay here."

Jake met that speech with more stony silence.

"Just tell me this. Are you planning to turn him over to a zoo or a sanctuary? That's the only thing I can figure out, since you were so hot to get rid of my carving. If you're giving up custody of the wolf, then you probably didn't want the carving that looks exactly like him, either."

He studied her for a moment longer. Then he sighed. "Ted Haggerty always said you have an incredible imagination. He must be right if you imagined that you saw a wolf waltz into my house. There's no wolf here. There never has been a wolf here. Now, if you'll excuse me, I have some things to do." He started to close the door.

"Don't you dare dismiss me!" She stepped over the threshold. Let him throw her bodily out if he had the guts to do it. "The wolf is not a figment of my imagination, and you damned well know it. Where is he?"

With a shrug that made all those yummy muscles flex, Jake stepped back. "Go ahead. Look around. Maybe this *wolf*"—he used air quotes to emphasize his mocking tone—"crept into my house without my knowledge. Maybe he's hiding under the bed. Search the place if that will make you happy."

"See? You know he likes to hide under the bed!" She was determined not to be distracted by all that bare skin. And where had he picked up those welts, anyway?

"Any frightened creature dives under a bed."

"If you think I won't look there because I don't want to seem crazy, forget it." She stormed past him. God, but he smelled good.

One quick glance around his combination living and dining room, which looked similar to hers in both layout and furnishings, convinced her that a large black wolf wasn't there. She noticed that the kitchen had a pocket door like hers, so she walked in there, thinking she might find a water dish and a food bowl on the floor. He wouldn't have had time to hide every bit of evidence.

The kitchen yielded nothing of interest. No food or water bowls. No dirty dishes in the sink. Either the guy was neat or he ate out a lot.

With one last survey to make sure she hadn't missed

any telltale signs of a wolf in residence, she left the kitchen and started for his bedroom. He came walking out of it, pulling on a plain white T-shirt.

She appreciated his decision to put on more clothes. After all the times she'd ogled his naked body through her binoculars, she had difficulty ignoring the up-close-and-personal view. This visit was about wolf welfare, not her infatuation with Jake's physique.

"I want to look in your bedroom."

He stepped aside and swept an arm in that direction.

"Thank you." Keeping her mind on her mission, she walked in. The bed, of course, was sinfully enormous. It was probably one of those super kings, which a man of his size needed.

A comforter in shades of green covered the thick mattress. He'd stacked four pillows against the rustic wooden headboard. An image of him sprawled naked on that magnificent bed popped into her rebellious brain and wouldn't leave.

"Don't care, don't care, don't care," she muttered, hoping she could make it be true. Dropping to her knees, she peeked under the bed. Empty. Damn it! She'd wanted to catch him in the lie.

Pushing herself upright again, she turned to find him leaning in the doorway, watching her. "Did you let him out again? I sure hope not, because he's wounded, or did you miss that little fact?"

"Sorry, but I haven't seen a wolf around here, wounded or otherwise."

She hated the way his direct gaze affected her, making her doubt what she'd seen with her own two eyes. "He's big and black, with green eyes. He fought a grizzly last night, I'm pretty sure to save me, and the bear raked her claws down his side."

"A wolf attacked a bear to save you? That sounds like something out of the tabloids. Are you sure that's what happened?"

"Of course I'm sure! I kept him overnight because I was worried the wounds would get infected. But I let him out tonight, and he came around the lake and opened your slider. I saw him do it."

"How could you possibly see such a thing?"

"I watched through my binoculars."

His dark eyebrows lifted. "Are you in the habit of watching my place?"

Dear God, now she was blushing. She felt the heat in her cheeks and glanced away. "No, not really." She wasn't good at lying when she was face-to-face with someone. "But tonight I was worried about the wolf."

"Now I'll tell you what really happened."

"Oh, because you know?" She retrieved her indignation and pulled it around her like a cloak. She didn't have to wonder where he got that bruise on his nose. Somebody had probably punched him for being so damned arrogant.

"The explanation is pretty obvious. You became very attached to this wolf, which supposedly saved you."

"Yes, I did, and it absolutely saved me!"

"Whatever. Anyway, after you let him go, he headed into the hills, like any self-respecting wolf would do. But you desperately wanted to see him again, so when a cloud overhead created a shadow on my deck, you convinced yourself the wolf was here in my house."

"That's not right." But the wolf was no longer in his house, so she'd have a hard time contradicting his story. She'd told Lionel to go home, so she was the only one who'd watched the wolf go through the slider. And she was famous in Polecat for her active imagination.

"You can continue to think what you like." He pushed himself away from the doorframe. "But if you'll excuse me, I have things to do."

"Why did you give Ted that carving?"

He looked straight at her. "Got tired of it."

Ouch. Well, she'd asked him after all. She couldn't complain if she didn't like the answer. "You could have sold it for a lot of money."

"Didn't want the hassle. Are we done here?"

"Yes." She'd taken about all the insults she could handle for one evening. "We're so done."

"Good." He walked into the living room and opened the front door.

She couldn't get through it fast enough.

"Have a nice night," he called after her.

Spinning around, she let go with a parting shot. "I know you're connected to that wolf, and somehow I'm going to prove it."

"No, you're not. Good-bye, Rachel." He closed the door.

She wanted to yell in frustration. But that wouldn't accomplish anything and might startle any wild creatures nearby, including, perhaps, the wolf in question. Climbing into her truck, she pulled onto the two-lane road. Instead of going back the way she'd come, she drove slowly the other way and peered into the woods.

"Are you out there, wolf?" She tried to tune in to his mind, but all she got was static. After being the most real thing in her life for twenty-four hours, he seemed to have totally disappeared.

Chapter 8

On his flight to San Francisco two days later, Jake vowed to put the incident with Rachel behind him. Talking about it might have helped, but he couldn't confide in any of his Were friends. He'd built a reputation as a crusader against Were-human mating, so how could he admit that a human had tempted him so much he'd almost blown his cover?

Besides, it wouldn't happen again. This trip away from Polecat and Rachel would allow him to refocus. Meeting with Giselle Landry, who shared his objections to Were-human mating, would help, too.

His plane touched down a few minutes past eight in the evening. As it taxied toward the gate, he called Giselle, even though their appointment wasn't until the next morning. "Is it too late to meet for a drink?" He hoped not. He'd been alone with his thoughts far too much in the past forty-eight hours, and he needed to get his mind off his problems.

"It's not too late." She sounded frazzled. "But I should warn you I'm not good company right now."

"Hey, if you'd rather not, that's okay." He tamped

down his disappointment. "I'll be at your office at ten tomorrow and we can talk then."

"Actually, the idea of relaxing over a glass of vino sounds wonderful. I just can't promise I won't start whining."

"You can whine all you want, Giselle. I'll catch a cab to the Fairmont and meet you in the bar."

"Meet me in the lobby instead, okay? I know a great little Were-owned place down by Fisherman's Wharf."

"Perfect." Jake's spirits lifted. Listening to Giselle's troubles, whatever they might be, would take his mind off his own. He also looked forward to a night surrounded by his own kind. His preference for being a lone wolf had its drawbacks and probably made him more vulnerable to temptation of the Rachel variety.

"Okay," Giselle said. "See you in about an hour."

"If you'll tell me what you're driving, I can wait outside for you."

"A Harley."

He laughed. "Excellent." Riding behind Giselle while she navigated San Francisco's hills on her motorcycle sounded like exactly what he needed. "See you soon." As he disconnected, he once again wondered if someday Giselle could be more than a friend. He made a promise to himself to keep his mind open to the possibility.

An hour later, he stood outside the Fairmont as the fog rolled in. Great night for a couple of werewolves. He scanned the area for a motorcycle, and here she came, materializing out of the mist. She'd gone with all black—jacket, pants, boots, and bike. He wouldn't have known for sure it was her until he noticed a stray lock of dark red hair that had escaped from under her black helmet.

She spotted him and veered in his direction. "Hi there, Jake!" She put down a booted foot but left the motor running as she reached behind her and came up with a second helmet and goggles to match hers. "Put these on."

"Thanks." Knowing he'd be a passenger on her Harley, he'd worn jeans and a sweatshirt over his T-shirt. After putting on the helmet and goggles, he climbed onto the cushioned seat behind her.

"All set?" she called over her shoulder.

"Go for it."

She took off with a roar, and he steadied himself by holding on to her waist. The ride sent a welcome surge of adrenaline through him. He tried to convince himself that touching Giselle had something to do with it, too.

But when he compared his reaction to Giselle with what he'd felt with Rachel . . . damn it! Was he doomed to constantly reference Rachel whenever he came in contact with another female? That would suck.

Well, even if he didn't feel any sparks with Giselle, he loved riding on her motorcycle. She turned the streets of San Francisco into her own personal roller coaster, something she obviously relished doing. She'd mentioned having problems, so this wild race through the foggy night might be helping her release some tension, too.

Jake was almost sorry when they reached the harbor and she parked the Harley. "That was great," he said as he climbed off.

"I took the long way. Hope you didn't mind."

"Nope. Loved it." After taking off his goggles and helmet, he glanced at the bar she'd brought him to, a cozy-looking place with a wooden sign announcing it was the Den. He smiled. "Clever name. No one would guess."

"No, they don't." She removed her helmet and shook out her wavy red hair. "They think it's just another bar. But even so, humans don't tend to stick around after they've wandered in. On some level they must realize these aren't their peeps."

"I appreciate you bringing me here. It's exactly what I need right now. I'm pretty isolated in Polecat."

She tucked her goggles inside her helmet and started toward the bar. "What about the Hunter pack?"

"It's based in Idaho."

"I guess I didn't realize that. Most Weres live where their pack lives, so I naturally thought you—"

"I like Alaska better." He opened the bar's wooden door and held it for her.

"So you really are a lone wolf."

"I suppose I am." He hadn't evaluated that in terms of taking a mate, either. As he followed Giselle into the dimly lit bar, he acknowledged that his isolation could pose a problem for most females. Werewolves were pack animals, and most of them preferred it that way.

A female often moved to her mate's pack, but sometimes it worked the other way and a male switched locations. Jake hadn't thought about it before, but how many Were females would willingly spend the rest of their lives as he did, distanced from any pack? He thought the spectacular setting created a decent trade-off, but would she? Maybe not.

The bar was fragrant with the scent of fine liquor, expensive cigars, and expertly prepared food. The Den's humble exterior disguised a venue that would satisfy the most discerning customer. Jake realized he was starving.

Giselle was obviously known here. Customers called out greetings and she stopped to introduce Jake as they made their way to an empty table in a far corner. When they reached it, he held her chair.

"Thanks." She gave him a smile. "Call me old-fashioned, but I love chivalrous gestures."

"Me, too." As he sat down opposite her, he wished to hell he found her wildly sexy. Objectively speaking, she was extremely attractive—tall, graceful, classic features, pretty hair. Logically he should want her, except he didn't.

And unless he'd lost all perspective, she didn't want him, either. She gazed at him with friendly interest but not a trace of smoldering lust. Well, good. If she'd shown any signs of being attracted, he'd have an awkward situation on his hands.

A waitress approached the table to take their order for drinks.

Jake glanced over at Giselle. "If you don't mind, I'm ordering food. I know I asked you to meet me for a drink, but—"

"I'm ordering food, too." She opened the menu and snapped it shut again before gazing up at the waitress. "Surf and turf for me." She looked at Jake. "It's outstanding here, and I haven't stopped long enough to eat a decent meal in days."

"Then let's make that two."

Giselle lifted her eyebrows. "Wine?"

"Let's order a bottle of red. I'm ready to stay awhile, but if you need to get back, just say the word."

"The Landry pack can do without me for a few hours." She pulled a cell phone from a pocket of her leather jacket. "In fact, I'm turning this off."

Jake checked the wine offerings.

"May I suggest the Paradigm Shift pinot noir?" the waitress said. "It's local."

"Sounds great." Jake handed back the wine list. The evening had all the trappings of a romantic interlude, except that it lacked the necessary chemistry. Once the waitress had left, he turned to Giselle. "You're now free to whine."

She hesitated, as if debating whether to get into it. Then she groaned and covered her face with both hands. "It's my big brother, although right now I feel years older than him."

"So what's he doing?" Jake felt a pang of envy that she had a brother to be upset with. He had no siblings and would have loved having them, but he was his parents' only offspring. That fact made him doubly determined to carry on the legacy of his mother's pack as best he could.

Giselle sighed and settled back in her chair. "Bryce is going crazy, apparently. He's in line to be the next Landry alpha, but last week he ran off to Vegas and has no immediate plans to come back."

"But he will eventually, right?"

"Who knows? He texts every day so we know he's alive, but he's not talking—not to me, or my parents, or Miranda, who'd agreed to become his mate within the next year. She's announced that she's free again, which only makes sense considering how he's behaving."

"What about his friends? Can't they get through to him?"

Giselle shook her head. "He's cut them off, too. The only clue I have is that he'd started reading Duncan MacDowell's blog, because he mentioned it to me and wondered what I thought about Duncan's ideas on Were-human mating."

Jake cursed softly under his breath. The Scottish Were had organized WOOF—Werewolves Optimizing Our Future—the previous year to promote MacDowell's belief that Were-human mating was inevitable and should be encouraged. He'd made serious inroads with that agenda during WereCon2012.

His popular blog continued to rally support for Were-human mating, and it looked as if he might have another well-placed convert. The heir apparent to the Landry pack would be a feather in Duncan's cap.

"I'm sure hearing that doesn't make you happy."

"Nope."

"I haven't told my parents about my suspicions because they'd hit the roof if they thought Bryce might consider a human mate. I hope his Vegas adventure is nothing more than sowing some wild oats and he'll come back ready to mate with Miranda and assume his responsibilities. But I don't know if he will or not."

"I'm sorry, Giselle. I wish there was something I could do."

"If I thought you could talk him into coming home, I'd beg you to go down there. But he has a stubborn streak, and he'd dig in his heels if he thinks we're coercing him in any way. I—" She paused as the waitress approached. "Good. We have wine."

"I didn't realize how much we might need that tonight."

Giselle chuckled. "I realized it. I'm really glad you suggested this, Jake. I've wanted someone to talk to. You were at that conference. You saw how charismatic Duncan MacDowell is."

"I did." Jake tasted the wine and signaled the waitress to fill both glasses. "He got Kate Stillman to change her tune, after all, and I thought she was firmly in the Were-Were camp. Hell, I even like MacDowell, myself. It's hard not to when he's so sincere. Misguided, but sincere."

"Well, let's drink a toast to my wayward brother and the possibility that he'll resist going over to Duncan's side."

Jake raised his glass. "To Bryce Landry. May he fulfill his destiny with Miranda, the Were mate he's pledged to."

"Hear, hear." Giselle touched her glass to his and drank. Then she put it down and picked up the bottle on the table. "Paradigm Shift is her parents' label. Among other things, the Randolph pack owns a winery in Napa, so naturally the Den will always recommend Were-made wine."

"They should. It's good wine." Jake took another swallow.

"It is, and until last week, Miranda's folks kept my folks well stocked with it. Understandably, the Randolph pack is being less generous with their wine. It's all a mess, and sad, too. My parents get along great with her parents, or at least they used to. Now everyone's tiptoeing around the subject of Bryce's defection."

Jake topped off their glasses. "If he comes back, can he fix this?"

"Probably. He can be a charmer."

"So he could show up and convince everyone to forgive him?"

"Oh, yes. But he could also mate with a topless Vegas dancer simply to prove a point. When we were children he'd go along quietly for months, and then something would hit him wrong and he'd blow his stack in a rather spectacular fashion. I thought he'd outgrown that pattern, but apparently not."

"I think we should blame it all on Duncan MacDowell."

Giselle laughed. "Wish I could, but we all have free will, Jake." She took another sip of her wine. "Let's change the subject. I happen to know you didn't fly all the way down here to talk about my brother. What's up with WARM?"

"It's growing." He briefly described the trips he'd made and the network he'd created. After their food arrived, she encouraged him to elaborate, and he became so engrossed in his subject that he barely noticed what he was eating.

When the waitress came to clear their plates, he realized that he'd talked nonstop through the entire meal. "Sorry about that, Giselle. It's a wonder I didn't put you to sleep with that monologue."

"I love listening to someone who's passionate about a cause."

"Yeah, for five minutes, maybe. After that it's overkill." He grinned at her. "I'm blaming Duncan MacDowell. The thought of that Were and all he stands for gets my blood pumping."

"Well, it sounds like he has a worthy opponent in you."

"Thanks for that. And now that I've bored you to death, can we stay for coffee so I can ask you what I came down here for?"

"Sure." Giselle caught the waitress's eye and ordered two coffees. Then she gazed across the table at Jake. "I'll bet I know why you're here."

"Wouldn't be hard to guess. I want you to head up the WARM organization here in San Francisco."

"I can't."

He didn't want to hear that. "Giselle, at least think about it."

"I have." She reached across and touched his arm as if in silent apology. "I knew that's why you were coming down, so I've given it plenty of thought, but ... I have several issues. One is that I'd have to resign from the council."

"I know." They'd served together on the council of the Worldwide Organization of Werewolves under Howard Wallace, the council's first president. Although Jake had resigned, Giselle was still a member.

"I believe in WOW, Jake. I think I can do some good by being on the council."

"I used to think that you could help balance the scales, but I'm not sure that's possible. Considering that Howard's two sons are mated with humans, we can guess how the organization is going to evolve."

"You might be surprised. Now that Kate and Duncan are mated, she's having a steadying influence on WOW and on Duncan, too."

"You're sure that's not wishful thinking?" Jake still felt betrayed by that union. Kate used to be a powerful leader in the movement to end Were-human sexual involvement. How she'd ended up with Duncan, who held the opposite view, was a mystery to Jake, and he didn't see how any good could come of it.

"I know he's still fire and brimstone on his blog, but privately he's less convinced he has all the answers. I know you think he's corrupted our Kate, but the sword cuts both ways. I also trust Howard not to send us off a cliff."

The coffee arrived, which gave Jake a chance to regroup. He waited until she'd doctored hers with cream before throwing out a revised suggestion. "Okay, so forget heading up the San Francisco division of WARM. You can work in the background and we'll put someone else in that position, someone you handpick." He lifted the coffee mug to his lips.

"I can't do that, either."

He set the mug back down without drinking. "Why not?"

"It's all tied in with my brother. Before he left, I had my hands full as the chief accountant for Landry Enterprises. Now I'm doing that plus some of the board duties Bryce handled. Both Mom and Dad had to step back into positions they'd turned over to Bryce, as well."

"You must be ready to wring his neck."

Her fingers tightened around her coffee mug. "Pretty much. But that said, I'm going to tone down my activism for the time being. Bryce might screw up and mate with a human, and if he does, I'll be the family peacemaker. I always have been. So I need to leave myself some middle ground to stand on."

Jake knew when he was fighting a losing battle. "I understand. But if you'd be willing to recommend someone else from this area, that would help me."

"Be happy to. I know who would be perfect. I'll introduce you to Evan when we take our run tomorrow night."

"Do you have time for the run? Sounds to me as if you're stretched thin." Concern for her schedule wasn't his main reason for asking. With the evening drawing to a close, he became aware of a growing urge to scrap the rest of his plans and hop on a plane bound for home.

When he'd left Polecat this morning, he'd been intent on putting distance between himself and Rachel. He'd accomplished that, but instead of relief, he was battling an uneasy feeling that he needed to be at home to keep an eye on things. He might have underestimated Rachel's determination to find that big black wolf.

"It's all planned, and I'd have some disappointed Weres if we didn't do it . . . unless you have to get back sooner. In which case, we'll run without you, I guess."

"No, no, I don't have to get back." He just felt compelled to. Maybe he was spooked for no reason. "I'd love to take that run. It'll give me a chance to talk with Evan."

"Then the run's a go. I didn't ask you how long you were staying. I hope at least a few more days, so you can enjoy the city."

"That would be nice, but my flight leaves the morning

after our run." That hadn't been his original itinerary, but it was now. Maybe he was being ridiculous to think Rachel might snoop around his place while he was gone. But he also couldn't remember locking his back slider.

Damn, he might not have, because he was so used to leaving it unlocked. Surely Rachel wouldn't consider actually going into his place uninvited, though. Yet he remembered her fury when he'd denied having a wolf on the premises. He hadn't lied. Strictly speaking, he wasn't a wolf. He only looked like one sometimes.

But she'd acted as if she thought he was hiding something, which he was. She also believed her "wolf" was being neglected. By him. Her love of wolves might cause her to do something uncharacteristic, like trespassing on his property.

Well, so what if she did? She wouldn't find a wolf or any conclusive evidence one had been there. But if she went so far as to dig through his stuff . . . that possibility made him as nervous as hell. Yeah, he needed to get back, the sooner the better.

"It's a shame you can't stay longer," Giselle said. "But if anybody understands tight schedules, it's me."

"Yep." Jake sipped his coffee. "I can't let anything slip through the cracks."

Chapter 9

Rachel had spent an inordinate amount of time driving around the lake, hoping to catch a glimpse of the wolf somewhere near Jake's cabin. Even so, she didn't immediately figure out that he'd left town. But when she phoned the general store at closing time to casually ask Ted about it, he confirmed that Jake was gone.

Ted had agreed to collect Jake's mail from the rural box by the road, as usual. "He went to Frisco for some reason," he informed Rachel. "Said he'd be home day after tomorrow. You need to see him?"

She was ready for the question. "I'm planning to take some day hikes for inspiration. I thought he could help me figure out the best options."

"I thought you were mad at him."

Trust good old Ted to come up with the significant point of the discussion. "I am, but he's an expert in this field, so I can't let my irritation keep me from getting good advice, right?"

"I suppose not. That's a very mature attitude to take, Rachel."

"Thank you. I thought so, too." Good thing she was on

the phone instead of looking straight at Ted. If he could have seen her face, he would have realized she was handing him a line of bull. Phones were an excellent invention. "Well, gotta go."

"Right. See you later."

She hung up quickly because she wanted to hotfoot it over to Jake's now that she knew he was gone. Too bad she hadn't tweaked to it sooner, but at least she had tonight and tomorrow to snoop. Somewhere on his property she would find evidence of a wolf. Then she would confront him with it.

Grabbing her backpack, she climbed into her truck and drove around the lake. But as she started to park in front of his cabin, she thought better of it. Several yards beyond his cabin, an old logging road wound back into the woods. That would work.

She passed his cabin, turned off there, and parked where her truck couldn't be seen from the road. Might as well not advertise her presence. Polecat was a small community and she'd rather not have anyone ask why she'd been at Jake's. Aside from not wanting to state her reason for being there, she wouldn't want anyone to think she was a friend of his.

She definitely was not. Although he had the gall to deny it, he was harboring a wolf, and not very humanely at that. Initially she'd told him that she wouldn't turn him in to the authorities, but he'd destroyed her goodwill with his arrogant attitude. The wolf was the only thing keeping her from calling the law down on Jake's head. She didn't want to cause that poor animal any more stress than it had already endured.

Maybe if she went over there, the wolf would come out of hiding. She wondered if Jake had made any provision for it before he jetted off to San Francisco. The more she thought about his cavalier behavior toward such a magnificent animal, the more she fumed.

With her truck tucked out of sight, she slipped on her pack and walked back to his cabin. She'd start in the back because she wouldn't expect to find the wolf anywhere near the road. She had dog treats in the backpack, along with a collar and leash. She'd bought the supplies the day after her run-in with Jake and had taken the precaution of driving forty miles to another small town's general store so she wouldn't arouse Ted's suspicions. She'd kept the dog treats and leash with her whenever she'd gone out searching for the wolf.

She hoped that the treats might convince the wolf to let her collar and leash him. Then she'd use more treats to coax him back to her truck. She had no compunction about stealing the wolf out from under the nose of an untrustworthy person like Jake, but the wolf might not cooperate. When she'd had him at her place, he had been hell-bent on getting back over here.

The wolf's devotion to a man who had only a casual interest in his pet's welfare stuck in her craw. Such unquestioning loyalty reflected well on the wolf, but he might pay dearly for it if Jake shipped him off to a zoo or a sanctuary in the near future. She couldn't bear the thought.

If she couldn't steal the wolf, she might have to negotiate with Jake to buy him. But first she had to get that infuriating man to admit he had such an animal. Every time she pictured him standing there stony-faced while he lied through his teeth, she felt like hitting something. Like him.

She was so wrapped up in her murderous thoughts that she almost stepped on an outstanding piece of evidence. With a soft cry, she leaped back before she crushed an imprint in the moist earth next to the lake. The paw print was large, and while it could have been made by a dog, she knew it hadn't been.

Stepping carefully, she discovered several similar paw prints. Taking out her camera phone, she snapped pictures of them before following the trail that led directly to Jake's deck. Let him deny *this*. She took more pictures to document what she considered concrete evidence.

Once on the deck, she glanced around. When she'd used her binoculars to scan the area, she hadn't paid much attention to Jake's outdoor furniture. He had an expensive gas grill and an elevated patio table surrounded by four tall chairs. Probably suited a big guy like him.

Finally she walked over to the slider and peered in. No wolf stood on the other side. No doubt the slider was locked, but she tugged on it anyway, for good measure. It glided open smoothly, as if recently cleaned and oiled.

Heart pounding, she quickly closed it. She was willing to trespass on the outside of his property, but going into his house when he wasn't home was a whole different level of invasion. On top of that, the wolf might be inside silently guarding the house.

She didn't *think* the animal would attack her after recently saving her life, but she would be encroaching on his master's territory. That might change the rules. Turning away from the unlatched slider, she studied the deck, not sure what she might be looking for.

There! Crouching down, she examined some bits of black hair caught between the deck's weathered gray floorboards. She took pictures of that, too. Unfortunately, Jake had hair just like it, so this bit of evidence wasn't so telling.

But he couldn't explain the paw prints, unless he had

the ability to change into a wolf and . . . She gasped and went very still. Now, there was a crazy thought — a completely impossible concept that had no business taking up residence in her brain.

Standing, she gazed out over the lake toward her cabin, as if the familiar sight of her house and her workshop would help ground her in reality and wipe out that scary idea she'd just come up with. If anyone could read her mind right now, they'd ship her off to a mental ward. Sure, legends were fun to think about, but nobody actually believed in such things as . . . *werewolves*.

Suddenly breathing became a real chore and her stomach didn't feel so good, either. She was letting her imagination run away with her again, of course. Werewolves existed only in books. They didn't live in cabins on Polecat Lake, drive trucks, and run trekking companies.

Except that would explain everything. She remembered the angry red welts on Jake's torso, welts that were on the same side as the wounds the wolf had received from the bear's claws. Jake's nose had been bruised, too, as if someone had hit him. *Someone with a baseball bat.*

The air was soft and warm on this summer evening, but Rachel couldn't stop shivering. No doubt this was a horrible nightmare and she'd wake up from it in a few minutes. She pinched herself, and it hurt like hell. So much for that remedy.

The cry of a hawk overhead caused her to glance up . . . and remember. Years ago she'd been obsessed with *Ladyhawke*, a movie about two lovers placed under a spell. At night he'd turned into a wolf and at dawn she'd become a hawk. Rachel's young heart had been captured by the love story, and she'd watched that movie over and over.

Had the story stuck in her mind and emerged now to create this wild scenario? Possibly. Her imagination could be her greatest asset or her biggest enemy. Even her friends said so.

And wait. Jake had a *grill*, for crying out loud. A werewolf wouldn't need a grill. So there. The grill and the patio furniture were both normal guy stuff that didn't fit with her goofy werewolf idea at all.

Also, she'd allowed herself to become too invested in the fate of Jake's pet wolf. Of course he had one, and it was either in his cabin or in hiding somewhere. Jake might not have any intention of sending it to a zoo, either. Yes, she owed that wolf a lot, but he seemed happy enough here with Jake.

She might want to start minding her own business. She had a commissioned work in progress, and her client would be expecting it to be finished and hanging in the lobby of his office building within the next month. Taking a deep breath, she started back down the steps of Jake's deck. Time to head home, brew a nice pot of tea, and get back to work.

Before she did that, though, she'd call her parents. She hadn't done that in a couple of weeks. Inviting them up for a visit sounded like a really good idea, too.

She imagined how great it would be to see her mom and dad again, and the fun they could have grilling outside, just like her neighbor Jake, who was certainly not a werewolf, while they enjoyed the view of the lake and the mountains. She was a good ten steps away from Jake's deck when she admitted why that image appealed to her so much.

She was scared to death. Scared and running away from something that might be outside the bounds of her experience. *Way* outside. Like a little girl, she wanted her mommy and daddy to make everything nice and safe again.

But damn it, she'd seen those welts on Jake's torso and the bruise on his nose. She hadn't imagined them, and she hadn't imagined a wolf that had shown up right when she needed saving from a bear. Maybe that hadn't been a coincidence, after all.

Jake had been careless enough to leave his sliding door open. Or maybe it was an ingrained habit. The wolf, who might or might not be Jake, needed an unlatched slider for easy entrance and exit.

She'd come this far. If she left now without checking inside his house, she might never learn the truth. She might search the place and find nothing conclusive, but at least she would have made use of this time while he was gone.

Retracing her route and climbing the steps back up to his deck took more courage than she'd expected. She felt like Belle in *Beauty and the Beast*. The wolf, an actual one, might still be inside the cabin, though, and she needed to be careful.

Then she thought of the message taught by the fairy tale. Despite his fearsome looks, that beast hadn't been dangerous. She had no reason to fear the wolf, either. The creature that had attacked the bear, whatever that creature was, had been intent on her safety, not her destruction.

But all that self-talk didn't stop her heart from beating wildly as she opened the slider. "Wolf? Are you in here?" Silence greeted her. "I'm coming in, and I mean no harm."

After listening for any telltale sound of toenails on the floorboards, a growl, or a snuffle, she stepped inside Jake's cabin. She didn't realize she was holding her breath until dizziness made her grab the back of an easy chair near the slider. Gulping in air, she stood beside the chair until she felt steady again.

"Wolf? Are you in here?" After spending twenty-four hours with him, she thought he'd surely come out to investigate when he heard her familiar voice. The utter quiet in the cabin told her the wolf was not here. *Maybe because he's in San Francisco.*

Swallowing her nervousness, she slipped off her backpack and left it on the chair. Then she took a deep breath and looked around.

The cabin seemed much as it had the other day—ordinary. The layout resembled hers, as she'd noted before. Her grandfather had said the two homes had been built around the same time. Furniture selection was limited in a place like Polecat, so it wasn't surprising that Jake's looked quite a bit like hers, too.

At first she moved tentatively through the house, afraid to touch anything. But within a short time, when no wolf appeared, she grew bolder. Starting with the kitchen, she opened cabinets and drawers in search of mysterious items.

Nothing turned up. A bottle opener with a wolf's head on it was the only slightly different utensil, but this was Alaska. Such things could be found in any tourist shop.

His canned goods revealed nothing, either. Apparently he liked organic cereal with dried fruit and nuts, because he had a supply of that. When she opened his freezer she discovered it was full of red meat, but that wasn't significant, either. Many guys built like Jake enjoyed their burgers and steaks.

She found fresh veggies in the refrigerator's bottom section—staples like potatoes, carrots, and onions. Obviously he didn't live on an all-meat diet. In fact, he had a good variety of food for being a bachelor. He'd stocked in eggs, milk, and cottage cheese, along with several bottles of Spruce Tip ale. She left the kitchen feeling no wiser than she had before, but calmer. So far there was nothing scary about Jake's place.

In the living room, she rummaged through his DVDs and discovered no werewolf movies in the mix. His bookshelf contained paperback mysteries, some science fiction, and a few nonfiction books on hiking trails in Alaska. Then she saw a book she recognized because she had one just like it at home. It was titled *Alaskan Artisans of Today*.

She was featured in that book, which was only about six months old. Why would he buy an expensive coffee-table book that included pictures of her and her work, yet be so determined to give away her original wolf carving? Maybe he'd read something about her in the book that had turned him off.

Flipping to the section devoted to her, she found a folded sheet of notepaper. It looked vaguely familiar, and when she opened it, she blinked in surprise. Instead of ignoring her note, as she'd imagined, he'd saved it. Even more astounding, he'd saved it for a couple of years before placing it in this book.

These weren't the actions of someone who was indifferent to her, or who had tired of having her work in his house. She didn't know if Jake was a shape-shifter or not, but he was definitely more complicated than she'd originally thought.

Replacing the book, she moved into his bedroom. The atmosphere here was so potently male that she caught her breath. Testosterone oozed from the oversized bed, with its massive peeled-log bedposts and huge mattress. She'd been drawn to it the first time she'd walked into this room, and now she had the luxury of being here without supervision.

Giving in to temptation, she walked to the side of the bed, leaned over it with her arms outstretched, and slid up onto the mattress. She let her feet dangle off the edge, but the bed was big enough that she could have laid crossways on it, no problem.

With her cheek resting against the soft comforter, she breathed in Jake's scent. Too bad her interaction with him had become so damned confusing and strange, because she'd felt chemistry between them from the beginning. Rubbing her cheek against the material, she imagined lying here with Jake as sexual awareness hummed deep in her belly.

Well, this was pleasant, but it wasn't getting her any closer to the truth about Jake Hunter. After levering herself off the bed, she smoothed the comforter back into place. Then she opened his nightstand drawer, fully expecting she might find a package of condoms there. Many guys kept them handy by the bed.

No condoms. But she found a notepad, a couple of pens, and underneath that, a slim paperback titled *Down with Dogma: Benefits of Were-Human Cooperation*. She held the book for several seconds as her heart thudded wildly and her brain struggled to make sense of what she was seeing.

With trembling hands, she opened the cover and scanned the first page. The word *werewolf* leaped out at her as if surrounded with blinking lights. She seemed to be holding a treatise of some kind that had been written by a werewolf.

Or perhaps the author, Duncan MacDowell, was *pretending* to be a werewolf. It could be a spoof. In fact, it probably was. She was panicking for no reason.

But as she thumbed through the pages, she discovered that the text had been marked up, apparently by Jake. Spoofs didn't usually prompt people to do that. They read the jokes, laughed, and passed on the funny book to the next person. They didn't underline and write notes in the margin.

Her heart rate picked up again. The book was for real. She wasn't sure what that meant, but she had some ideas. Sinking down to the bed, she drew in a quivering breath and began to read.

Eventually that position became uncomfortable, but she couldn't stop reading. Her eyes still glued to the pages, she nudged off her shoes, turned one of Jake's gigantic pillows on end, and scooted up on the bed. She leaned back. Much better.

She was halfway through the book when a soft sound penetrated her deep concentration. She glanced up and nearly fainted from shock.

Jake stood in the bedroom doorway.

She stared at him for what seemed like forever as adrenaline pumped through her veins and flushed her skin. He looked every inch a man—an extremely virile, travel-rumpled man. He'd pulled his dark green shirt loose from the waistband of his jeans, as if he'd needed to be more comfortable on the drive home from the airport.

Concern was etched on his rugged face, but she saw no menace in his expression. He didn't seem angry to discover her trespassing on his property. She had the odd thought that of the two of them, he might have more to fear than she did.

Slowly she closed the book before sliding to the edge of the bed and putting both feet on the floor. Then she swallowed in an attempt to remove the metallic taste from her mouth. "You're back early."

"So it seems." His voice sounded as rusty as hers felt.

Looking into his green eyes, she searched for answers. "Who are you, Jake?"

"Your across-the-lake neighbor."

"And?"

"You tell me." But his resigned expression indicated he knew the game was over.

She felt light-headed as she balanced on the brink of a truth she'd never imagined could be possible. "I think . . ." She paused to lick her dry lips. "I think you save careless women from ferocious mother bears."

"Maybe."

She sucked in a breath. He hadn't denied it. "Instead of asking *who* you are, should I ask *what* you are?"

That sparked the anger she might have expected earlier when he'd first caught her in his home. "I'm still a *who*, Rachel. Regardless of what form I take, I'm a creature with a soul and a conscience. I'm a thinking being at all times. I'm no monster."

She'd hurt him. What an astonishing thought. "I'm sorry. That wasn't very sensitive of me to say." She gripped the book tightly in both hands, needing something to hold on to. "But give me some credit for not becoming hysterical, okay?"

"I wouldn't expect that of you. Anyone who leads a full-grown wolf into her bedroom and dresses his wounds isn't the hysterical type."

Her pulse quickened. "So you really are a . . ." She couldn't make herself say it. The idea seemed too preposterous, even with the evidence all around her.

"A werewolf. Yes, I am."

She took several quick, shallow breaths and managed not to faint. "Wow." She didn't really believe him. Not yet, anyway. Such things took a while to sink in.

"And I would give anything, all I possess in this world, if you'd never found that out."

Fear skittered up her spine for the first time since he'd arrived. "Because you're going to kill me?"

"No! God, no. I could never hurt you."

Her shoulders sagged. "That's a relief." Her laughter was edged with the hysteria she'd denied feeling seconds ago. "I was afraid you might walk over here and break my neck with one easy twist."

"Damn it, I saved you from the bear! How could you think I'd hurt you?"

"Because I know too much. It happens all the time in movies. You might not *want* to kill me, but it's the only way to guarantee my silence. It's not, by the way," she added quickly. "I can keep a secret."

Jake sighed. "You might think so, but this is one hell of a secret. Keeping it won't be easy, and the repercussions if you don't . . . Let's say the stakes are extremely high."

"I'll bet."

"You have no idea. This kind of security breach isn't supposed to happen. We take great care to make sure humans have no idea we exist."

"Just how many of you are there?"

He squeezed his eyes shut. "Damn."

"How many, Jake? Six? Twenty? Thousands?"

When he opened his eyes, his gaze was bleak. "The less you know, the better, so I'm not going to answer that question." He hesitated, as if choosing his words very carefully. "This really is not good, Rachel. I blame myself, but unfortunately, you'll suffer the consequences, too."

The fear returned. "Like what?"

"I don't know yet." He rubbed the back of his neck.

"If you don't, who does?" She'd been so pleased with her relatively calm reaction to finding out her neighbor was a werewolf, but his uncertainty about her fate was creating a panicky feeling she might not be able to control much longer.

"Never mind. But whatever happens, I promise I won't turn you over to the Were Council."

"There is one?" Her voice went up an octave.

"Shit. Forget I said that."

"Does this Were Council kill people?"

"*No.* For God's sake, quit talking like that. Weres don't kill. We have a bad reputation thanks to horror novels and Hollywood, but we're not killers. We're protectors."

She *really* wanted to believe him. "But you mentioned something about me paying the consequences. Forgive me if I'm a tad bit worried."

"Then let me explain, at least a little. Now that you've discovered I'm a werewolf, I can't let you waltz out of here as if nothing happened."

She nodded. "Exactly, so the easiest thing is to wring my neck. But you don't seem to want to, so what's the alternative?"

"One option is taking you as my mate."

"What the hell?"

"I didn't say I was going to do that. It's one option."

Heat sluiced through her. She couldn't tell whether it was from indignation or sexual excitement, but she chose anger over arousal. "Sorry, buddy, but that doesn't happen in my world. In my world, the woman has a choice in the matter, and no male, no matter how hairy, gets to declare that he's going to *take* me. Got that, Jake?" His proposal was primitive and it was wrong. But not without appeal, damn it.

"I get it, Rachel. Believe me, I'm no more eager to choose that option than you are."

"Why not?" Now she was insulted.

"I have a deep and abiding conviction that Weres should never mate with humans."

Yes, she truly was insulted. "That's not what Duncan MacDowell says." She held up the book she'd been reading. "He thinks it's a swell idea."

"Duncan MacDowell is an idiot."

"That explains all the notes in the margins. You were marshaling your arguments."

"I was." He cleared his throat. "So mating with you is out, which means we have to come up with a different solution."

"Great." Putting MacDowell's book on the bedside table, she grabbed one of her shoes and began loosening the laces so she could get it back on. "Let's sleep on it. I'll be in touch."

"You misunderstand." His large frame filled the doorway, blocking her exit. "Until we come up with that solution, you're staying with me."

Her jaw dropped. "You're holding me *prisoner*?"

"I'd rather say I'm detaining you for your own good."

"How is holding me prisoner going to be for my own good?"

"Let me put it this way. You know enough to be dangerous. If you were to escape, I'd be obligated to report that to the Were Council. They would dispatch other Weres to find you and detain you."

"You mean hunt me down?" Breathing grew difficult as she imagined being chased by werewolves.

"In a sense."

She shuddered.

"I'm assuming you'd rather stay here with me than go through that."

"Well, *duh*. How about I leave and you don't report

me because you trust me? I'm a very trustworthy person. Ask anyone." She got one shoe on and started working with the laces of the second.

"Can't."

"I'll take an oath, sign in blood. I have some pictures of me naked in a wading pool. You can have them for blackmail purposes. The idea that you'd show those pictures around will keep my lip zipped forever, guaranteed." She tied her second shoe.

A hint of laughter flickered in his eyes. "How old were you in those pictures?"

"Four."

"I'd like to see those sometime."

"Let me run home and get them!" She stood. "I'll leave my wallet here as collateral. I'll—"

"Sorry. You're not going anywhere. Not until I figure out a plan."

She blew out a breath. "This is freaking unbelievable." That tiny flare of humor in his gaze made her feel a little bit better, but not much.

He shrugged. "I'm not any happier about it than you are."

"Sounds as if we're in for a lovely evening, then."

"It is what it is."

"Guess so." *Be careful what you wish for,* she thought as she gazed at him. She was about to spend several hours in lockdown with the man of her dreams, and he hated the prospect. Also—small detail—he wasn't a man.

Chapter 10

Jake had been in tight spots before, but he'd always figured a way out of them. This fuck-up with Rachel could turn out to be the granddaddy of all exceptions. Although he did his best to project calm acceptance of an unfortunate situation, he was a mass of nerves.

On top of that, he was hungry—for food, mostly. But the minute he'd walked into his house and discovered it was filled with Rachel's scent, he'd become hungry for something far more complicated, something a simple dinner wouldn't take care of. Finding her propped up on his massive bed had tested his willpower more than anything had in years.

He needed to get her out of his bedroom, pronto, before he did something really stupid and seduced her. She might not be seducible, of course, but he had a gut-level feeling that she was. His instincts were sharply honed in that regard, and Rachel was giving off little sparks of interest in between her bursts of outrage. Her scent had changed subtly, too, ever since he'd confronted her.

Having her stay with him for the next few hours

would be easier if he kept them both far, far from that bed while they worked on a solution to this gigantic problem. He took most of the responsibility for the mess they were in, but she sure as hell hadn't helped.

Damned nosy woman. But he'd been afraid she'd grab the chance to poke around his place looking for the wolf. He should have anticipated that and locked his door. He couldn't help admiring her tenacity and concern for another creature, though, even if she had landed them both in hot water.

Hands on her hips, she stood watching him. "Now what?"

"I could use some dinner. Have you eaten yet?"

"No."

"Hungry?"

She paused as if thinking about it. "A little."

He turned from the doorway. "Then let me thaw a couple of steaks for us."

"Um, you know, I'm really not that hungry, after all."

He pivoted to face her again. "Would you rather have something else? I think there're some chicken breasts in the freezer, or I could—"

"No, you go ahead. I'm more tired than hungry. You eat, and I'll stretch out on your bed for a little while and rest." She sat on the edge of the bed and untied her running shoes.

He gulped. "Don't do that."

"Do what?" She glanced up.

"Take anything off. I mean . . . don't take a nap . . . on my bed."

"I won't mess it up, Jake. I admit I rearranged your pillow while I was reading, but I'll put everything back the way I found it. Sheesh, I didn't know you were such an anal neat freak. It's not like I'll get under the covers, if that's what you're worried about. Never mind. I'll just . . . relax in the living room."

"I'm not worried that you'll mess up the bed." If only she knew how much he wanted to mess it up with her. He switched back to the safer topic of food. "It's just that I thought you were hungry, and suddenly you're not. It's kind of late, and you said you haven't had dinner, so surely you want something to eat."

She leaned down and fussed with the laces of her shoes. She made a big production out of it, almost as if she needed something else to concentrate on so that she didn't have to look at him. "Maybe I'll have something later."

"Want me to grill your steak so you can have a steak sandwich when you're ready?"

She finished with her shoes and stood. "Please don't fire up the grill on my account. Go ahead and eat. I'll have some of your fruit and nut cereal if I get hungry."

So she'd checked out the contents of his cupboards while she was at it. But that wasn't the most significant thing she'd said just now. He finally understood her reluctance to eat with him, and he was both horrified and amused. "You think I'm going to eat my steak raw, don't you?"

Keeping her expression carefully neutral, she nodded. "But there's nothing wrong with that," she added quickly. "You should be allowed to eat whatever way you want in your own home."

He couldn't blame her for thinking such a thing. He'd devoured both raw steak and raw hamburger over at her place. She didn't know that had been under duress. "I prefer my meat cooked," he said.

Her eyes widened. "You do? But you're a—"

"Shape-shifter. Maybe it'll help to use that term instead of werewolf. I'm not, strictly speaking, a wolf at all. I can take that form, but I'd rather not eat once I've shifted. That is, unless I have no alternative."

"Oh." Her cheeks turned a soft pink, which made her quicksilver eyes even brighter. "Sorry about that. I didn't know."

"No need to apologize. I was grateful for any food, raw or cooked." God, she was beautiful. He'd need a bigger vocabulary just to describe all the rich shades of brown in her shoulder-length hair. The last time he'd stood this close to her, he'd been half-crazy with pain, but now he was free to enjoy every second of close proximity.

He breathed in her almond scent, which had become like an aphrodisiac. How in hell would he make it through this night without doing something foolish? Maybe he was destined to act like a fool and pay the price.

"I knew you were famished," she said. "I used it to trick you so I could keep you captive longer." She hesitated. "Now I have to wonder. Would you have been better off if I'd simply left you alone?"

He hesitated to give her the answer, both because it might make her feel bad and because he really did want to limit her knowledge.

"You would have been better off." Regret laced her words. "I can tell by your expression."

"Shifting helps me heal." He could say that much without causing more problems.

She groaned. "And I thought I was helping."

"That's all that counts." He resisted the urge to cup her face as he said that. "You were nothing but kind to me during that twenty-four-hour period. I'll never forget how caring you were."

"You'd saved me from that bear, so of course I wanted to take care of you. I didn't know I was doing it wrong."

"You couldn't know that."

"I was so grateful to you. I'm still grateful, in spite of . . . well, everything." She paused. "But how did you happen to show up in the nick of time?"

That was a topic he'd rather not discuss, either. "We can talk about it over dinner." Maybe by then he'd have come up with a great cover story. "That is, if you're willing to share a meal with me now that you know I have decent table manners."

She smiled. "I am willing. More than willing. I'm starving, and I'd love a steak."

"Good." Fixing dinner would give him something to concentrate on besides his recurring fantasy of rolling around with her on that big bed. He headed for the kitchen. "How do you like your steak?" he called over his shoulder.

"Barely pink."

"Got it." He liked his steak rare, but after this touchy conversation, he'd cook his a little longer so it looked the same as hers. He might not be able to erase her image of him in wolf form tearing into the raw meat she'd offered him days ago, but he'd sure as hell like to.

As she followed him through the living room, a cell phone rang, and it wasn't his.

"Don't answer," he said quickly.

"Sorry, but you don't get to decide that." She pulled her phone from the backpack she'd left sitting in his easy chair. "Hi, Ted. What's up?"

Jake clenched his jaw. He should have known she wouldn't accept a barked order. If he'd said *please*, she might have responded better. And now she was on the phone with Ted, and no telling what she'd say to him.

"Yes, as a matter of fact, I'm at his cabin right now, but thanks for letting me know, anyway. I happened to be passing by and saw his truck was here, so I stopped."

Jake shook his head in frustration. When he'd stopped at the general store on his way home to pick up his mail and let Ted know he was back early, Ted had mentioned that Rachel wanted some advice on hikes in the area. He'd known then that he might have trouble, and sure enough—she'd wanted to make certain he was really gone so she could case the joint, and the hiking thing had been a smoke screen.

"Yes, Jake's been extremely helpful. He's offered to take me out hiking tomorrow, in fact."

Jake stared at her. What in God's name was she doing telling Ted they were going on a hike together?

"Uh-huh. Should be a good day for it. Anyway, thanks for letting me know he was back. Talk to you soon. 'Bye." She disconnected the call and tucked the phone into her pack.

"Would you care to explain that?"

She faced him, her expression unapologetic. "I made up a story for Ted that I needed hiking advice so I could find out how long you'd be gone."

"So you could nose around. I realize that. But what's the point of telling him we're going hiking tomorrow?"

"Just planning ahead. In case you hadn't noticed, we have a big issue to resolve."

"Trust me, I noticed."

She crossed her arms and gazed at him with those amazing silver-gray eyes. "What if we don't get it figured out tonight?"

At the moment he didn't want to figure out anything. He wanted to walk over there and haul her into his arms. "We have to." Because the longer he was locked in this dance with her, the less control he'd have over his raging libido.

"And that"—she uncrossed her arms and pointed at him—"is *exactly* why we might get stuck. Too much pressure. We could freeze up."

Or burn up. That seemed more likely. "I won't let that happen."

"Then great, we'll 'cancel' the hike." She used air quotes to make her point. "But if for some reason your magnificent brain stalls tonight, we don't have to avoid everyone we know while we hole up in this cabin struggling to find an answer. We can leave on the hike I just mentioned to Ted. That might not be a bad way to clear our heads, anyway."

"I hope it won't come to that."

A hint of vulnerability shadowed her expression. "Can't wait to get rid of me, huh?"

Yes, but not for the reason she thought. "Nobody likes to have problems, and you present one. It's not your fault . . . well, some of it is. If you'd resisted the urge to come over here and investigate, we wouldn't be in this situation."

"I owed it to the wolf."

"Who, it turns out, was me."

"Yes, but I didn't know that. And my debt is actually to you. When you put it that way, I guess if I help find a solution to our problem, that would be a way of me settling up with you."

"I'll accept that as a fair trade. And I hope for both our sakes we can come up with a workable plan."

"As you said, we have to."

"Right. And I don't know about you, but I can't think very well on an empty stomach. I'm going to start dinner." He started toward the kitchen.

"Good idea." She followed. "Can I help?"

He wondered if having her sweet body in the kitchen would help or hinder. Probably hinder. "Tell you what. How about if you set the table out on the deck? I'll bet you know where all the utensils are." He gave her a knowing glance as he opened the freezer door.

Instead of looking guilty, she laughed. "I do. I searched your kitchen for anything strange and only came up with a wolf's-head bottle opener."

"I bought that in Anchorage as an inside joke." He took the wrapping off the steaks and put them on a plate in the microwave. "Speaking of the bottle opener, what would you say to opening a couple of bottles of Spruce Tip ale?"

"I can do that." She went straight to the right drawer and took out the opener.

He took a couple of bottles from the door in the refrigerator and handed them to her. "Even though you've been through all the drawers and cupboards, I'm impressed that you remember where the bottle opener was."

"Good memory." She popped the top from a bottle and gave it back to him.

"I'll keep that in mind."

"It doesn't mean I blurt out everything I remember, though. Just so you know." After opening her bottle, she raised it in his direction. "Here's to solutions."

"I'll drink to that." The ale tasted good shared with Rachel. He thought about his dinner with Giselle. The air hadn't crackled when he and Giselle were together, but it certainly crackled now.

Rachel opened the utensil drawer and gathered up what they'd need for the meal. "Are you sure you trust me to go out on the deck by myself? What if I try to escape?"

He'd been crouched in front of the bottom bin of the refrigerator while he chose a couple of potatoes to bake in the microwave after he'd thawed the steaks. He glanced up at her. "You wouldn't get far."

She met his gaze. "I might. I'm pretty fast."

"Not as fast as I am." Holding two potatoes in one hand, he stood.

"What, you have some sort of Were speed?"

"Something like that."

She shrugged. "I wouldn't try it, anyway. You'd just call that Were Council and I'd have Were police on my trail."

"And then the entire Were community would be involved. I'd rather keep this to ourselves if we can."

"Contain the damage?"

"Exactly."

"I'm good with that. I won't try to run away." Her hands full of utensils, place mats, and napkins, she left the kitchen.

But shortly she was back to retrieve her bottle of ale. He put her to work scrubbing carrots and was mesmerized by the way her breasts shifted beneath her T-shirt as she did that chore. So he looked away, but he couldn't block out her scent, her body heat, or her soft breathing. Everything about her called to him.

Because he was attuned to her breathing, he noticed that it picked up whenever he came close. That could be because she now knew he was a werewolf, but he thought it was more than that. She wanted him, too. That knowledge was good for his ego but bad for their chances of keeping the evening from getting out of hand.

After about ten minutes of effort, the potatoes were in the microwave and the carrots steaming away in a saucepan. They'd moved on to their second bottle of ale apiece, and Rachel carried those out to the deck while Jake brought the platter of steaks, a long-handled fork, and his basket of spices.

"You're obviously used to cooking." She set both bottles on the elevated patio table and climbed up onto one of four tall swivel chairs grouped around it.

"I like doing it." He adjusted the heat on the gas grill. "When I take groups out on the trail, it's a fun challenge to prepare them a decent meal in the middle of nowhere. It's one of my selling points."

"Do you ever . . . cook for other werewolves?"

"Sometimes." He put on the steaks and came over to join her at the table. "Look, it'd be better if you don't ask questions. As I said before, the less you know—"

"I disagree. What you want from me is loyalty and trustworthiness, right?"

What he really wanted from her was something he wasn't supposed to have. He tipped his bottle and drank some ale before he answered the question. "Ignorance would be preferable."

"Too late. I know you're a werewolf and that there's a werewolf council out there somewhere. You threatened me with werewolves who would hunt me down if I tried to run away from you. I'm envisioning an entire shadow community living alongside the human population. Am I right?"

"I'm taking the Fifth on that."

She blew out an impatient breath. "Look, I'm pretty smart, Jake, and I'll probably figure a lot of this out on my own."

"You're certainly free to do that, but I don't have to supply any more details."

She sipped her ale and gazed at the mountains in the half-light of an Alaskan summer evening. A breeze ruffled Polecat Lake, causing small ripples to lap against the shore.

Through all that, he could almost hear Rachel thinking. Almost. They'd had a mental connection for a brief time after he'd shifted into wolf form, but he wasn't as psychic in human form.

He could certainly feel lust in the air, though. The aroma of grilled steak teased his nostrils. That smell, combined with the tang of the ale he'd consumed and the almond scent of a female he wanted, aroused him to a level he hadn't reached in a long time. Considering the trouble he was in, he shouldn't allow himself to enjoy this sensually rich moment with Rachel. But he couldn't seem to help himself. She was potent.

At last she spoke again. "I've been thinking."

"I'm sure." He wondered if any of her thoughts had to do with the sexual tension building between them.

"I mean, does it matter whether I know a few details or a lot of details? In a case like this, there's no such thing as a small leak."

He had to admit she had a point.

She tilted her bottle, took a drink, and swallowed, her delicate throat moving seductively, making him long to nip that slender column. Then she looked over at him. "I'm just glad you're not planning to have me rubbed out."

He had a mouthful of ale when she said that. Because he didn't want to spew it all over her, he choked instead. She left her chair to pound him on the back, which was of no help.

Finally he was able to breathe again.

"You okay, sport?" She resumed her seat and peered at him.

"Yeah." He grinned and shook his head. "*Rubbed out.* Where do you come up with things like that?"

"I watch a lot of movies. I love the world of the imagination. And FYI, now that I know werewolves exist, I think it's plain mean for you not to tell me all the juicy details. Like I said, a leak is a leak."

"I'm only thinking that you can't blab what you don't know."

"You say that like somebody's going to put thumb screws on me and force me to talk. They're not, Jake. We live a fairly isolated existence up here, and when I travel for work, I guarantee nobody will ask me what I know about werewolves. If I keep my mouth shut—and I will—the subject won't come up."

He studied her. "I want to believe that you can keep your mouth shut." He shouldn't be discussing her mouth, though, because it made him think of what fun he could have exploring it.

"I can absolutely do that. I understand the issues. I may understand them better than most because I have such an active imagination. But I have to ask, are werewolves planning to take over the world?"

"What?"

"It's a fair question. In the movies, the nonhuman creatures usually take over the world and enslave the humans. Why wouldn't werewolves want to do that?"

"Because it's not our nature to be aggressive." He almost added that Weres were lovers, not fighters, but thought better of it.

"But you're organized enough to have a council, and apparently you look out for each other, even if you don't always agree, like in the case of you and Duncan Mac-Dowell. In his book, Duncan referred to extensive business interests. Do werewolves have a lot of money?"

Jake put down his empty bottle and stood. "I need to check the steak."

She seemed undeterred by his attempt to change the subject. "Because if they have a lot of money, they might be planning an economic takeover. Or maybe they *already* control huge chunks of the economy. If that's so, then—"

"Steaks are done. Let's eat."

"Don't think you can stop me from asking questions by keeping my mouth busy with food."

Naturally that comment made him think of another way he could keep her mouth busy. He loaded the steaks on a platter and set it on the table. "Can't blame me for trying."

"I'm just warning you it won't work." Straightening in her chair, she eyed him with defiance.

Just his luck, he found her attitude extremely sexy. "Then I'll have to use more creative ways to shut you up."

"And what's that supposed to mean?"

He allowed himself a very slow, very male perusal of her body. "Use your imagination."

Chapter 11

Whoa. Rachel hadn't been born yesterday, and she recognized a sexual gauntlet when it had been thrown down. Jake had just served notice that he had testosterone and he wasn't afraid to use it.

After all those nights of watching him skinny-dipping, she was more than primed for whatever he cared to dish out. Desire gripped her tight, warming her skin and dampening her panties. She wanted him bad.

Sure, he wasn't quite who she'd imagined during those nights of spying on his naked-swimming routine. He had another, rather unusual, side to him. But she could ignore that aspect, because at this moment in time he was the built-for-sin man she'd admired through her binoculars. *Bring it on, big boy.*

She was more than willing to abandon the meal and have a close encounter right here on the deck, or up against the railing, or spinning on one of the swivel chairs surrounding the table. Nobody else was around except a few geese on the lake and the occasional fish leaping out of the water. They wouldn't mind.

Jake's gaze met hers and he swore softly. But instead

of grabbing her and ripping her clothes off as she'd fantasized he might, he took a deep breath. "That's some imagination you have."

Her pulse raced. "You can read my mind?"

"Don't have to. It's all there in your eyes." He groaned. "God, Rachel. I can't . . . we can't do this."

"But you want me." If his expression hadn't told her so, the fit of his jeans would have.

"Yes. And that's a problem." He turned away. "I'll get the rest of the food. Help yourself to a steak." He disappeared into the house.

During the brief time Jake was gone, Rachel had a moment to decompress and think about what had just happened. She'd read enough in Duncan MacDowell's book to know that for Weres, sex wasn't the same as mating. She and Jake could have sex without making a lifetime commitment, and that seemed to be what he was morally against.

Yet he'd said wanting her was a problem for him. She'd have to ask him to explain, because she didn't understand. She also wondered how long he'd been nurturing this case of lust. There was that telltale note of hers tucked inside a book with her picture in it. How ironic if he'd wanted her as long as she'd wanted him.

By the time he returned with the potatoes and carrots, she'd made up her mind. "There's no way around it, Jake. You have to level with me."

"I know." He took the chair opposite hers but didn't pick up his fork. "I decided the same thing while I was in the kitchen. Ultimately, I started the whole thing when I bought your carving. That was my first mistake."

"Mistake?" She stared at him. "Are you kidding me? You inspired me to give up on becoming a vet so I could devote myself to my art. I don't just owe you my life. I owe you my career!"

"No, you don't. Someone else would have bought that carving. Then you would have them to thank. And we wouldn't be in the middle of this big mess."

"I don't agree with that logic. Hearing your positive comments about the carving was as important as the sale, maybe more important. I was meant to be in that store when you walked in. You have no idea what a boost your comments gave me. In fact, I wrote you a note to that effect. You probably don't remember, though." She was a devil to mention it, but she couldn't resist.

A dull red stain crept up the back of his neck. "I seem to remember a note."

She didn't push it. She didn't want to embarrass him by pointing out his sentimentality. "I'm just saying that sale was a significant event that helped encourage me to become a full-time carver."

"There would have been different inspirations. You're very talented. You would have made it with or without that moment in Ted's store. Now, eat your food before it gets cold."

"You sound like my mother."

He smiled. "No cook wants food to sit around after they've fixed it. Dig in."

"But you promised to tell me everything."

"I will." He cut into his steak. "Between bites. It's a long story, so I need to keep up my strength. And so do you."

"Okay." She sliced into her steak, which was grilled exactly as she liked it. She couldn't resist glancing over at Jake's, which was the same shade of pale pink inside. She thought that might be on purpose. "Now, start talking."

He did, pausing sporadically to eat. He told her about his father, the actual wolf she'd photographed and immortalized in wood. He mentioned that his parents had died in a skiing accident but didn't dwell on that part of the story. He did admit, though, that after buying her carving, he'd become fascinated with her and had fallen into the habit of late-night runs over to her place.

Which explained why he'd kept her note. She finished her last bite and put down her fork. "Are you saying that we wasted three years when we could have been . . ." She trailed off, not sure what the relationship might have developed into.

He shook his head as he finished chewing and swallowed. "No, we couldn't, not without me becoming a hypocrite."

"How's that?"

"Think about it. The obvious way to halt Were-human mating is to end Were-human sexual encounters. If a Were never has sex with a human, he or she won't be tempted to consider mating with one."

"So you've never had sex with a human?"

"Nope." He picked up his ale and took a drink.

Because she was watching him very closely, she noticed that his hand quivered ever so slightly.

"Ever been tempted?"

He set down the bottle and glanced at her. "You mean, other than you?"

"Right."

"Maybe a little, but I could always shrug it off." He looked out over the lake. "If I hadn't bought that carving, I might have been okay. But you put a part of yourself in that piece, and I felt it drawing me. That's why I had to get rid of it."

"You make it sound like the carving's possessed."

"It is." He gave her a half smile. "By you."

"Jake, I've sold carvings to lots of people, including many single guys. Not one of them has insinuated that my work makes them want to take me to bed."

"Maybe they're more polite and civilized than I am. It might affect them that way, but they don't want to offend you." He leaned both elbows on the table. "None of your clients have propositioned you, though?"

"No. Partly because I never give them the chance."

He nodded. "Makes sense. You don't want to mix business with pleasure."

"Actually, I'd be happy to mix business with pleasure, but none of my clients have appealed to me in that way."

"So who have you been dating?"

"None of your beeswax!"

"Probably not, but I want to know. I assume you're not hooked up with someone now, or you wouldn't have given me the green light a while ago. But I'll bet there's been a guy. You're too beautiful to stay celibate."

"Thank you for that. I was beginning to think without my carving I'd have no sex appeal at all."

He laughed. "Oh, my God. You're kidding, right?"

"You have been raving on about that carving and the effect it had on you."

"Then let me set your mind to rest on that score. The carving is the icing on the cake, but the cake is plenty rich without it. Sad to say, I'm on a sugar-free diet."

She polished off her ale. "Aren't you the least bit curious about how sex with a human would be?"

"Oh, I'm very curious, but I'm also not a fan of hypocrisy. I've set myself up as the standard-bearer for the cause. All my traveling since last October has been to promote the organization I founded, Werewolves Against

Random Mating. That's why I was in San Francisco, on business for WARM."

"Warm?"

"It's an acronym."

"Oh. Like Duncan MacDowell has WOOF, Werewolves Optimizing Our Future."

Jake frowned, clearly unhappy that she'd brought Duncan into the conversation. "Yes, he does, damn it. Plus he wrote a book that I felt compelled to buy and read. If you hadn't found it in my nightstand drawer, you'd still be in the dark about all this."

"I guess you don't believe that things happen for a reason."

He gazed at her. "I guess you do."

"I take after my Grandpa Ike, and he was a big believer in that. I'm sure he'd say you were supposed to be my first customer and that we were destined to have this connection."

"Are you saying he would have been happy that you're connected to a werewolf?"

"He might have, if he'd had enough information. Don't think I've forgotten your promise to tell all. You still have a lot of ground to cover."

"I'll tell you more after you've answered the dating question you've continued to dodge. I'm sure you could have your pick, so do you go for corporate types? Other artists? Jocks?"

She thought about how to answer. Maybe, all things considered, he deserved the truth. "I haven't been dating."

"Really?"

"Yes, really. At first I was too busy with work, and then I was worried that someone would be attracted to the fame and fortune instead of me, personally. So at the suggestion of my girlfriends in Fairbanks, I signed up for a couple of online sites about six months ago."

"And?"

"Nada. Can't get worked up about any of them. I'm dateless in Polecat."

"Damn. That sucks."

"Fortunately I have an active fantasy life involving my neighbor."

Jake's eyes widened. Leaning back in his chair, he raised both eyebrows and pointed a finger at his chest.

"Yes, you, Aquaman. Thanks to your regular skinny-dipping schedule and my grandfather's excellent binoculars, my fantasy life is doing fine."

Adorably, his face turned red. "Didn't know I had an audience."

"A very appreciative audience, I might add."

Jake scrubbed a hand across his face, as if he could wipe off the embarrassment. When he finally looked at her, chagrin had been replaced with the ever-present glow of desire. "Ah, Rachel. What are we going to do about this crazy situation?"

She'd been thinking of little else all through the meal. "Well, I'm already the keeper of one big secret."

"Right." His green eyes grew wary.

"Why not make it two?"

He took a shaky breath. "I was afraid you were going to say that."

"Were you afraid, or were you perhaps hoping I would?"

He hesitated. "Probably both. Ever since I walked in and found you in my bedroom, I've wondered how the hell I'd make it through this without cracking. And now I discover you've been fantasizing about me, too."

"So are you about ready to crack?"

"Yeah. 'Fraid so."

Her pulse skyrocketed. "Oh."

"And now that I've admitted that, it's time to take this discussion inside."

Heat danced through her veins as she helped him gather up the dishes. They'd found no long-range solutions, but they might have hit on a short-range one.

Jake wanted to blame Rachel's confession for sending him over the edge, but then again, it wouldn't have taken much. He'd been teetering for a long time. Now that he was about to fall, he couldn't wait.

Carrying the empty meat platter and their ale bottles, he followed her into the kitchen. "Just dump everything in the sink. We'll worry about it later."

She followed his instructions and turned back to him. "I forgot the place mats."

"Let 'em blow away. I don't care." Shoving the platter and bottles onto the counter, he pulled her into his arms. *At last.* With a sigh, he lowered his head for the kiss he'd been dreaming about for three years.

Incredibly, she put her hand to his mouth, halting his forward progress. "Wait, Jake."

Capturing her wrist, he tugged her hand away. "I'm through waiting. I want you so much I'm dizzy."

She started to say something else, and when her mouth was open he took it as a golden opportunity to kiss her. Ahh. Warm, moist, soft . . . a velvet playground.

The thought that she was human, not Were, drifted through his mind and was gone. She was . . . Rachel, and kissing her felt like coming home. He groaned with delight when she pressed her fingers into his scalp and kissed him back.

God, she felt great pressed up against him, her breasts

tight against his chest, her pelvis cradling his erection as they undulated together, two halves of a whole. He began undressing her without thinking about it. All he knew was that her clothes were in the way, and he wanted them gone.

She seemed to want his gone, too, and that was fine with him. She kissed him with even more urgency as her fingers flew down the row of buttons holding his shirt together. The kitchen filled with the sound of rapid breathing and soft murmurs of joy.

Then came Jake's muted oath of frustration when he realized he had to deal with her running shoes before he could slide off her jeans. Grasping her hips, he hoisted her up on the counter. The platter and bottles he'd put there earlier tumbled with a crash into the sink. He ignored them and dropped to his knees so he could yank at the laces of her shoes.

"Forget untying." She gulped for air. "Just . . . pull them off."

He did, followed by her jeans and her gratifyingly wet panties. As he stood, he realized he loved having her at counter level. Extremely convenient. Cupping her face in both hands, he leaned in to kiss her again. He already knew he'd never tire of doing that.

Once again she tried to say something, but it was muffled against his questing mouth. Moving aside the lapels of his shirt, she flattened her palms against his chest and began a sensuous massage. Her touch was heaven, but he wished she'd unfasten his jeans and unzip his fly. He could do it, but then he'd have to stop stroking her silky breasts, and he was entranced with those.

Cradling their sweet weight, he kissed his way down the smooth column of her neck and over the slope of one breast. When he circled her taut nipple with his tongue, she gasped with pleasure. That tiny gasp made him eager to create more like it.

Closing his mouth over her nipple, he rolled it between his tongue and the roof of his mouth. He was rewarded with a soft moan. That moan, predicting more to come as he continued to love her, sent a message straight to his cock. It swelled painfully inside its prison of briefs and denim.

Lifting his mouth, he murmured his request against her damp skin. "Unzip my jeans." Then he went back to nuzzling her beautiful breasts.

"Do you have a condom?"

He paused in midnuzzle, confused as to why she'd ask him that. He didn't need condoms. Never had. Never would. Then the truth of the situation penetrated his hormone-soaked brain.

She'd asked because she was human. Humans needed condoms to prevent unplanned pregnancies and disease. Rachel didn't know anything about werewolves, so she didn't know they didn't have to worry about either. They were immune to diseases and could reproduce only with their bonded soul mate. But because he'd never had sex with a human before, he hadn't realized she wouldn't understand any of that.

Reluctantly leaving the erotic contemplation of her plump breasts, he raised his head to look into her gray eyes. They reminded him of storm clouds heavy with rain, begging for release. He wanted to give her that release, and very soon, too.

He'd rather not have to take time for a lengthy explanation about werewolves and birth control. "Weres don't use condoms."

Lightning flashed in her storm-cloud eyes. "If they intend to have sex with me, they do."

He definitely intended to have sex with her, but he didn't have a single condom in the house. If he'd had one, he would have used it to forestall an argument. But he'd never bought one in his life.

He tried to keep the explanation concise. He had things to do, orgasms to give. "We're disease resistant and we can't get a female pregnant unless we've been through the mating ritual."

"I've heard that line before and I didn't buy it then, either."

He sucked in a breath. "From a werewolf?"

"No, from a guy who didn't like wearing little raincoats on his pride and joy. He claimed to be disease-free and sterile. I kicked him out of bed."

"I'm different."

"I won't argue that point, but the part about not getting me pregnant sounds fishy." She looked him in the eye. "We need to rethink this."

He wanted to howl in frustration. They'd been so close! More than close, actually. She was completely naked and he could be naked in no time. Except she didn't trust him without a condom in hand or, more precisely, on his cock.

Time for a compromise. He stroked her thighs. "At least let me make you come."

"No." She grasped his wrists. "That could be a trick. You give me a lovely orgasm, and while I'm feeling all loose and accommodating, you get busy."

"I'm insulted that you'd believe that of me."

"Anyone who tries to have sex without a condom is suspect in my book." She shoved at his bare chest. "Go on, now. Move away so I can get down and put my clothes on."

"What can I do to convince you?"

"I don't know, Jake. I'm not an easy sell on this point." She hopped down from the counter and began gathering her clothes.

"It's not like I can run up to the store and buy some. Ted's closed up for the night, and besides, I wouldn't dare buy them from him when he knows we're hanging out together."

"Yeah, that would be a bad idea." She shrugged. "Oh, well. I know you have ice cream in your freezer. Shall we have some dessert?"

Her nonchalance about this irritated him to no end. He ached from not following through on what they'd started. She must be in bad shape, too, but she wasn't willing to let on.

Now she wanted to act as if a bowl of chocolate ice cream would suit her in place of a mind-blowing climax. That was insulting to his abilities as a lover. He could give her way more pleasure than that stupid ice cream.

He blew out a breath. "That's a damn poor substitute for the dessert I had in mind."

"Maybe so, but we can both enjoy it without worrying about consequences other than a sugar high."

"I'll dish it up." He buttoned his shirt as he stomped over to the freezer. He was already thinking of a way he might be able to prove to her that he didn't need condoms when they had sex. But it would involve breaching Were security even more than he already had.

How far was he willing to go to satisfy this craving? Pretty far, apparently.

Chapter 12

Bitterly disappointed in Jake, Rachel sat in his easy chair eating ice cream and wishing he could have been the wonderful lover she'd imagined he would be. She'd tried to settle the condom issue early on, but he hadn't let her talk to him. Then he'd been ready to blow right past the subject with some weird mumbo jumbo about werewolves not needing them.

Yeah, right. Maybe next he'd try to sell her oceanfront property in Arizona. She might be running a sexual deficit these days, but she wasn't bankrupt enough to chance a condomless encounter with Jake Hunter, no matter how gorgeous he was.

While she sat in the easy chair, he paced the living room, eating from his ice cream bowl as he roamed around. Probably walking it off—*it* being the large erection she'd felt when they'd been so close together she wouldn't have been able to slide a DVD between them.

Pausing in his circuit of the room, he faced her. "You wanted to know more about the werewolf community, right?"

"Sure." He was trying to get on her good side, and she had to admit he was going about it the right way. She was dying of curiosity. She suspected that Duncan's book wouldn't be available at a normal bookstore or online outlet, but she wanted a copy. If Jake fell asleep, which he'd have to do eventually, she'd go read the rest of it while she had the chance.

"Naturally Weres can't use the Internet without being found out, so we've created our own digital communication system that only Weres can access. Duncan has a blog on it. I have a website for WARM there, too. We also have a version of Twitter, only we call it Sniffer."

Rachel couldn't help smiling. "That's funny."

"Want to see it work?"

She gazed up at him. "You know how to tempt a girl, don't you, Jake?"

He didn't deny it. "I could get in huge trouble for showing you this, but . . ." He shrugged. "I'm already in huge trouble, and you'll learn more about us this way. Maybe that's a good thing, like you said."

She wasn't fooled. "You're going to round up some support for your claim about not needing condoms while you're on this Sniffer thing, aren't you?"

"It's a thought."

She fell into a fit of giggles. "Were or human, male animals are all the same. They think with their dicks."

"Hey! I've wanted to seduce you for three years! I've controlled that urge because it was inappropriate. I didn't give in until you were right under my nose. You're damned right I'm focused on my cock."

"Fair enough." She glanced around. "Where's your computer? I don't remember seeing one when I . . . when I was here earlier."

"What you meant to say was you didn't see one when

you invaded my private space late this afternoon. Isn't that right?"

She finished the last of her ice cream and scraped the bowl with her spoon. "I felt justified."

"Want more ice cream?"

"No, thank you." She stood and walked into the kitchen with her bowl. "FYI, you have some broken dishes in the sink." She thought about why they were broken and sexual excitement curled within her.

"It was almost worth it."

She walked back into the living room. "Smart-ass. It's not my fault that you came to the party without a present."

"I don't need a present for that particular party, but you won't believe me." He set his ice cream bowl on an end table and walked over to the duffel bag that still sat in the entry. "Let's go on Sniffer and see what information we get on the subject."

"I just realized you haven't unpacked from your trip."

"I've been busy." Crouching down, he unzipped the duffel and pulled out a laptop. "I should thank you, by the way. Until you managed to coax the powers that be to lay cable up here, I was dead in the water when it came to going online. That was going to be a big problem for gathering supporters for WARM. You helped the cause."

"Oh, goody." She wasn't sure how she felt about his cause. It sounded elitist to her, but then, she wasn't a werewolf living in fear of discovery. She should remember that before passing judgment.

After crossing to his bookshelf and turning on a modem tucked in with the books, he sat on his sofa with the laptop. Soon he'd booted it up. "Come on over. I'll show you what Sniffer looks like."

Unable to resist, she sat on the sofa next to him. He was giving her entrée into a secret society, and that was the stuff of novels and movies. Unfortunately, she wouldn't be able to tell anyone about this, ever.

As Jake typed his log-in and password, she thought about how her parents would react if she tried to tell them about Jake and his underground community. She wouldn't, of course. She would keep this secret forever, and once Jake believed that, they could go about their separate lives.

But it was still interesting to imagine what sort of response she'd get from her folks. Her dad would think she'd gone stir-crazy up here in the woods. Her mother would want to believe, but she might eventually side with her husband and decide Rachel was imagining things again.

Realizing that she'd never convince her closest family members comforted her. A secret wasn't particularly fun to tell if nobody believed you and instead hustled you off for a psychiatric evaluation. Jake might be worried about exposure, but Rachel didn't think it was all that likely.

"So here we are. This is Sniffer." He pointed to a screen that closely resembled Twitter. "Let's see what I can dig up without alerting anyone as to why I'm asking."

"Because you have your reputation to protect?"

"Exactly." He typed in "Researching origins of condom-free Were sex. Was it always this way?" Then he hit the Send button and sat back.

"I see you're following Duncan MacDowell on Tw—I mean *Sniffer*."

"Have to. He's a lunatic and I have to keep track of what madness he'll suggest next." Jake seemed to relish the idea of going toe to toe with MacDowell.

Rachel took note that Jake, like many of the human males she'd known, enjoyed the challenge of a worthy opponent. Duncan seemed to fill the bill. His posts were funny and intelligent, just like his book. She'd like to meet him someday but doubted she ever would.

She watched in fascination as messages popped up on the screen accompanied by a little snuffling sound. Sniffer, indeed. Werewolves seemed to have a sense of humor. "Who's @Kate Stillman? Duncan references her a lot."

"His mate. She's being groomed to take over the alpha position in the Stillman pack, which is based in Denver. That's where the first annual conference was held last fall."

"A werewolf conference?"

"Yep."

"Denver was full of werewolves and nobody knew about it?"

Jake glanced at her. "We're very big on security. Kate organized the conference and did a great job. The sad part is she hooked up with MacDowell during that conference and changed her stripes. She used to be firmly aligned with us, the conservative contingent. Now that she's MacDowell's mate, she's more wishy-washy."

"Fascinating." Rachel could have been listening to a politician from a red state talking about a turncoat colleague, except, once again, Jake was discussing werewolves. "But how can Kate serve as the Denver pack alpha when her mate Duncan's from Scotland? I read his bio in the front of his book, and he lives in some place called Glenbarra."

"He's relocated to Denver, which doesn't please me. He's charismatic and he's liable to do more damage in person over here. I wish he'd stayed in Scotland."

"I see." As they sat huddled over the laptop, Rachel didn't miss the coziness of the setup. Jake's big warm body next to hers had a predictable effect. She scooted sideways but stayed close enough to read the messages.

"Afraid of me?" Jake didn't take his attention from the screen.

"You're too damned sexy for your own good, Hunter."

"Thank you." He swore under his breath. "Now Mac-Dowell's suggesting private nightclubs where humans and werewolves could meet. What a moron."

"If he's so big on mating with humans, why did he choose a werewolf, and a budding pack alpha, at that?"

"He didn't intend to, but he fell for her, and that was that." Jake typed something to @DuncanMacDowell on the subject of Were-human nightclubs. "Aha! There's a Sniff responding about condoms. And there's another one. Three more. Looks like a popular topic."

"Let me see." Rachel leaned closer as the computer erupted in a chorus of Sniffs directed to @JakeHunter.

Thank God Weres don't need those blasted things!

Another reason for Were-Were sex. No explanation needed.

Ready to give up on human chicks. They all insist on one. Yuck.

No offspring until I was mated. Great system, eh?

The Sniffs kept coming, piling on top of each other. Rachel finally stopped reading and leaned back against the plump cushions of Jake's sofa. It seemed that he was telling her the truth—werewolves didn't need condoms.

And why wouldn't it be true? She'd fallen down the rabbit hole and discovered an alternate universe where *anything* could be true. The world she'd thought she knew reasonably well was nothing like she'd imagined.

She'd just been introduced to a Were-only digital messaging system called Sniffer. Jake had casually mentioned that someone named Kate Stillman was being groomed to be the alpha for a pack in Denver. A blogger named Duncan wanted to set up private Were-human nightclubs.

And last, but certainly not least, she was sitting within a few inches of someone who looked like a man but could turn into a big black wolf. She should ask him more about the logistics and timing of that maneuver, too. If they were going to spend quality time together, and it looked as if that might be in the cards, she didn't want to wake up and find herself in bed with the big bad wolf.

"Convinced?"

She nodded. "Yes." Standing, she began her round of pacing. They had more to discuss, and she needed to put some space between them while they talked. Earlier she'd let herself be swept along on a tide of lust, but that was when she'd thought sex with Jake, as long as he stayed in human form, would be like sex with any man.

But if he had built-in birth control and some sort of natural shield against disease, what else was in store if they got friendly between the sheets? She needed full disclosure before she got naked again. Any smart woman would demand that, even from a hottie like Jake.

He turned off his laptop, shut the lid, and set it on the coffee table in front of him. "So if you're convinced that we can have sex without a condom, why are you pacing like a caged animal?"

"Because I'm finally beginning to understand how different you are, both inside and out, and I don't want any unpleasant surprises."

His smile was pure sin. "How about nice surprises? Are you okay with those? Because I have some moves that I think you'll—"

"Stop it, Jake. Don't flirt with me when I'm trying to get important information. It's distracting."

"God, I hope so. If not, I'd be worried that I'd lost my touch."

"Be serious! I want to know about this shifting thing."

His teasing expression vanished and his green gaze grew kind. "Okay, sorry. Ask me anything."

"Is shifting spontaneous or can you control it?"

"I can control it, but I had to learn how. We develop our shifting ability during puberty, and at first it's very spontaneous, which means we have a rougher adolescence than human kids."

"No kidding!"

"Each of us reacted differently, of course. For some the stress of a big test would bring on a shift. For me it was females, especially the beautiful ones." He winked at her. "I outgrew it. Just FYI so you're not insulted because I didn't spontaneously shift once I got you naked."

"That would have terrified me."

"Understandably so. But I'm not dangerous to you. I hope you believe that."

She nodded, although if he changed into a wolf right in front of her, she might still scream. "Did you go to a special school so no one would notice when you suddenly sprouted hair?"

"The pack usually homeschools young Weres for a couple of years until we get the hang of how to manage our shifts."

She became conscious of staring at him the way she might stare at an alien who'd stepped out of a spaceship. That was rude, and she glanced away. "Do you ever wish . . ." She paused, thinking even her question was rude. "Never mind."

"That I wasn't a werewolf?"

She met his gaze. "Do you?"

"Never."

"Why not? Wouldn't life be easier if you weren't?"

"Maybe in some ways, but it wouldn't be a good trade-off. You already know about our built-in birth control. Our immune system is far superior to a human's, and my sensory perception is wolflike, even in human form. I don't know if a guy with normal twenty-twenty eyesight would have seen that bear from across the lake. I used binoculars to make a positive ID, but I didn't really need them."

"Okay, what else?"

"Stamina."

"You mean like for running and stuff?" Sexual excitement curled low in her belly.

"Yeah. Running and . . . stuff." His eyes lit with amusement.

"You're flirting again."

"Just answering your question."

"And implying something about your staying power, I might add."

"You can interpret it any way you like." He leaned forward and pinned her with a look. "The truth is, I'm big and I'm strong, which isn't bragging on my part, because most Were males are. So the answer is no, I wouldn't trade places with a human male and give up the advantages I've inherited. I'm grateful to be Were."

Once again, she hesitated to ask something he might consider too personal.

"Rachel, I can see the questions in your eyes. I said you could ask me anything, and you can. I won't be offended."

"What's it like to shift?"

Leaning his forearms on his knees, he let his big hands dangle between them as he stared at the floor.

"See, I have offended you."

"Not at all." When he lifted his head, his eyes glowed. "I was trying to think how to explain it in a way that wouldn't sound too sappy. But it's like being reborn. My human body stretches and transforms into a powerful animal with more grace and presence than I will ever have looking like this."

Personally she had trouble imagining how anything could improve him. His broad shoulders stretched the cotton seams of his green shirt in a most impressive way, and his worn jeans lovingly hugged his taut thighs. He had the narrow hips of a well-conditioned athlete and the strong neck and square jaw of Superman. His black hair was so glossy it seemed almost blue in the light from the midnight sun coming through the window.

"So you like shifting, then?"

"Love it. What a rush. And then, if I can go for a run afterward and give those muscles a workout, there's nothing like it." He glanced at her with another half smile. "Almost nothing."

He sure did have the ability to make her juices flow. One look, one tiny smile, one suggestive remark, and her motor revved. But all this discussion of his prowess put her somewhat in awe of him.

She wanted him more than ever, but he was used to having sex with Weres. They'd possess all the characteristics he did and would probably be a better match.

They'd be able to keep up, whereas she hadn't even done well in gym class.

Facing him, she cleared her throat. "Maybe I should tell you a little bit about me."

"I'd love that."

"In school I had a reputation for being nerdy and quiet. I wasn't into sports because, frankly, I'm not that coordinated. I spent most of my time either reading or roaming around outside looking for interesting animals to draw. Once I was old enough to learn carving from Grandpa Ike, I'd lose myself in that."

Jake nodded. "It's your gift."

"All that is to say that I'm not a great physical specimen. I'm probably not up to your—"

"Hold it right there. Apparently you weren't listening when I said that ever since I saw you in Ted's store, I've wanted you with the heat of a thousand suns."

"Yes, but—"

"But nothing." He stood, all six foot and several inches of him. "In the three years I've been dreaming about you, I've tried my damnedest to get interested in Were females. I even took one of them to bed. She was magnificent—athletic, coordinated, tireless."

"That's what I'm saying! I'm none of those things!"

He came around the coffee table and walked toward her. "Maybe not, but you're Rachel, the most talented, beautiful creature I've ever met. Knowing we have no future tears me up inside. But that doesn't stop me from wanting you in every way I can think of having you."

Her heart beat so fast she thought she might pass out.

He stood inches away but didn't touch her. "I want my mouth on every inch of your skin. I want my tongue dipping into all your secret nooks and crannies."

She gulped for air.

"I want my cock in your mouth and sliding between your breasts, but mostly I want to sink it deep inside that hot, juicy channel that leads to your womb. And then I want to stroke you until you're wild with pleasure and begging for release. Then I'll watch the fire in your eyes as you come."

She gazed up at him, mute and trembling, her pulse hammering like bongos.

"So you see, Rachel . . ." He reached out and traced a finger across her quivering lower lip. "You don't have to be anything more than you already are to be everything I've always wanted." He took a deep breath. "Now, will you please come into the bedroom?"

With a supreme effort, she forced her vocal cords to deliver the only response any sane woman could possibly have to an invitation like that. "Hell, yes."

Chapter 13

Jake had never waited so long or worked so hard to seduce a female. But to be fair, he'd spent three years focused on *not* seducing her. To realize she was here and willing, to understand that he only had to grasp her hand and lead her into his bedroom in order to have all that he'd ever wanted from her, was surreal.

Because he didn't expect to have another night like this, he decided he'd be wise to weave in all the fantasies that had swirled through his fevered brain for three years. That meant beginning differently from the way he'd approached her in the kitchen. Then he'd been so overwhelmed by the prospect of having her, so intoxicated by the scent and feel of her, that he'd rushed it.

"I have a favor to ask." His voice, rasping in the stillness of the bedroom, revealed his burning lust and just how tightly it was leashed. Squeezing her hand, he let go and stepped back.

"What?" Her reply was breathy with anticipation.

"When I was in your bedroom after being wounded, I crawled under your bed."

"And I wondered why."

"The razor. I couldn't let you shave me. I had a forest run with other werewolves scheduled in San Francisco, and I didn't want to explain to them why I was shaved."

Laughter danced in her eyes. "Oh."

"But when I was under the bed, I couldn't watch you undress."

"Is that the request? To watch me take my clothes off?"

He nodded.

"Such a simple thing." Backing away a little more, she nudged off her shoes.

"Not to me. I've imagined you here stripping down because you can hardly wait to show me what I so desperately want to see."

"But I'm just an ordinary—"

"Shh. You're a goddess. Your skin is like satin. I know that now because I've touched you, but somehow I've always known."

She'd taken hold of her T-shirt hem, but she paused. "I need to do this right." Releasing her hold on the shirt, she reached behind her back and slid both hands under the shirt to unhook her bra.

Once it was free, she whipped off both her bra and the shirt in one dramatic motion. He caught his breath. In the kitchen, he'd been too intent on caressing her to really look. Now he did.

She was lush, ripe, tantalizing almost beyond his ability to control himself. Saliva pooled in his mouth as he imagined swirling his tongue over each of her raspberry-tipped breasts. He would take his time, cup them in his palms, and savor the pebbled texture while she moaned with pleasure.

But she was not content merely to present her treasures for his viewing. No, she had sweet torture in mind.

Sliding her hands up her rib cage, she cradled her bounty, lifting and massaging her breasts for several long seconds.

She couldn't know that her massage intensified the sweet aroma of her skin, a powerful trigger for a creature with a heightened sense of smell. Her preference for almond lotion and soap had always drawn him, but now he breathed in her essence, that pheromone-laden scent that was unique to her and the most compelling aphrodisiac he'd encountered in any female, ever.

His cock swelled in response. He clenched his hands, determined not to grab her like some savage. But with each breath, a red haze of lust threatened to overwhelm his control. When she squeezed her nipples between her thumbs and forefingers, he nearly came. The effort not to made him groan.

Her eyes lit with mischief. "Am I creating the fantasy you had in mind, Jake?"

"Mm-hm." Coherent speech had deserted him. He hadn't counted on her vivid imagination, but he should have after admiring her carving wizardry all these years. She might not have his physical stamina, but she was miles ahead of him in the fantasy department.

"I'm glad I'm pleasing you." Slowly moving her hands down her torso, she reached for the fastening on her jeans. She held his gaze as she undid the metal button and inched the zipper down.

He expected her to wiggle out of the jeans once they were loose enough to slide over her hips. And then . . . then she would be his, every sweet-smelling inch of her. His nostrils flared.

But instead she slipped one hand under the elastic of her panties and eased it down, down, until . . . dear God, she was pleasuring herself.

Earthy and primitive, the scent of her arousal was more than he could take. He held his breath to block it. But he had to breathe, and when he did, his heart kicked into overdrive and the crotch of his jeans felt like a vise squeezing his privates.

She moved her hand faster and with obvious intent as her lips parted and her breathing quickened. Her nipples puckered in response to her impending climax.

"Don't come." He gulped for air and fought the animal instincts that urged him to take her *now*.

Her question came out as a short gasp. "Why . . . not?"

"Because . . ." Wrenching his zipper down, he closed the gap between them and pulled her hand from her panties. *Because I'll pass out or go insane if I have to wait another second.* Pushing her jeans to the floor, he lifted one of her legs from the confining denim.

That was all he needed, one leg free. He backed her against the nearest wall, not even caring which one, knowing only that he needed a surface that wouldn't give way as he drove into her. At last he could breathe, because at last he could satisfy the pounding need she'd unwittingly escalated beyond all endurance.

The rich scent of her was a banquet and he was taking his seat at the table. Grasping her sleek bottom in both hands, he lifted her and propped her against the wall.

"I'm not athletic," she said breathlessly.

"That's okay. I am." He found her pulsing wet center and surged forward. As he buried his aching cock up to the hilt, he cried out in triumph. Nothing had ever felt this good. Nothing.

She might not be athletic, but she obviously understood the basics of this position. She wrapped her legs around his waist and clutched his shoulders as he began to move. He could have supported her without that extra help, but he was willing to accept it because it allowed him to relax and enjoy the ride.

And that meant relishing her response when she came, and if he was very lucky, when she came a second time. Once they were both steady, he looked into her eyes. "How's that?"

For an answer she tightened her pelvic muscles and squeezed his very happy cock. "How's that?"

He closed his eyes for a few seconds while he fought against coming immediately. "Dynamite. Keep that up and this will be over in a jiffy."

Her low chuckle was the sexiest laugh he'd ever heard. "What about your famous stamina, big boy?"

When he opened his eyes, she was smiling at him. "You sabotaged it, you sexy woman."

"I wanted to fulfill your fantasy."

"You did. And then some." Later he might tell her how far she'd pushed him without even knowing it. He eased back and slid home again. "What about your fantasy?"

"This . . ." She gasped as he pulled away and pushed in tight. "This handles it."

"Too bad." He began to pump faster. "I was hoping you'd want another round."

"I might. Mm. I just might. You're very convincing, Jake."

He stroked faster as the smell of good sex whirled around them. "I like it when you say my name."

"I like your name." She whimpered and arched her back, allowing him deeper access.

"Say it again."

"Jake." She murmured it at first. Then his name became a chant, then a wild cry as she came, her spasms gripping his penis, massaging it relentlessly, coaxing him to pour himself into her.

With a groan of surrender, he did. With one more deep thrust, he erupted. His seed spilled out in a rush of such pleasure that he was left gasping her name.

Rachel. Rachel. Rachel.

As long as he lived, he would remember this moment. And this woman. This very human woman.

Rachel discovered she liked being with a physically fit male creature who could carry her around. After experiencing the most shattering climax of her life, she didn't have the strength to stand, let alone walk over to the bed. Jake carried her there. Problem solved.

He even managed to slide the covers out from under her limp body so that she was lying on the soft bottom sheet. Jake obviously favored a high thread count. She did, too, but his concept of luxury bedding was even more evolved than hers. She liked that in a man ... er ... werewolf.

In her postorgasmic haze, she wasn't particularly concerned about Jake's alternate persona. He was behaving like a strong and very solicitous lover, which certainly worked, no matter what he became in his spare time. He finished undressing her so that every inch of her could appreciate the softness of his sheets, which were pale green and had a masculine scent that reminded her of sage.

The room dimmed as he closed curtains or blinds or both. She didn't look to find out. She was still riding the smooth wave of the climax he'd given her and wasn't interested in the details of anything other than this huge, incredible bed ... and huge, incredible Jake.

When he climbed in beside her, the mattress didn't shift much at all. A firm, strong bed with luscious sheets turned out to be a seductive combination. Slowly Jake began stroking her with his big hands. Her eyes still closed, she stretched like a cat under his lazy caress.

"It's late," he murmured. "I should probably let you sleep." But as he outlined each curve with the tips of his fingers, he didn't seem inclined to do that.

Opening her eyes, she discovered that he was following the tracing motion of his hands with his gaze, almost as if he was finger-painting a pattern on her skin and wanted to get it right. She'd never had anyone focus so intently on her body.

She wondered why she wasn't self-conscious under his close scrutiny and decided his attitude had everything to do with it. She was willing to lie there and let him explore because his appreciation made her feel beautiful, cherished, and sensual. A girl could get used to that.

She wouldn't let herself, though. He'd suspended his moral code on an extremely temporary basis. This blindingly erotic encounter would be brief and all the sweeter for that, probably.

As he continued mapping her body, he trailed his fingers down her thigh to her calf, which was as far as he could reach without changing position. Pausing, he lifted his head to look into her eyes. "Do you want to sleep?"

"No." Reaching for him, she cupped his cheek and felt the slight bristle of his beard. "I can always sleep, but I won't always have a chance to lie in this bed with you."

Regret flashed in his eyes. "No, you won't. That's why I'm memorizing you."

She brushed her thumb over his jaw. "Am I different from your Were lovers?" She understood that her novelty might be part of his fascination, but that was okay. If he allowed himself to have only one human sexual partner, she was happy to be his choice. "I mean, of course

I'm different. I can't become a wolf. But if you compare me with a female werewolf in human form, am I any different?"

"Yes," he said without hesitation.

That surprised her. "How?"

"The biggest difference is your scent." Capturing her hand, he turned his head so he could kiss her palm.

"Werewolves don't like almond?"

He tickled her palm with his tongue. "This werewolf loves it. The smell of almonds will always remind me of you. It gets me hot. But that's not what I meant."

"Then do explain, Professor Wolf."

"Okay." Releasing her hand, he swung one leg over her hips and was soon braced above her on his forearms and knees. "But I can talk and kiss you at the same time."

"Really? Now you're a ventriloquist, too?"

"I meant I'd be butterfly kissing your body, not French-kissing your mouth." Leaning forward, he started with her forehead. "Like this." His lips brushed lightly over her brow.

"Nice."

"And this." He touched his lips to the end of her nose. "But I'm skipping that sexy mouth. You kiss like a porn star."

She wasn't sure whether to be insulted or not. "How do you know? Have you kissed one?"

He laughed. "No. Just watched the video." He nuzzled her throat. "They give it their all, and so do you. If I let myself get involved with your mouth, I'll never finish paying attention to the rest of you."

"I'll take that as a compliment, then."

"I meant it to be." He moved slowly across her shoulder and down her left arm, dropping kisses along the way.

It seemed innocent at first, but as her skin began to tingle, she realized how potent this seemingly low-impact caress could be. He was seducing her a millimeter at a time.

"The thing about werewolves," he said as he moved to her other shoulder to give it the same treatment, "is that of the five senses, smell is our most acute. If a Were in human form walked into a room, you would never know. But I would by the scent." His warm breath touched the places he'd moistened with his lips.

"Oh." Now she was tingling and deliciously shivery, too. "Do males and females smell different?"

"Yes, but not a lot different." He kissed the tips of her fingers and paused. "Plus each individual varies in scent. Humans, on the other hand, smell altogether different from Weres. And they have as many individual variations as werewolves do."

When he paused, she expected him to move back up her body to her collarbone and work down from there. But instead he slipped to the end of the bed and began kissing her toes. "That tickles."

"Then I'd better hold you still so you don't kick me in the face." He grasped both ankles as he took his time placing his mouth on her toes, her heels, and the arch of each foot. She'd never realized the arch of her foot was an erogenous zone. Judging from the zing of sensation between her thighs, the arch of her foot was prime sensual real estate.

"In other words," he continued, "I have a very sensitive nose, and I know what I like. The almond scent is a nice touch, but your own special aroma, the one you don't even realize you have, drives me crazy." He began his journey from her ankles up her calf toward her knee.

Her breathing grew shallow. "Speaking of driving

someone crazy, you're having quite an effect with those little kisses, Jake."

"I can tell." He kissed the back of her knee and took a deep breath. "You smell more delicious by the second."

"Are you going to eat me up?"

He laughed. "How did you guess?"

She knew what he meant and wasn't frightened in the least. As he kissed his way along her inner thigh, his destination obvious, she trembled with anticipation. Chances were he'd be very good at what he was about to do. She was in for a treat.

Apparently, so was he. Until now she'd been kidding herself that he was no different from any guy she'd had sex with. Sure, he had a few more muscles and could carry her to bed without breaking a sweat, but that only meant he was in great shape, not that he was different.

Ah, but he was different. His senses were sharper than any human's. Every physical experience he had would be enhanced as a result. It stood to reason that his sensual appetites would be highly developed to match his greater capacity for enjoyment.

Now she recognized him for what he was, a creature not of her kind. She felt it in the grip of his strong hands as he steadied her for his purposeful assault. She heard it in the rasp of his breathing, saw it in the fierce joy lighting his eyes before he dipped his head to take what he wanted.

She surrendered to pleasure that whispered of primitive cravings and untamed desire. At last she understood that with every moment in his embrace, she'd slip farther from the civilized world and deeper into the wild place that Jake called home. Although he appeared to be a man, beneath his muscled chest beat the heart of a wolf.

Chapter 14

Jake knew the exact moment when Rachel fully realized who and what he was. He saw it in her silver eyes right before he captured her in that most intimate of kisses. If he'd seen fear in her gaze, he would have released her.

But instead of fear, he saw excitement. She knew him as a werewolf, and she wanted him anyway. No, that was wrong. She didn't want him in spite of his shape-shifting nature, but because of it. His wildness spoke to something wild in her, and she welcomed it, and him.

Her complete acceptance was more than he'd ever hoped for, and it meant he could give her so much more. He could call to that primitive part of her that longed to loosen the polite bonds of society. He could teach her to grasp the power of raw hunger instead. And he could start now.

Gone were the butterfly kisses. He thrust deep with his tongue, invading her most private spaces without giving her time to think or even to breathe. He applied relentless suction and she came in a heartbeat, arching off the bed and pressing herself against his mouth. Her panting cries filled the room.

He went deeper, pushed her harder, and she writhed on the bed in ecstasy. When she came again, she swore so colorfully, he laughed. The vibration of his laughter sent her spinning out of control again as she moaned and thrashed in his grip. He loved turning her inside out.

He bore down again as she gasped and begged for mercy. But he knew her now. She didn't want mercy. She wanted one more climax, the kind that would leave her half-crazed with the majesty and wonder of it, the kind that stripped her down to the basics of what it meant to be a sexual animal.

Her skin was slippery with sweat and her breathing was no longer ladylike and prim. She dragged in air through her mouth and uttered cries that had no resemblance to speech. But they spoke to him.

Joy exploded within him at her willingness to shoot past the barriers and follow him to this place of uninhibited ecstasy. With a sound wrenched from the depths of her being, a sound more growl than groan, she surged over the precipice in one final, glorious orgasm.

Slowly he lowered her hips to the bed, but he stayed with her, savoring her juices, calming her with slow swipes of his tongue. She quivered as the aftershocks rippled through her body, and then she lay still. The room was quiet again except for the gentle sound of their breathing.

Jake matched the rhythm of his breath to hers and relished the sound of that. His cock, thick and hot, reminded him that she'd had multiple orgasms but he had not. He would wait. When he took her again, he wanted her eagerness. Even Rachel, as sensual as she had proven to be, wouldn't be eager for him now.

He smiled as he replayed her unbridled response to his lovemaking. Because they had no future, he shouldn't

"You're what?" She leaned forward, as if that would encourage him to finish the sentence.

But he couldn't finish it. Exhaustion and booze claimed him. He fell asleep with the delicious sensation of her hand moving over his fur.

Rachel sat beside Jake for a long time. Normally she would have bandaged a wound like this, but she'd promised not to shave him, and besides, she wasn't sure what would happen if he woke up and wanted to shift. Could cause major problems. So she held the pressure bandage in place.

Eventually the bleeding stopped and she set the bandage aside, although she continued to stroke his fur. It felt so incredibly soft under her fingertips, and she doubted he would have allowed her to pet him under normal circumstances. He would bristle at the idea of being treated like a dog. But now he was injured, drunk, and fast asleep.

The last time he'd been in her bedroom, which seemed like years ago, she'd thought he was a semitame wolf. That still wasn't a bad description of Jake—part man, part wolf, all male. In a few short hours of fabulous lovemaking, he'd ruined her for anyone else.

Nice job, Jake. Well, it wasn't over till it was over. She hadn't given up on her campaign to change his rigid beliefs. But if that proved impossible, she was pretty sure she'd be losing the love of her life. Unless he could see that, though, they were both doomed to settle for second best. What a shame.

As her own weariness made her yawn, she decided to grab a pillow and blanket so she could sleep on the floor next to her patient. That way she could be aware if he moved. Moving could make the bleeding start again.

First she tidied up the area and carried everything except some extra gauze pads into the bathroom. Then she changed into a tank top and pj bottoms so she'd be more comfortable. Jake didn't stir. She wasn't surprised. She hadn't slept much the night before and he hadn't slept more than an hour or two at most.

Now that she was up, she felt hungry. Worry over Jake had stolen her appetite earlier, but now she wanted . . . a candy bar. Perfect. Maybe two candy bars. Lionel would have a fit if he knew. Not only was she harboring the wolf, but she was compounding her foolishness by snacking on sugar.

She walked around lowering all the blinds in the house while she ate the first candy bar. No sense in giving anyone, especially Lionel, a peek into what was going on in her little cabin in the middle of the afternoon. He probably wouldn't bother her, though, because he thought she was having a hot love affair.

He'd blushed when she'd mentioned wanting to catch up on her sleep today. Then he'd asked if Jake would be by later, and she'd said he might. Sure enough, he had come by and was currently in her bedroom recovering from the bullet Lionel had pumped into him.

The poor kid had thought he was saving her life, and she couldn't blame him for that. But she couldn't let him see the wolf again under any circumstances. As far as Lionel would ever know, that wolf had lit out for the tundra.

Lionel obviously didn't like Jake, the man, either. He believed Jake had been careless in his guardianship of the wolf, which meant he wasn't the guy for Rachel. Lionel hadn't looked happy to hear that Jake might spend the night at her house. But at least the prospect of that would keep Lionel away until morning.

As she folded a blanket and laid it next to Jake, she leaned down to inspect his wound. Still looked okay. He whined in his sleep and his legs twitched, but that didn't cause him to bleed, so maybe he'd be fine until he recovered from his drinking binge and could shift.

Plopping the pillow down, she stretched out on her back and unwrapped the second candy bar. As she ate it and listened to Jake breathe, she felt calm for the first time since the awful moment when Lionel had found them on the trail.

She was gradually becoming used to the idea that her lover was sometimes a big black wolf. Then again, he might not be her lover anymore. Maybe by trying to convince him that they should consider mating, she'd made him too wary of her. He needed her now, but once he healed, he had no reason to stay. Well, except the biggest reason of all—they belonged together.

He wouldn't have to stick around to monitor her behavior and make sure she didn't leak werewolf info. After this incident, he couldn't doubt her trustworthiness. And his days of running through the woods of Polecat were over. Everything pointed to Jake Hunter selling his cabin and moving somewhere else. Where would that leave her?

She had no answer for that, but at least Jake was okay. That was the main thing. As she drifted off to sleep, she thought about all the Wild Turkey he'd lapped up and wondered if werewolves had hangovers.

Sometime later, she got her answer when he began to groan and whimper as if he would die any minute. She leaped up and crouched next to him, her heart pounding. "Is it your shoulder?"

No, it's my head! Evil gnomes with hammers and chisels are excavating my skull!

She pressed her lips together so she wouldn't laugh. He wouldn't appreciate that. "You have a hangover, Jake."

This is no hangover. I've had hangovers, and this is way worse. My brain is bleeding.

"Wild Turkey packs a punch. Maybe if you tried to shift, you'd feel—"

What if I shift and my head explodes? What about that?

"It won't."

How do you know? When was the last time you shifted?

"Never, but I recognize the symptoms of a hangover, even in a werewolf. I thought shifting might help."

Can't shift. The top of my head would come off.

She gave up arguing the point. "Do you want to try and swallow some ibuprofen?"

I guess. Rachel, my head really hurts. I mean really, really.

"I'm sure it does." She kept her smile to herself, but he was pretty funny. Her big bad wolf, who'd fought a bear and survived being shot, had been brought low by a bottle of Wild Turkey. "I'll get you some ibuprofen and an ice pack for your head. Don't thrash around while I'm gone or you'll start bleeding again."

Okay.

In the kitchen cupboard she searched around and finally found what she was looking for. Grandpa Ike had loved his Wild Turkey, and on some mornings he'd needed an ice pack. He had the old-fashioned kind—a soft-sided bag that unscrewed from the top.

She filled it with ice, ran a bowl full of water, and carried both into her bathroom, where she picked up the bottle of ibuprofen. Armed with her hangover remedies, she returned to kneel beside Jake, who continued to moan.

"I need you to lift your head so I can put the pills into the back of your mouth."

Don't want to.

"Come on. You'll feel better once you get these down."

With another anguished groan, he lifted his broad head and opened his mouth. She set two pills on the back of his tongue. "Now swallow. I have water here to help wash them down."

He closed his jaws and gave her a baleful glare. *Those damned gnomes are trying to kill me.*

"I know. Swallow."

His eyes closed and his throat moved.

"Good. Now drink a little water."

Moving very slowly, he lowered his head to the bowl and took a couple of laps. *That's plenty.* He sank back onto the quilt.

"Now hold still. Let me position the ice pack." She settled it between his ears. "How's that?"

He sighed. *A little better.*

"Good." She picked up the bowl of water and left quickly, afraid she'd start laughing any minute.

Oh, for a camera, although he'd be horrified if she tried to take his picture. She'd never be able to show the picture to anyone, though.

Maybe she didn't need a camera, after all. As she'd told Lionel, she had a good memory. The image of her scary werewolf lying on her flowered quilt with Grandpa Ike's old-fashioned ice pack on his head would stay with her forever.

Chapter 18

When Jake woke the next time, the evil gnomes had put away their hammers and chisels. Something soft and squishy rested against his forehead, and when he tilted his head back, it sagged down into his eyes, covering them. He smelled water inside.

Oh, yeah. Rachel had fixed him up with an ice pack. He'd caught a glimpse of it before she'd laid it on his head. He'd seen that kind in cartoons, but never in real life. He'd probably looked like a cartoon wearing the silly thing.

But it had worked like a charm, and so had the ibuprofen. He felt a hundred percent better. *Thank you, Rachel.*

No response. Yet she had to be close by. The air was filled with her scent.

Nudging the ice pack away from his eyes, he lifted his head to see where she was. Ah, right there beside him, sound asleep and clutching a candy wrapper. He was touched that she'd made a bed on the floor so that she could be close in case he needed her.

She lay curled on her side facing him, strands of her

rich brown hair lying across her cheek. She had a smudge of dark chocolate there, too. If he were a man, he could lean over and swipe it clean with his tongue.

Sure, he could do it as a wolf, too, but it wouldn't be the same. It couldn't lead to other activities. Gazing at her in the skimpy tank top and cotton pj bottoms, he was motivated to change his designation and change it fast.

Speeding the healing process was a very good reason for that, but he could think of another one. Making love to her again wouldn't be particularly smart, though. The smart thing would be to wake her up and ask her to pick up some clothes from his house. He could shift while she was gone.

Yep, that's exactly what he should do. Time to start wrapping up this project. She wasn't going to blow the whistle on him and the Were community. It wasn't in her nature, and as she'd said, no one would believe her, anyway. So he had no excuse for hanging around.

What a depressing line of thought. But it made perfect sense, and he was supposed to be an intelligent being. He'd stayed long enough to neutralize her shocking discovery about him. He could go now.

On the other hand, how would it look if he left abruptly? After all she'd done for him, wouldn't that be rude? He certainly didn't want to leave her with the impression that he was an ungrateful jerk who accepted her kindness and then took off.

So he couldn't go yet. He should ease into it. He liked that reasoning so much better. He could shift now and . . . see what developed. Maybe he could show his gratitude in a way that would make them both happy.

But first he had to shift. After the way she'd reacted to it out on the trail, he didn't want to risk having her wake up in the middle of the action. Leaving the room wasn't a good option, either. The less he moved his shoulder before he shifted, the less likely he'd make it bleed.

He needed to wake her up. So maybe he would give her cheek a little lick, after all. By stretching his neck, he could just reach her with his tongue.

She woke up with a gasp. "Jake! You scared me. Are you okay? You look better."

I'm lots better. You cured my hangover.

"I'm glad." She pushed herself up on one elbow. "I should check your shoulder."

It'll be fine. I'm ready to shift, but I . . . I wanted to warn you before I did.

She looked into his eyes. "Thank you."

You can leave the room if you want.

"I want to stay right here." Her gaze didn't waver from his.

You're sure?

"Yes."

Then here goes. Lying back on the quilt, he closed his eyes and willed his shift. It would take longer than usual because he was weakened by the bullet wound, but once he'd accomplished it, he'd regain most of that strength.

For the second time in his life, he was shifting in front of a human. He'd never expected to do it once. This morning he'd been desperate to shock her, and she'd admitted to being freaked-out.

She was obviously still unnerved by the process. He could feel her nervous energy, and it distracted him. But he had to admire her courage. She could have left the room and she'd chosen not to.

Taking a deep breath, he blocked his awareness of her as best he could and concentrated on his transformation. He'd shifted hundreds of times, maybe even thousands, and he was good at it. Adverse conditions no longer affected him. He could shift anywhere, anytime.

Except now. Opening his eyes, he gazed at her.

"Jake? Is something wrong?"

I can't do it.

"You can't shift? You mean your shifter is broken?"

Not permanently, I hope. I think . . . it's you.

"Me? But you did it in front of me this morning."

I was in a different mood then. I was trying to prove something. Now I'm not.

Her silver eyes grew troubled. "Then I guess you want me to leave the room, huh?"

She sounded so disappointed that he didn't have the heart to send her away. It would be like denying her fireworks on the Fourth of July. *No, please stay.*

"But I'm making you choke. You're having shiftus interruptus."

You make it sound like erectile dysfunction.

"It sort of is, right?"

I beg your pardon. I don't have those problems.

"Then why aren't you shifting?"

He thought about that. Maybe, although it was counterintuitive, he needed her to be even closer to him so that he didn't think of her as *other*. He decided to give that a whirl.

I want you to touch me while I shift.

"Touch you? Won't that make it worse?"

Maybe not. Put your hand on me. Let's see what happens.

She scooted closer and rested her hand on his paw. "How's that?"

Good. If it works, I'll end up holding your hand. Now help me concentrate.

"Want me to close my eyes, too?"

That would miss the point of you being able to watch, wouldn't it?

"Oh, yeah. Guess so."

Okay, here we go again. He closed his eyes. Instead of trying to block Rachel, he focused on the connection— her hand resting on his paw. He drew on that connection and felt a surge of energy rush through his body.

She gasped but didn't move her hand. Her touch was light, allowing the shift to happen under her fingertips, but he felt something resembling an electrical charge pulsing at that point of contact. Muscle and bone responded with a speed and grace he'd never felt before. His heart ached with the beauty of it and the joy of sharing this moment with her.

And then it was over. Dazed and breathing hard, he lay on the quilt. Her fingers rested on the back of his hand instead of the back of his paw. Without opening his eyes, he turned his hand over and laced his fingers through hers.

She squeezed his hand.

He started to say something and realized emotion clogged his throat, preventing him from talking. The past two minutes had been the most emotionally moving of his entire life.

"Are you okay?" she asked softly.

He nodded, still struggling with the enormity of his feelings. He might have seriously miscalculated. He'd meant to solve a simple problem of shifting blockage. But he'd created an even bigger problem.

Less than twenty minutes ago he'd been calculating how soon he could leave her. But during this shift, he'd forged a bond so strong he couldn't imagine ever doing that. And he would have to.

"Jake, you're worrying me. Is your shoulder bothering

you? It looks really good from here, but if you have a lot of pain, then—"

He opened his eyes and gazed at her. "I'm fine." He cleared his throat. "But that was the most intense shift I've ever had."

"You were glowing pretty bright. There was heat, too."

Still holding her hand, he rolled to his side to face her. "I'll bet."

"Why do you think it was so intense?"

"You were touching me. Your energy shot through my system and I felt supercharged." He held up their clasped hands. "I can still feel the tingle."

"So can I. I thought it might just be me, though."

"No, it's both of us." As he gazed at her, the energy coursing between them took a sensual turn.

Although only their hands touched, her pupils darkened as if he'd begun stroking her breasts and thighs. Her lips parted and her breathing changed tempo. Her throat moved in a slow swallow, and beneath her thin tank top, her nipples thrust against the material.

His body responded immediately. His balls tightened and his cock grew hard. "Lie with me, Rachel."

She moistened her lips in an unconsciously provocative gesture. "I will." Her voice was low and sultry. "But first, I'm going to touch you. I'm going to worship this body that just appeared before my eyes. You're such a mystery to me, Jake. I want to know you."

He inhaled sharply, from both excitement and a dash of apprehension. He wanted her touch, wanted it desperately. Perhaps too desperately. He couldn't shake the feeling that they were crossing some sort of line, one that he hadn't meant to cross at all.

But no red-blooded male could resist the promise in

Rachel's silvery eyes as she gently slipped her fingers free and rose to her knees. In an instant she'd disposed of her tank top. Then she slid out of her pj bottoms.

"Lie back," she murmured.

Holding her gaze, he did as he was told, his heart hammering as she crawled onto his makeshift bed. Her eyes smoldered with repressed heat. Straddling him, she started with his mouth.

Her kiss held nothing back. She plundered his mouth with her tongue and nipped his lower lip with her teeth. Last night he'd stripped away her civilized veneer, and now that wild creature was back, ready to do the same to him.

He was used to being in control, but she didn't seem inclined to allow that. When he reached for her, she grasped his hands and pinned them beside his head. He started to resist, and she lifted her mouth from his and tightened her hold.

"I know you could overpower me easily. But let me be in charge, werewolf." Leaning down, she brushed her taut nipples over his chest.

His breath hissed out as he fought the urge to grab her and drive his rigid penis into her waiting warmth. He knew she was ready for him. His sense of smell told him all he needed to know.

But she'd made a request. Although it scrambled his brain to turn over control, especially to a human female, he would do it because she deserved that. She'd proven herself strong and true. If she wanted to be in charge, she would be.

As if sensing his complete surrender, she laughed softly. "Good. Now we'll have some fun."

With that, she proceeded to turn him inside out. Using her lips, her tongue, her teeth, her fingers, and her breasts, she caressed him without mercy. She turned him into a seething mass of frustration, and all because she carefully avoided touching his aching cock and throbbing balls.

Her laughing eyes found his. "How are we doing, werewolf?"

He growled. He wasn't proud of making that sort of primitive sound, but it fit his mood perfectly. Only one part of his body remained untouched, and he wanted her mouth there. Now. Or five minutes ago would have been even better.

"Ah, you seem a little upset. Maybe I can do something about that." She placed her lips where he'd been longing to have them and gave him a sweet kiss right on the tip.

He groaned.

"More?"

"Rachel, so help me . . ."

"I want to help you, Jake. Is this what you had in mind?" She ran her tongue from base to tip. And stopped.

He gasped. "You're making me crazy."

"That's my goal."

"Do you want me to beg?"

"Sure."

He gulped for air. "Rachel, please take my cock into your sweet mouth. Please."

"Be glad to." And she did, while fondling his family jewels at the same time. Her attentions were so thorough that he almost came. Twice.

"That's . . . enough." He sucked air into his tortured lungs. "I'm right on the edge."

"Me, too." With one last swipe of her tongue she released him. "And I want this, too." Straddling his hips, she took what he offered and moaned softly as she slid downward.

The sensation was so great he simply reveled in it for several long seconds.

She leaned forward and brushed her lips over his. "You good?"

"More than good," he mumbled.

"I'm going to move."

"Please do."

"You can join in if you want now."

He hesitated. This was her show, after all. "You're sure?"

"Absolutely." She began a rhythmic motion with her hips. "Participation is welcome."

That was all he needed. Bracketing her hips with both hands, he synchronized his movements to hers. Beautiful. The pressure mounted within him, but it was a sweet pressure. A welcome pressure. He'd tried to hold it back for too long.

But now he felt her reaching for her climax, and at last he could let go. With a cry of triumph, she took him deeper and found her nirvana. He followed her over the edge as he drove upward and abandoned himself to the wonder of loving Rachel.

Afterward, she slumped against him, her breath labored and her skin slick. Wrapping his arms around her, he eased her down, coaxing her to relax and let him support her. He felt her go boneless with contentment.

He should probably be worried about the close bond developing between them. But when he was filled with joy and satisfaction, he had a tough time being worried about anything. Maybe someday he'd regret his openness with Rachel. But this wasn't that day.

They lay there together for a long time, and he was

content to let her choose the moment they would move. Her body was warm and comforting against his, and he could have stayed that way without complaint for hours.

Eventually, though, she stirred and propped herself on her elbows to gaze at him. "I like being in charge."

He chuckled. "I noticed."

"No, really. I understand that you're probably an alpha male who expects to be in command of the situation, but I congratulate you on holding back."

"Alpha male? Where did you come up with that term?"

She smiled and traced the line of his jaw with one finger. "I had some time on my hands while I was pacing the floor worrying about you, so I got on the computer and researched wolves."

"I'm not a—"

She laid a finger over his mouth. "I know you're not a wolf, but you have packs the way wolves do, and surely there are some similarities."

"Yes, there are."

"You mentioned that Duncan MacDowell's mate is in line to be the alpha of her pack."

"She is." He found her interest flattering. "But what makes you think I'm an alpha? I'm not in command of any pack."

"That's true." She cupped his face in one hand and gazed at him. "But I have the distinct feeling you would like that, Jake Hunter. You're a born leader. You'd be very good as a pack alpha."

"It's a nice compliment, but I'm not going to challenge my pack alpha, a Were named Keegan, who happens to be doing a great job."

"You have a pack?"

"Sure. All werewolves do. I belong to the Hunter pack based in Idaho."

She looked puzzled. "That's not very close. Do you ever see them?"

"Sometimes." He shrugged. "I've always felt more like a Wallace, I guess, although the Wallace pack doesn't exist anymore in Alaska. The Were community maintains the Wallace museum near Sitka, but that's about all that's left. Anyway, I like it here. It feels right to me."

"Hmm."

"What?"

She propped her chin on her fist. "I'm sure I'm not telling you something you don't already know, but sometimes, in the wolf world, a young alpha goes off and starts his own pack."

"Yeah, so?"

"Why not do that, Jake?"

It was a stunning concept. As much as he enjoyed his independence, he'd thought about the advantages of having his own pack nearby. He'd wondered if his mate, whoever she turned out to be, would go along with staying here, even though his pack was in Idaho.

"It's a good idea, isn't it, Jake?"

"I don't know. I'm still thinking about it." A pack of his own. The beginning of a dynasty. Yeah, he liked it. She was right about him. He was an alpha, which might be one reason he'd organized WARM.

But WARM was not a pack. It was a social movement. Rachel was suggesting a true wolf pack, of which he would be the alpha. He couldn't create a pack without a mate, however.

He gazed into her silver eyes and knew exactly what she was thinking. But it violated every belief he held. She might have come up with a life-changing idea, but that didn't mean she should be a part of it.

Yet she was the only one he could imagine by his side.

Enough. It was past time to end a discussion that had nothing to do with her and gently disentangle himself from a situation that could go nowhere. He wouldn't leave abruptly, but he would leave.

"You've given me a lot to think about," he said. "Thanks for that."

"You're welcome."

"I don't know about you, but I'm starving."

"Sure. Let's eat." But the sparkle had faded in her eyes. She obviously knew he'd changed the subject on purpose because he didn't want to continue discussing his future plans with her.

And so their parting would begin. Maybe he should leave abruptly, after all. Quick might be more merciful than slow. Perhaps she should have a say in that.

"Rachel, you know how this is going to end, right?"

"I know how you plan for it to end."

He kept his gaze locked with hers. "It will end with me leaving Polecat. I'll put my cabin up for sale, but I don't intend to stick around and wait for a buyer to come along. I'll let a real estate agent handle it for me."

She swallowed but didn't say anything.

"I'm telling you this straight out because I . . . care about you. A lot."

"I care about you, too." Her voice was husky.

"I know now I can trust you not to breach werewolf security."

"Thank you for that."

His voice softened. "I've never really thought you would, but my knee-jerk reaction was to keep you close until I was sure."

"So I'm free now to go about my life?" Her smile was faint.

"We both are. So I'm asking you . . . would you like me to leave right now?"

"You can't, unless you can fit into my jeans."

He laughed. It was a damned serious situation, and yet he couldn't help it.

Then she started laughing, too. "God, I'd love to see that!"

They laughed until the tears came. It felt good. And finally, they both stared at each other with silly grins on their faces.

She wiped her eyes and sniffed. "Tell you what. I'll drive over to your place and bring you some clothes."

"I'd appreciate that."

"But if you don't mind, I'd rather you didn't leave just yet."

"You're sure? Because I don't want to make this any worse than it already is."

She looked into his eyes. "When you leave, it will be the worst day of my life. It doesn't matter if that's today, tomorrow, or a week from now. I'll hate that day because it'll be the last time I'll ever see you."

He nodded slowly.

"So can I be greedy and ask for a little more time?"

"Yeah." He leaned forward and kissed her. "Because I want to be greedy, too."

Chapter 19

Rachel missed Jake the minute she drove away from her cabin. She'd have to get over this intense desire to be with him, or at the very least to maintain contact, because she wouldn't be able to for much longer. But she'd left him her cell number and had insisted on digging his phone out of her backpack and turning it on. Knowing she could call him, or vice versa, gave her comfort for the time being.

She had two errands to run—clothes for Jake at his house, and a pound of coffee at the general store. She hadn't told Jake about the coffee because he might have objected to her making contact with Ted. But she wouldn't take long, and she just had time to drop by the store before Ted closed up for the night.

She was almost out of coffee, and a day without caffeine wouldn't work for her, especially considering the stress she was under. She'd meant to pick up a pound a week ago, but she'd been distracted by a sexy werewolf.

Jake was in charge of cooking dinner while she was gone. He'd do a far better job of it than she would. When she'd left him in her kitchen, he'd been whistling as he concocted a barbecue sauce for the ribs she'd taken out of the freezer and stuck in the microwave.

She had to admit he did a lot for the decor of her kitchen, although he'd chosen not to be completely naked while he worked in there. He'd said that sharp knives and hot liquids made him nervous about his family jewels. So he'd protected his privates with a towel slung loosely around his hips. With his dark hair and ripped body, he'd looked like a primitive warrior wearing a loincloth. The faint red marks from the bear's claws and his bullet wound only made him look more manly. And, bonus, he could cook.

Yes, she wanted him. She'd run through all the reasons why she shouldn't want him, and none of them amounted to a hill of beans. Because he trusted her, she could live the way she always had, except she'd have a man in her life. Jake passed for human all the time. Around her friends and family, he'd continue to do that.

The issue of children had given her pause at first, but she believed that two parents who were devoted to each other were such a gift that a little thing like uncertain genetic patterns became unimportant. Her kids would never know anything different, anyway, and they'd be loved, no matter if they turned out human or Were. She'd help them deal with whichever species designation they'd inherited.

Sadly, she probably wouldn't get the chance, because Jake wasn't buying what she was selling. She didn't delude herself on that score. Not anymore. He had every intention of walking out of her life forever.

After that, he'd mate with some lucky werewolf and start his own pack. She'd seen how he'd lit up at that suggestion of hers. It was her idea, damn it. She'd hoped he'd make the obvious leap of faith and ask her to share that dream with him.

But he hadn't. There'd been a moment there, a milli-second of optimism when something in his expression had told her he was thinking about it. In the end, he'd rejected that possibility.

As she drove around the lake to his cabin, she won-dered whether she should simply hand him his clothes and tell him to hit the road. He could take a doggie bag full of the food he'd cooked. Or a wolfie bag. If she hadn't changed his mind by now, after she'd taken care of his wounded self twice and they'd enjoyed stellar sex many times, chances were she wasn't going to change it.

Would keeping him around longer, knowing she couldn't win, make the end more devastating? Maybe, but she'd also have more memories to warm her on cold winter nights. Those memories would make finding a re-placement for him extremely difficult, though. She couldn't do much about that. She'd had the best and was now stuck with the rest.

The parking lot of the Polecat General Store was empty except for Ted's truck and a late-model SUV with, of all things, Idaho plates. The dusty, mud-spattered ve-hicle had obviously traveled the Alaskan highway to get here. Rachel hesitated before pulling in, but she really needed that coffee.

She'd be okay unless the visitors could ID her on sight. Some could do that because she'd been featured on a few news shows in the lower forty-eight. Once someone pin-pointed her location here in Polecat, she would have to increase her security measures in both her cabin and her workshop. She'd like to avoid that if possible.

Reaching for the faded navy baseball cap she kept tucked behind her visor, she shook it out, put it on, and pulled her hair through the opening in back. Without makeup and wearing old clothes, she didn't look much like the internationally famous wood-carver from Alaska's interior. The baseball cap finished off what she hoped was a successful disguise.

Opening the screen door, she set off the jangling bells that Ted had hung there as a cheap alert system. Ted was behind the counter talking to an attractive middle-aged couple. They were both tall and athletic looking, with good bone structure.

Rachel had been in contact with enough wealthy people in her new career to recognize that these folks had money. That could mean they were collectors searching for her. Although they seemed harmless enough, she couldn't trust them not to brag to others and give away her exact location.

Tugging her baseball cap lower, she headed down the aisle toward the coffee. Ted wouldn't announce her presence, and she could wait until they left to approach the counter and pay.

Then Ted called her name. "Hey, Rachel!"

She froze in place. What in the hell was Ted doing, indentifying her like that? Cautiously she turned around.

"These folks are looking for Jake." Ted gave her a reassuring smile as if to say that all was well. The visitors didn't want her, after all.

"Oh?" Alarms went off in her head. *Idaho.*

"They knew his folks and wanted to stop and say hello, but they didn't find him at home. I thought you might have some idea where he is. Weren't you two going hiking today?"

"Um, yeah." She thought fast as she tried not to stare at what had to be a mated pair of werewolves. And they looked so completely normal, too. But then, so did Jake. "Jake, um, hurt himself on the trail, so he's over at my place." She could feel the couple studying her. They knew she wasn't Were. Jake had said werewolves could smell the difference.

"I hope it's nothing serious," the woman said.

But this visitor wasn't a *woman*, Rachel reminded herself. She was a female werewolf. Rachel began to sweat. "No, not too bad. Took a fall, has a bit of a sprain, but he'll be fine. How long are you here for?"

"We're staying at a place about an hour back down the road," the male said. "We tried to call his cell, but it just went to voice mail, so we thought it would be fun to surprise him."

They must have tried to call while Jake's phone had been turned off at the bottom of her backpack. "I'm sure he'd love to see you." Rachel did her best to sound enthusiastic. God, she didn't want to get Jake in trouble. For all she knew, these two belonged to his anti-human-mating group.

Even if they weren't part of that group, they were certainly from his pack. They had to be wondering why he was laid up since he had the ability to heal himself through shifting. Maybe they assumed he was trapped with her, a human, and couldn't shift. But why not? She'd left him to go shopping, so by all rights, he'd be fine when she returned.

All this complication for a pound of coffee! If only she'd bought some last week. "I don't think he's up to company tonight," she said. "But tomorrow would probably work. Do you want to leave me your phone number so I can give it to him?"

The female hesitated. "If you're sure he can't see us tonight, we can do that."

"It's been a long day for him." Now, there was an understatement. "Tomorrow would be much better." She sounded like a protective girlfriend and couldn't help that. She wasn't about to invite these werewolves to her house. Something about them gave her the creeps, and she hoped it wasn't a newly discovered prejudice.

Then she realized that if anyone was displaying prejudice, it was these two werewolves. When they looked at her, there was no warmth. Apparently they judged her as unworthy simply because she was human. Unfortunately for them, she controlled access to Jake, and they'd come to see him.

"Then let me give you our information," the female said. Opening her designer purse, she pulled out a small notepad and a jeweled pen. "I'll write our names down, too."

"It's been years," the male said. "But he'll remember who we are."

"I'm sure he will." Rachel took the slip of paper. Above the number, the female had written *Ann and Bruce Hunter.* Rachel could have predicted that the last name would be Hunter.

"Give him our best," the female said. "We'll wait to hear from him."

"I'll be sure to. Have a good night."

"Thanks for stopping by!" Ted called after them. Then he glanced at Rachel. "Did I screw that up? They weren't looking for you, just Jake. And they seemed to know him really well. They had his address and cell phone number, so I thought—"

"It's okay, Ted."

"Is he really hurt? Or are you two enjoying some alone time?"

"Both. He did have a small accident, but he'll be right as rain in the morning." Especially if he shifted once more while she was running errands. "But we ... I guess you could say we hit it off better than I thought we would."

Ted beamed. "That's wonderful. Here I thought you two were destined to be bitter enemies."

"No." Rachel blew out a breath. "Not enemies. Hey, I came in for coffee, so I should probably buy it so you can close up."

"Don't be silly. Take your time." His eyebrows rose. "I'm a nosy old man, but you blush every time you talk about Jake, and it sounds as if he's settled in at your place instead of his . . ."

"He'll be staying over." Even though she'd known Ted for years and shouldn't care if he knew she was getting cozy with someone, she felt shy admitting it.

"Ah. No wonder you don't want those people barging in on your private evening. I'm glad you held them off."

They're not people, Ted. They're shape-shifters. But she couldn't tell this sweet man that, not now and not ever. If she'd needed a demonstration of what her life would be like if she hooked up with Jake, she was in luck. Ann and Bruce Hunter were testing her ability to deal with two different realities.

She wasn't crazy about the maneuvering, but if the reward was Jake Hunter, who was presently preparing food in her kitchen wearing only a skimpy towel, she could deal. He, on the other hand, probably would be horrified to find out she'd had a conversation with Ann and Bruce of Idaho.

Getting back to her cabin took on greater urgency. "Let me get my coffee."

"Need more candy bars?"

"Oh, sure, why not?" After grabbing a bag of fresh-roasted coffee beans, she detoured past the candy aisle and scooped up several of her favorites. Chocolate was a known mood elevator, and she might require a little mood enhancer in the near future.

Placing the coffee and candy on the counter, she dug in her purse for the small mesh bag she always carried for impulse buys. A random thought crossed her mind. She'd had several rounds of mind-blowing sex with Jake, but she didn't even know if he recycled.

He'd said werewolves were protectors, so she figured he would include the Earth under that umbrella. After all, a wolf couldn't run through the woods if someone cut down all the trees. A wolf couldn't drink from a stream that had been polluted with chemicals. Being wild would seem to focus a creature on sustainability.

But she didn't know that, and she was curious. She should make a list of all the questions she had so that she could ask them while there was still time. When Ann and Bruce came to call tomorrow, he'd want to distance himself from her. It might be the end of her acquaintance with Jake.

Ted put her candy and coffee in the bag she handed him. "Did you ever find out why Jake was so hell-bent on giving away that carving?"

Well, yes, she had. She gave Ted a piece of the truth. "He's been attracted to me for a long time, but he didn't think we were right for each other. The carving was a reminder of me, and so he wanted it gone." That story would play nicely into their inevitable breakup. Jake's belief that they weren't right for each other would prove to be true.

"Huh." Ted rubbed a hand over his balding head. "Guess he was wrong about that."

She smiled at him. "Time will tell. It's early days, yet." She handed over the cash for her purchase.

"Good point. My advice—go slow. Margie and I met and decided to get married in a matter of weeks. We should have waited a while to make sure getting married was the right decision."

"Do you miss her, Ted?"

A hint of vulnerability shadowed his blue eyes. Even

the glare from his thick glasses didn't hide it. "Sometimes. The winter nights can be long."

"Then for your sake, I hope a nice woman shows up one of these days, Ted. You deserve that."

He laughed. "That would be great, but I'm not counting on it. It takes a special kind of person to want to live in Polecat, Alaska." He gazed at her. "Like you. And Jake, for that matter. I hope it works out for the two of you."

"Thanks." Her heart ached with the knowledge that her chances of that were slim to none. "We'll see. Have a good night, Ted." Grabbing her bag, she left the store. She heard the lock click behind her. Ted would go home, but no one would be waiting. Maybe in a few days she'd suggest that she and Ted check out the Internet dating scene together.

Moments later, she parked in front of Jake's cabin. He'd told her the back slider was open as usual, so she walked around to the deck. This was where it had all started. The first time she'd set foot on this deck, she'd thought she was tracking Jake's pet wolf.

Glancing around, she remembered the meal they'd shared sitting at his elevated table. That reminded her that she was extremely hungry and Jake was cooking another fabulous meal on the other side of the lake. Gazing across the water, she imagined him inside, the small towel flipping back and forth as he moved around her kitchen. Mm. So she was hungry for more than food.

Opening his slider, she stepped into his living room, closed the glass door, and headed directly for his bedroom. Previously she'd rummaged through his house uninvited while she looked for clues, but this time she had permission to open drawers and closets. He'd given her instructions as to where everything was kept.

She piled things on his bed and tried not to get

wrapped up in the memories the bed evoked. Chances were she wouldn't share this bed with him again, so she might as well shut down that train of thought. She chose two of everything with the hope that he might stay more than another twenty-four hours.

But she didn't really think that would happen now that Ann and Bruce were in the neighborhood. The timing of their visit couldn't have been worse from her standpoint, but she believed things happened for a reason. She'd have to go with it.

Once she had everything gathered, she took his duffel bag from the closet and piled it all in there. Before they'd left this morning he'd unpacked from his San Francisco trip, so the duffel was available. She started to zip it and paused.

One more thing in this bedroom called to her. She wouldn't keep it, of course. But as long as she was transporting items from here to her cabin, she might as well include Duncan MacDowell's book.

Jake wouldn't appreciate her bringing it over, of course. But Duncan was on her side, and she would give anything to talk to him. After all, he'd converted Kate Stillman to the cause. Rachel wanted to know how he'd done it.

Tucking the book into the bag and zipping it up, she was about to leave Jake's bedroom when her cell phone rang. When she answered, she found herself talking to Jake himself.

"Where are you?" He sounded uneasy.

"Sitting on your bed in your bedroom. Why?"

"You need to leave ASAP. I just checked my messages, and damned if some old friends of my parents aren't headed to Polecat. What are the chances?"

"I've met them."

"Oh, boy."

"I stopped by the store for coffee and they were there, asking Ted if he knew where you were. Naturally, because he thinks we're hanging out together these days, he turned to me for information."

"What did you say?"

She took a breath and rolled her shoulders. "I did the best I could under the circumstances, Jake."

"I'm sure you did. I'm sure you handled it well. But I need to know my lines for when I talk with them."

"I said you'd been laid up following a small accident on the hiking trail. A minor sprain."

He greeted that with silence.

"I wanted to stall them off. I didn't want them coming to my house, Jake."

"Were they rude to you? Because if they were, I'll let them know that I don't appreciate—"

"No, they weren't rude. I could tell they were a little suspicious of me, but they were polite."

"Unless they've changed, they're conservatives like my folks were. They probably suspect a relationship and don't approve of it."

"I think you're right. And it was weird, Jake. I'm not used to being judged as not good enough because of something I can't change."

"I'm sorry, Rachel. They probably *are* prejudiced against you for being human."

"And it's pretty obvious you and I have been spending quality time together." She sighed. "I know you didn't want anyone in the werewolf community to know about us. I hope I haven't compromised you in some way."

His warm chuckle soothed her. "You've compromised me in every way possible, and I've loved it. Don't worry about them. I can smooth it over."

"I hope so. Are they members of your WARM group?"

"No. They're not activists."

"That's a relief. I imagined them ratting on you for being involved with a human."

"I'll ask them not to. They're old friends, so I'm sure it'll be fine."

"Thanks. I feel a whole lot better about this. And the good news is, I have coffee for breakfast."

"And clothes? I could use some clothes. I'm having a hell of a time keeping this towel on."

"And that's a problem?" Her mood improved dramatically as she anticipated the evening they were about to have. The next day could be a real letdown, but until then, she'd enjoy herself.

"You wouldn't be so cavalier if I ended up steaming something far more critical than the rice."

"No, I wouldn't. Take care of yourself. I'll be there soon."

"Good. The cabin is empty without you. I— Shit! I smell something burning. Gotta go." He disconnected.

Rachel started to put her phone back in her purse, but it blinked, indicating a text. It was from Lionel. Heart pounding, she opened it.

Found clothes that look like Mr. Hunter's. Went by his place. Truck was there. He wasn't. Thought about it. Suspect foul play. Headed for your cabin.

She started to respond, but that would waste valuable time. She could call Jake, but that wouldn't really help matters, either. Shoving the phone in her purse, she grabbed the duffel and ran out through the open slider.

She'd rather not imagine a scene between Lionel and a seminaked Jake. But explaining why his clothes were in the bushes would require some creative storytelling. She didn't know if her presence would help or hinder, but she knew she had to get to the other side of the lake as fast as she could.

Chapter 20

After Jake had steamed the rice, he'd decided to sauté it with some olive oil and spices he'd found in Rachel's cabinet. After getting that going, he'd unearthed his phone, retrieved the messages from Ann and Bruce, and called Rachel.

He didn't know how he was going to spin his association with her so Ann and Bruce wouldn't blab to the entire Hunter pack that Jake, who railed against Weres having sex with humans, was a hypocrite who'd done exactly that.

But he didn't want Rachel to feel responsible. This lapse was his fault, not hers. He hoped that the Hunters wouldn't make a big deal out of it. Because they'd known his folks so well, maybe they'd let it go.

But his conversation with Rachel had distracted him from his cooking long enough for the rice to burn and set off the smoke alarm. Grabbing the smoking pan, he put it in the sink, where it hissed angrily and gave off a miserable stench. The smoke alarm continued to screech, so he opened the kitchen window to let out the smoke. So much for his famous cooking skills.

Not five minutes later, someone pounded on the front door. "Anybody in there?"

Jake recognized Lionel's voice and groaned. The kid meant well, but he was becoming a total pain in the ass.

"Miss M!" More pounding. "Miss M, if you're in there, your house is on fire!"

Jake stood in the kitchen in his towel debating his next move. By now most of the smoke had cleared and the smoke alarm had stuttered to a stop. Maybe Lionel would just go away.

Or not. The front door opened, and Jake belatedly realized Rachel wouldn't have thought to lock it behind her. And why would she? He was here and there was no crime in Polecat, anyway.

"Miss M!" Lionel called out again. Then he paused. "Well, guess I'd better check things out," he muttered, obviously to himself. "Could be serious."

"Lionel, I'm here." Left with no choice, Jake stepped out of the kitchen.

Lionel's eyes got huge and then his face turned red. "Uh, hi there, Mr. Hunter." He looked everywhere but at Jake. "Thought nobody was home. Miss M's truck is gone."

"She's . . . running errands." Jake resisted the urge to clasp his hands in front of his groin, but then he might disturb the delicate balance of the towel.

"Oh." Lionel glanced toward the kitchen. "So what's burning?"

"I was sautéing some rice. I got distracted."

"Ah. Must be fixing dinner for you and Miss M." Lionel nodded and darted a quick glance at Jake.

"Yes. She's not here right now."

"I figured. I, um, have your clothes."

For a moment Jake was disoriented. Rachel was sup-

posed to have his clothes. Why would Lionel have his . . .
Oh. *Those* clothes. He'd forgotten to ask Rachel what
she'd done to keep Lionel from noticing them in the first
place.

"They were sort of scattered under a bush out on the
trail. I was afraid you'd been murdered or something.
Although I couldn't figure out why they'd take your
clothes off and shove them under a bush."

"Well, obviously I'm fine." Jake scrambled for a rea-
sonable explanation and came up empty.

"Yep. That's good." Lionel surveyed the room with
great care, as if he'd never seen it before. "I didn't know
you were a nudist, Mr. Hunter."

"I'm n—" Jake caught himself. Maybe that was as
good a cover story as any. Once he left Polecat, it
wouldn't matter whether word got out that Jake Hunter
was a nudist.

"It's okay if you are," Lionel said. "I think people can
be anything they want. It's just that sometimes families
take their kids out on those trails, and I don't know how
it would work out if they came upon a naked man running through the woods. They might call the cops on
their cell phone, and then you could get arrested."

"Thanks for the warning. I'll keep that in mind."

"And the bad part is, when you got arrested, you'd be
naked."

Jake coughed to keep from laughing, and the towel
trembled dangerously. "That's true. I would be naked."

"Not the best way to be when you're hauled off to
jail."

"I suppose not."

"Listen, not to change the subject or anything."

Jake swallowed the laughter that kept bubbling up
from his throat. "Oh, please do."

"I hate to tell you this, but sometime while he was being transported to the sanctuary, your wolf got out of his cage."

"Uh-oh."

"Uh-oh is right!" Lionel took a deep breath. "I checked the news, and thank God there's no story about a wildlife transportation team being mauled by a black wolf, so maybe he just managed to slip out without hurting anyone."

"He's a very smart wolf."

"Well, I shot at him." Lionel's gaze moved away from Jake again. "I'm sorry to have to tell you that because I'm sure you care about him, but he was ready to attack Miss M, and I think he would've if I hadn't shown up."

"I can guarantee that wolf wouldn't hurt a hair on her head."

"Ha. You didn't see what I saw. He was going after her."

Jake couldn't argue with that. He'd been going after Rachel for some time now, only not in the way Lionel thought.

Lionel's glance skittered past Jake again. "So do you want your clothes? I have them out in my truck. I didn't expect to see you here, or I would've brought them in with me." Lionel blushed again. "I mean, it's obvious you don't want them *now*. You have this whole nudist thing going on. But they're nice clothes. A little dusty, but nice."

"I'd like them back," Jake said. "Thanks."

"All righty!" Lionel swung his arms back and forth. "I'll just go out and get them." He started toward the door right as Rachel came through it.

Jake was relieved to see that she'd left his duffel in her truck. All she carried was her purse and a mesh bag containing what looked like coffee and candy bars.

"Hey, Lionel!" Setting her purse and mesh bag on an end table, she gave Lionel the biggest, fakest smile Jake had ever seen.

"Hi, Miss M. I see you've been buying candy bars again."

"Well, yes, I have." She looked over at Jake with a wide-eyed, innocent expression. "I see Jake's been keeping you company while I was gone. How nice."

"Yeah." Lionel shoved his hands in his pockets. "We've been having a conversation. I told him it was fine with me if he wants to be a nudist."

Rachel coughed and ducked her head. When she looked up again, her eyes were swimming with tears of laughter. She swiped at them with the back of her hand.

Lionel glanced at her, his brow puckered. "Are you okay, Miss M?"

"Yeah, fine." She nodded vigorously. "Just swallowed wrong. You were saying?"

"About this nudist thing. I think Mr. Hunter needs to be careful out on the trail. He could get arrested."

"Mm." She cleared her throat. "Well, that's good advice, don't you think, Jake?"

"Excellent advice."

Her eyes twinkled. "Can't have a naked man running around scaring the kids."

"Exactly!" Lionel smiled in triumph. "That's what I told him." He peered at her. "You're not a nudist, are you? Wait. I don't want to know the answer to that. If you are, don't tell me. I don't want that mental image."

"I'm not a nudist, Lionel."

"Whew." His shoulders sagged. "That's good to hear. Well, I'll go get Mr. Hunter's clothes and . . ." He glanced from Rachel to Jake. "Uh, how about if I just leave them by the front door? You two probably want to be alone."

Jake decided to put an end to this party. "By the door would be great, Lionel. Thanks for picking them up for me."

"No prob." Lionel started out again but paused and turned around. "About tomorrow morning . . ."

"Come at your regular time," Rachel said. "Jake has some friends in town and he'll be meeting them in the morning. I'll be out in the workshop, as usual."

That plan made sense, but Jake couldn't help feeling sad that he wouldn't be spending the morning with her. He'd come back after meeting with the Hunters, though. Wouldn't he?

"Then I'll be here in the morning." Lionel hesitated, his manner suddenly shy. "I have that piece of wood nearly carved. Should finish it up tonight. I could bring it over tomorrow if you want."

Rachel gave him a genuine smile this time. "I would love for you to do that. I can hardly wait to see it."

"Then I'll bring it." Lionel's natural good cheer had returned. He grinned at both of them. "See you later." Head held high, he walked out the door.

Rachel glanced at Jake and dissolved into laughter. "A nudist?"

Jake gestured toward his towel-draped body. "The guy finds my clothes under a bush and walks into the house while I'm wearing nothing but a towel. I thought it was a brilliant deduction on his part."

"I suppose so." She continued to chuckle. "So you just agreed with his conclusion and let it go at that?"

"I started to contradict him, but then I realized he'd handed me the only logical explanation, so I rolled with it. Better to be thought a nudist than a werewolf."

"There's that." Her gaze roved over him. "You'd make a pretty impressive nudist, though."

"Thanks. Not my thing. As I've said, I was raised in a conservative household. Even our shifting was done in private."

"And yet, you stripped down in front of me in broad daylight. That seems out of character, now that I think about it."

"Oh, it was." He walked over to her. "But when I'm with you, I get sort of wild and crazy, in case you hadn't noticed."

"I've noticed." She lifted her face to his. "And I like that in a werewolf."

"Good." He cupped her face in both hands. "Because I think it's about to happen again." His lips hovered over hers when a rap sounded at the door. "Damn. I thought he was going to leave them and go away."

"Me, too."

The rap came again.

Rachel sighed. "Let me go see what he wants. He's only trying to be helpful, after all."

"I'll go check the ribs. They should be about done." Jake reluctantly let her go and walked into the kitchen. The towel started to fall and he knotted it more securely.

Had he been the nudist Lionel thought he was, he would whip the towel off and discard it, because the major part of the food preparation was over. But being a nudist was the last thing Jake would consider. The more he thought about his behavior on the trail, the more he marveled that Rachel could get under his skin and make him do something so uncharacteristic.

He heard the front door open. Sure enough, it was Lionel.

"Sorry to bother you again, Miss M, but I forgot to ask if you've seen that wolf. I still don't trust it not to come back around here, and I don't think Mr. Hunter understands that it's a dangerous animal. He talks just like you, like it's no problem."

Rachel's reply was filled with kindness. "I know you're worried, Lionel. I promise if I'm threatened by that wolf I'll call you right away."

Jake smiled. Instead of lying to the kid, she'd managed to dodge the question entirely. Nicely done.

"Make sure you do call me," Lionel said. "Anyway, you might as well take the clothes since you're standing here."

"Thanks."

"Okay, now I really am leaving."

"Good night, Lionel."

"See you later, Miss M."

The front door closed and Rachel approached the kitchen. "I'm sure you heard all that with your super-duper ears."

Jake walked out to meet her. "I did. You handled it well."

"I left your clothes just inside the front door. They definitely need washing. Assuming the coast is clear, would you like me to bring in the duffel bag?"

"Yes, please. And as much as I feel like ravishing you, I'm really, really hungry. And the food's ready."

"Then let me get your duffel so you can get dressed and we can have dinner." Her silver eyes held the promise of what was to come. "No rush. We have all night."

The way she said it almost made him reconsider having dinner first. But he hadn't eaten since breakfast, and he'd expended a lot of energy since them. While Rachel went out to her truck to grab the duffel bag, he went back into the kitchen for the bowl of salad he'd tossed earlier.

As he located place settings and opened a bottle of

red he'd found in her wine rack, he anticipated the pleasure of sharing another dinner with Rachel. Although he cooked for trekking clients out on the trail, he ate most of his meals at home by himself. He hadn't thought he'd minded, but now that he'd experienced having Rachel around for this daily ritual, he'd miss her enthusiastic presence.

By the time she returned with his duffel bag, he'd put all the food on the table and had even located a couple of candles and candlesticks.

She laughed in obvious delight when she noticed the flickering tapers. "I'd forgotten I had those."

"You don't eat by candlelight?"

"It seems sort of silly if you're by yourself." She set down the duffel and glanced at him. "Especially in the summer when it's bright as day."

"I know. We don't really need the light, but I've always liked the look of candles. Werewolves are drawn to fire."

She seemed intrigued by that idea. "Do you eat by candlelight?"

"Hey, do I strike you as the type of male who lights candles before diving into his solitary meal? I hope to hell not."

"Well, no." She grinned. "That doesn't conjure a picture of a manly man, or, in your case, a rugged werewolf."

"That's right. So the answer is no, I don't eat by candlelight. I make do with firelight on camping trips. But in some situations, candles are perfect. And this is one of them. I'm glad you had a couple of tapers in your cupboard."

"Me, too. Well, here's your stuff. I don't know if you want to get dressed here, or—"

"I'll take it into the bedroom."

"Right. You like privacy."

"I do. Go ahead and pour the wine. I'll be right back."
He picked up the duffel and carried it into her bedroom.
Then he came back out and scooped up his clothes lying
by the front door. "If you have a plastic bag, I'll stick
these in my duffle."

"Sure. Hang on." She set down the wine bottle and
popped into the kitchen. Soon she was back with a plastic grocery sack. "I don't have many of these. I take my
own bags to the store."

"I'm with you on that."

She smiled as if that meant a lot to her. "Glad to hear
it."

He dumped everything in the bag but on an impulse
pulled out the shirt. "Good thing I didn't lose this. It's my
favorite T-shirt."

"Yeah? I hate to admit I didn't notice your shirt this
morning. Let me see." She held it by the shoulders.
"Wow, nice."

"I found it several years ago on a trip to Idaho." The
T-shirt was black, imprinted with an image of wolves sit-
ting around a campfire. Underneath was lettered *The
Gathering*.

"I can guess why it's your favorite. It's a pack."

She was right, of course, but until now, he hadn't understood why he'd been so drawn to the graphic on this
shirt, other than the obvious—it was wolves and fire,
both of which he liked.

"You may live like a lone wolf, but that's not who you
are," she said gently. "You need a family."

"Guess so." Embarrassed by the catch in his voice, he
covered it with a laugh. "Damn, we're letting the food get
cold. You know how I hate that. Be right back." Turning
quickly, he walked into her bedroom. He didn't realize

until he got there that he'd been in such a hurry to escape his own emotional reaction that he'd left her holding the shirt.

She understood him in a way that no one ever had. Naturally he'd had guilty fantasies about building a life with her. Now she'd unearthed his deepest desire, one he hadn't admitted to himself until now. He longed to create a mighty werewolf pack in the heart of Alaska, where the legend had begun. And she was the one he pictured by his side. There was only one problem with that dream. She wasn't Were.

Chapter 21

Even without the rice, the meal was incredible. Rachel gazed at Jake over the rim of her wineglass. "You're one hell of a cook."

"Yeah, if you ignore the rice disaster that set off your smoke alarm."

She waved that aside. "Things happen. It's hard to concentrate on your rice when long-lost members of the Hunter pack show up. You probably need to call them. I told them you would."

"I should." He didn't look eager to grab his phone.

"They seemed nice enough, Jake. And they were close friends of your parents, right?"

"Yes."

"It might be really great to talk about your folks with someone who knew them back when. The Hunters probably have some good stories you haven't heard."

"Maybe. In fact, I'm sure they do." He poured himself more wine and started to give her some, too.

"That's okay." She placed her hand over her glass. "I'm not as big as you and I don't want anything to interfere with—" She started to say *our last night* because she thought it probably would be. But she decided not to put that into words, which would depress both of them. "Our fun and games," she said, finishing on a positive note.

Jake set down his wineglass. "In that case, maybe I'll leave this for later." Heat flared in his eyes. "Afterward."

"Jake, you need to make that call."

"Right." With a sigh, he pushed back his chair and stood. "If you don't mind, I'll take my phone out on the deck, in case they want to talk longer than a couple of minutes. There's nothing more annoying than being subjected to someone's one-sided phone conversation."

"True." She didn't say what she really felt, that listening to him interact with his own kind would be fascinating. She didn't want him to think she was a voyeur, peeking into the intimate life of his species.

Yet when he took his phone outside, she felt excluded. She didn't like being reminded that she wasn't a part of his world, but in fact, she wasn't. Not only that—he didn't want her to be.

Truth time here. She could rave on all day about her willingness to adjust to his culture, but he hadn't asked her to do that. Instead he constantly emphasized his opposition to bringing her into the werewolf community. If she didn't shut up about it, she would start to sound pathetic, like a werewolf groupie.

Gathering the dishes, she carried them into the kitchen and loaded them in the dishwasher. She wasn't much of a cook, but she was an excellent galley slave. Within ten minutes she had the food put away, the kitchen sparkling, and the dishwasher running.

Inching her living room window blind aside, she was able to see Jake pacing her deck while he talked on his phone. He didn't look particularly relaxed. Having the Hunters show up seemed to have put him on edge.

She got that. Living up here, far from her parents, she was used to being her own person. She'd left California to move to Alaska partly for that reason, to establish herself as an individual.

Jake's motivations for leaving Idaho seemed very similar to hers. But now Idaho had come to him, and that sense of freedom might be slipping away. She certainly experienced that whenever her parents came to visit, much as she loved them.

With nothing more to do, she walked into her bedroom. His duffel bag sat on the floor in a corner, but Duncan MacDowell's book, which she'd taken without permission from his bedside table, lay on the bed. She hoped he wasn't upset that she'd tucked it into the duffel.

Because she'd drawn all the blinds earlier in the day, the room was fairly dim except for the light from her bedside lamp. Nudging off her shoes, she propped pillows against the headboard, picked up Duncan's book, and settled down to read.

Several pages later, Jake's voice broke her concentration.

"I can't let you keep that." He stood in the doorway, and the scene wasn't terribly different from the time he'd first caught her reading this book, except they were in her bedroom and not his. His expression, though, was completely different. He looked at her with deep caring and more than a little concern.

"I know I can't have it," she said. "But are you upset because I brought it over here?"

"Not upset, exactly. Worried, maybe."

"Why are you worried?" She wished he'd come over to the bed so they could be closer while having this conversation, but she wasn't willing to ask him to do that.

He leaned against the doorframe. "I don't want you to become fascinated with the Were culture."

That hit her wrong. Who was he to say what should fascinate her and what shouldn't? "Too late." She heard the defiant tone of her voice but couldn't help it. "I'm already fascinated."

"That's Duncan's gift. He has charisma, which is why he has so many female followers. And he makes the life of a werewolf appear to be a glamorous alternative to the ordinary existence of humans."

"That's not so difficult to do, Jake. I've discovered that urban Weres glide through the city in chauffeured limos and have private jets at their disposal. Duncan describes a world of wealth and privilege. I'm beginning to wonder how many of my clients are werewolves."

"From what I know, quite a few."

She stared at him. "What do you mean, *from what you know*? Have you been keeping tabs on me?"

"I didn't tell you that?"

"No, you did not." She was secretly thrilled that he'd been paying such close attention to her and her career.

"You built your reputation on your rendering of a certain wolf who looks quite a lot like me. Don't think the werewolf community hasn't noticed."

"You're kidding."

"Nope."

"Are you telling me they *recognized* you in my carvings?"

"They did. Most humans think all wolves look alike, except maybe for some different coloring. But we don't, and a few Weres are convinced that you're reproducing versions of me."

She was stunned. "Are Ann and Bruce Hunter convinced of that?"

"They might be. We didn't get into that, fortunately. If push came to shove, I could point out that the wolf is actually my dad, not me. They'd probably take a closer look and agree, since they knew him so well. But I have to be careful not to sound defensive, as if I have something to hide."

"And you didn't used to, but now you do."

"It seems so."

She hated asking the next question, but she had to hear his answer. "Do you regret knowing me, then?"

"No." His low, urgent response was all she needed. Pushing away from the doorframe, he came over to the bed. "I'll never regret what we've had, Rachel."

She noticed the past tense but didn't want to dwell on it. She gazed up at him. "You had a nice long chat, though. You must be happy to reconnect." She had a hunch about the telephone conversation because his whole manner had changed in subtle ways.

"Yeah." He shoved his hands in the pockets of his jeans and glanced at her. "The Hunters aren't on vacation. They were sent by the pack as emissaries because their past ties with my parents made them the werewolves with the best chance of convincing me."

"To do what?" She scooted over and patted a spot beside her. "Come sit with me. Don't be a stranger."

Jake gave her a faint smile and sat down, angling his body to face her. "Keegan Hunter, the pack alpha, has asked to be relieved of his duties. He forced himself to lead the pack because he was next in line, but he's a werewolf historian who loves his studies more than he loves the daily job of running the pack. He's done well, but he isn't happy."

"And they want you to take over." Her heart thudded as she saw all hope of a future with Jake disappear. "Jake, that's a wonderful opportunity!"

"I have to admit it sounds pretty good."

"It sounds *perfect*." She pushed aside her own grief so that she could be happy for him. He might love Alaska, but he loved the idea of his own pack, too, and here was his chance to have that. He wouldn't have to start from scratch. The pack would be in place, and although Idaho wasn't Alaska, it had its own rugged beauty.

"Anyway, that's why Ann and Bruce are here." Jake met her gaze. "They didn't like the idea of presenting such a major proposition over the phone, but they ... well, after meeting you, they had a sense of urgency."

"Because I might be a threat to their plan?"

He nodded.

"I'm not a threat, Jake. I would never stand in your way. You know I wouldn't."

"I told them that, but they're hardwired to be suspicious of all humans."

"But as long as they don't know that I know, we're good, right?"

"Right. And they'll never find out that you're in on the secret."

Rachel told herself not to buy trouble, but she couldn't seem to keep herself from asking the question. "Let's say that they somehow *did* find out that I know. Would they have me killed?"

"No, of course not."

"But if they think I might destroy the entire werewolf community, why wouldn't they?"

"Because, as I keep trying to tell you, we're peaceful. We don't kill people. We don't even kill the traitors within our ranks, and we had one last year."

She swallowed. So there was a system of punishment. "If you didn't kill him, what did you do with him?"

"He'll be imprisoned for a long, long time."

"So I wouldn't be killed. I'd just be thrown in a dungeon deep under some castle, chained to the wall, and fed maggot-infested bread once a day."

"Good Lord." Jake shook his head. "You and Lionel come up with the most incredible doomsday scenarios. First of all, no one's going to find out you know anything, but even if they did, you wouldn't end up in a dungeon."

"Okay."

"Look, you'll be fine, but if someone suspected that you knew about us, I would never let anything happen to you."

"That's easy to say, Jake, but if you take this offer, you'll be in Idaho."

He gazed at her silently for several seconds. "Doesn't matter. I would still know if you're in trouble. I'd sense it."

She drew in a sharp breath. That meant more to her than he would ever realize. He'd acknowledged the soul-deep link between them.

But soul-deep link aside, he'd still be in Idaho. "Even if you sensed something was wrong, you couldn't get to me in time. I appreciate the sentiment more than I can say, but I don't see how you can protect me from Idaho."

"Of course I can."

"How? Are you going to send your personal bodyguards? Because that's not how I live, Jake. I don't even like the alarms I had installed. Secret agent–type werewolves with sunglasses, buzz haircuts, narrow black ties, and little curly wires hanging behind their ears would freak me out."

He stroked her hair back from her face and smiled at her. "You are so adorable."

"Don't patronize me. I mean it."

"I'm not sending bodyguards, but even if I did, they wouldn't look like that. Way too obvious."

"I don't care if they look like Betty White. I need my creative space. I realize that makes it harder to keep me safe, which is why I'm wondering how you would do it."

"You're assuming any of this will be necessary, which it won't. But okay, if you want to play worst-case scenario, if it comes out that you have knowledge of us, then I will guarantee to the Were community that you're completely trustworthy."

"And the powers that be will just accept that?"

"Yep."

"Is your word that powerful?"

He shrugged. "It's pretty powerful, but I'd also put up everything I own as collateral. Well, and they'd have me. So you'd never have to worry."

"Oh." She let out a breath. "Then I guess it's a good thing that nobody knows what I know."

"Yes, it is."

"But what a nightmare if they found out." Everything he owned, and even Jake himself, would be held hostage to guarantee that she'd keep her mouth shut. She'd always known the stakes were high, but this laid it out for her in detail. "You don't have to worry, Jake. I will never let you down."

"I know that." He gazed at her tenderly as he combed his fingers through her hair.

"Not even under torture. At least I hope not. I've never been tortured, so I might crack right away."

"Fortunately, I can't imagine why anyone would torture you, so I think we're okay there. But wow, you do have quite an imagination."

"So you say, but it took me several days to figure out you were a werewolf."

"But you did figure it out. I should have realized you would, with the way your brain works."

She studied him. "You know how in the cop shows it often turns out that the criminal really wants to be caught?"

"I guess. I don't watch much TV."

"Me, either, but I've picked up on that common thread. Anyway, my point is that you secretly wanted me to find out about you."

"No." He frowned. "No, I definitely didn't."

"Are you sure? Search your heart, Jake, and tell me you weren't hoping, even though you didn't want to admit it to yourself, that I'd break the code."

He hesitated, a reluctant smile on his lips. "Okay, maybe. I'll give you a maybe. That's not easy to confess, but if I'd really wanted to eliminate the temptation of you, I could have moved away from here three years ago, or anytime since then."

"Exactly." She took a deep breath. "So."

"So."

"You'll become the Hunter pack alpha." She forced herself to say that with enthusiasm. She was feeling a little better about all of it. His gentle touch had soothed the turbulent emotions rolling through her.

"That's the way it looks. And until you mentioned it, I wasn't aware that I wanted to lead a pack. The thought hadn't crossed my mind, even though something made me buy that T-shirt. I didn't analyze why I liked it so much. That insight came from you." Warmth glowed in his green eyes. "Thank you for that."

"So it all falls into place." She was determined that he wouldn't know that her heart was breaking. "Maybe that was my role, to make you aware of what you were missing in your life. Then when the opportunity came along, which it has, you can take it because you know it's the right decision."

He lightly massaged her scalp. "For me. But what about you, Rachel?"

Laying the book on the bedside table, she leaned forward and placed her hands on his broad shoulders. "I come out smelling like a rose. I have a career because your father posed for a picture and you bought the first carving inspired by that picture. I don't have a single complaint."

"But that happened years ago." He cupped her face in his big hands and stroked her cheeks with his thumbs. "Then I charged into your life uninvited and turned it upside down. I feel as if I'm leaving a mess."

"No, you aren't. You saved me from getting mauled by a bear. A bear attack could have ended my career, and maybe my life. So there's another reason for me to be eternally grateful to you."

"I just . . . want to make sure you're going to be okay."

She squeezed his shoulders. "Of course I'll be okay. Better than okay." She soldiered on, because he was damn well *not* going to feel sorry for her. "Your role wasn't that different, really. You allowed me to see what I was missing in my life."

"I did?"

"You bet. Thanks to you, I'm planning to find a worthy partner to share my bed. I deserve that." And didn't that sound spunky and proactive? Damn straight. "If it takes a while to come up with someone as wonderful as you, then so be it. At least I'm motivated to search him out."

He was quiet for a moment as his gaze probed hers. Finally he sighed. "Am I allowed to hate that idea?"

Ah, knowing that he'd be jealous felt *so* good. "Only if I'm allowed to hate the thought of you hooking up with some perfect little werewolf who will give you pure-bred werewolf children."

His smile had a touch of sadness. "Fair enough."

"I don't suppose you could bite me and turn me into a werewolf?"

He shook his head. "That's another myth."

"I figured. Just thought I'd ask." Her chest felt tight, as if someone had shoved her into a straitjacket. "So it's decided. You'll go to Idaho and become the Hunter alpha," she said again. Maybe repeating it would make it easier to bear.

"Yeah, I think it's the right thing to do. They need me."

She recognized the powerful appeal of that. She needed him, too, but she wasn't about to compete with an entire werewolf pack. "How soon?"

"They don't want to take any more time than necessary. I told them to give me until tomorrow to decide. But assuming I agree, which I'm planning to, they'd like me to pack up my truck in the morning and drive in tandem with them back to Idaho."

The suddenness of that shocked her, but she worked hard to make sure he didn't notice. "What about your cabin?"

"I'll contact an agent first thing in the morning and sell it furnished."

She wanted to cry. She'd sat on that sofa, eaten dinner at his patio table, made love in his bed. She couldn't imagine strangers moving into his place. Knowing he lived across the lake, even before they'd become lovers, had given her life a little extra shine.

That was about to change, and she wasn't sure she could deal with it. She would, though. If this was what Jake wanted, then she would send him on his way with a cheerful smile and a joyful heart. That was what you did when you loved someone.

Chapter 22

It couldn't end any other way. Jake had known that from the moment he'd met Rachel three years ago in the Polecat General Store. He'd known it and he'd fought the attraction until finally he couldn't fight it anymore.

And now they'd come to this—last kisses, last touches, last words murmured in the silky half-light of Alaska's midnight sun. They undressed each other slowly, peeling back layers of clothing to stroke skin heated by a desire that would leave each of them burning for days, weeks, perhaps the rest of their lives.

But the Hunters' arrival, right when he was struggling with his feelings for Rachel, had an inevitability about it. They were supposed to come and give him a reason to leave her. But he wasn't leaving yet, and her long, lithe body beckoned him.

Once all her clothes were gone, she stretched out on the bed and opened her arms. Jake silently accepted her invitation. Gliding over her, he breathed in the intoxicating scent that had beguiled him from that first day. Lying beneath him, touched by the golden light from the bedside lamp, she was more beautiful than he ever could have imagined on that fateful day three years ago.

He'd fantasized about her for three long years, but nothing he'd imagined had been as potent as the woman herself. He knew she would haunt his dreams for a very long time. But his path was set, and it didn't include her. That was better for both of them.

Still, his heart wept at the thought of leaving her. Leaning down to kiss her eyes, her cheeks, and her lips, he murmured his thanks for all she'd given him. She'd allowed him to love her, and she'd willingly accepted the limits he'd placed on that loving. While he'd had limits, she'd had none.

If he asked her to go with him, she would. She'd put up with the disapproval of werewolves like Ann and Bruce, just to be by his side. If he didn't ask—and he wouldn't—then she would let him go without a single word of protest. She was a proud woman, and he cherished that about her, too.

"I'll miss touching you here," he murmured as he brushed his mouth over the hollow of her throat. "And here." He pressed his lips to her full breast, right above her heart. He could feel it beating as he nuzzled her velvety skin and tugged on the firm peak of her nipple. Each caress made her heart beat faster.

She spoke his name on a sigh, then drew in a long, quivering breath and shuddered beneath him.

Returning to her lips, he drank the sweetness of her exhale. Her eyes remained closed, as if she couldn't bear to watch their story end. Or maybe she didn't want him to see the sadness in those stormy depths.

So he wouldn't ask her to look at him. If she wanted to hide, he understood. Trembling with the need to sink into her, he nevertheless held back. No one had ever welcomed him the way she did, and he suspected no one ever would again. He wanted to take his time.

"And I'll miss this most of all," he said. Gently he probed her moist center with the blunt tip of his cock, but he resisted the urge to push forward. "I love the anticipation right before I thrust, when I'm balanced above you and your heat reaches out to me. Your scent drives me crazy right now, but I'm going to wait."

Her eyelids fluttered and she moaned.

"I'm going to wait so that I can admire the flush on your cheeks. Now it's moved to your breasts, and your nipples have tightened even more. Your skin is glowing with a special sheen, like early-morning dew."

With a soft whimper of need, she moved restlessly beneath him.

"Soon, very soon. But this is my favorite moment of making love to you and I don't want to rush it. Not tonight. My climax is a wonderful moment, too, and yours is even better, but . . . this is the best, right now, before it all begins."

Her eyelids lifted, and he sucked in a breath. Instead of being shadowed with misery, her silvery eyes blazed with light.

Cradling his face in both hands, she locked her gaze with his. "That's the most beautiful speech I've ever heard."

"I meant every word of it."

"I could tell. And here's my response. I love you, Jake Hunter." She said the words clearly, as if she didn't want him to misunderstand. There was no request buried in those words, no expectation lurking in those magnificent eyes. "I thought you should know."

He was humbled by her courage. Declaring her love now, when she knew it was over, took guts. But it didn't surprise him. Her next words did.

"And you love me." She said it with the same strong conviction. "But you don't want to tell me because you think it makes no sense to say you love someone when you're leaving for Idaho."

His heart ached. "How come you're so smart?"

"It doesn't take a genius. You aren't willing to lay down your fortune and your life for some person you sort of care about."

"No."

"You may not think you can say the words, but your actions are pretty darned obvious. The thing is, you can love me and still go to Idaho. They're not mutually exclusive."

He looked into those amazing eyes of hers for several long seconds and wondered how in the hell he would leave her tomorrow. "I do love you," he said softly. "And you're right. I didn't think I could say it."

"But see? It's okay. You can."

"So I can." Joy poured through him at being able to speak the words that had been hammering at his heart. "I love you, Rachel Miller." And he drove deep with a groan of pure happiness.

"Told you so."

What followed was an enthusiastic bout of wild, loud, and celebratory sex. Jake lost count of how many times he told Rachel he loved her. He even lost count of how many orgasms she had, but it was quite a few.

When he finally came and they collapsed in a sweaty heap, she rocked him in her arms while she crooned *I love you, Jake Hunter* over and over. But at last, she nestled quietly in his arms and closed her eyes. Her breathing slowed and she sighed in obvious contentment.

Jake's heart ached more than he'd ever thought possible. He wanted to hold her tight and never let her go, but that was not to be. In his agony, his soul sent out a message. *I'll love you forever, Rachel. No one will ever take your place in my heart.*

Her eyes fluttered open and she gazed up at him. "There will be no one else for me, either, Jake."

He went very still. "What did you say?"

"No one will take your place in my heart, either. Just like you said to me."

"But I didn't say anything."

She frowned. "Yes, you did. I heard you distinctly. I was starting to drift off to sleep, and then you said—"

"I only thought it, Rachel." His throat went dry and his heart began to pound. "I didn't say it out loud. Somehow, you heard what I thought."

She didn't seem particularly impressed with that information. "I would believe that. It was sort of the way I could hear you when you were in wolf form."

"You don't understand. As a wolf, I can mentally communicate with wolves and other wild creatures. Amazingly, I was able to communicate with you, too, after I shifted, which I'm pretty sure is rare. But I have never been able to form that same mental link when I'm in human form. Not with Weres or with humans. I've never heard of any werewolf who could."

"You look a little freaked-out about it, Jake. Is it a problem?"

He tried to get a handle on what had just happened. "Not a problem, exactly, but definitely a phenomenon."

"I'm not surprised that I can hear your thoughts, no matter what form you take." She stroked his face. "I've never bonded with anyone the way I have with you."

"Same here." Dazed as he was by this discovery, he had to know if it went both ways. "Let's test this. I want you to try and send me a message. Not about us, or anything I would guess easily. Make it more of a challenge."

"Okay." She focused her gaze on his.

And he heard *Ted desperately needs to find a girlfriend.* Jake repeated the message he'd heard.

"That's it! Word for word."

"My God." Jake looked at her in amazement. "This could make werewolf history, but no one will ever find out about it."

"Oh, well."

"Is that true? Does Ted need a girlfriend?"

"Oh, Jake, he does. He puts up a good front, but he's lonely. I'm going to get him signed up for one of the dating sites after . . . after you leave."

"Good. But I'd rather not think about the leaving part, if you don't mind."

"I don't want to, either, but after you move to Idaho, we'll be able to communicate with each other and no one will ever know. Isn't that cool?"

"Yeah." He leaned over and kissed her, because he didn't want to dim the sparkle of excitement in her eyes. "It's very cool." But he wondered if this was more of a curse than a blessing. The temptation to keep in touch this way would be constant.

And yet, if it was all they had, if they could never hold each other, never share their laughter and tears, then what was that mental connection worth? For their own sanity, they might have to give it up.

But in the meantime, she was still here, and her kisses made him forget that she wouldn't always be with him. Seeking oblivion, he melted into her.

They didn't sleep much that night, which was how Rachel wanted it. Buying a pound of coffee the night before had turned into a three-act play. After all that she'd gone through to get the coffee, they might as well make use of it to counteract their lack of sleep. Loving Jake was far more important than getting a good night's rest, anyway.

They showered together, which involved more sex, but once they were dressed, the mood shifted. Rachel knew they wouldn't be getting naked again, and that meant the good-bye scene was coming up soon. She went into survival mode.

Jake contacted the Hunters to let them know he'd made his decision and he'd be over at his place within the next hour. Because Rachel needed something to do while he made that call, she threw together an omelet to go with the coffee she'd brewed.

All the blinds were up now because they had nothing to be secretive about. When Jake made his call to the Hunters out on her deck, she was able to sneak glances at him while he talked. He still looked tense, which was a shame if he was about to live his dream.

When he came back in, he seemed surprised to see food on the table but covered his amazement quickly. "Terrific, Rachel. Thanks for fixing breakfast."

"You didn't think I could, did you?"

His smile was apologetic. "I didn't because you kept telling me you weren't much of a cook."

"I'm not, but I have to feed myself and I can't exist totally on candy bars, so I've mastered a few basics. Go ahead and sit down. I'll bring you some coffee."

"Okay, thanks."

Although her nerves were stretched tight, she congratulated herself on behaving like a relatively sane person. That was until she almost poured the coffee down the drain instead of carrying it into the dining area. Maybe she wasn't as cool about this as she liked to think she was.

But Jake wouldn't have to know that. She'd stopped

herself before dumping the coffee in the sink, so she carried it out of the kitchen and poured each of them a steaming mug.

"Smells great."

"Thanks." She returned the pot to the kitchen and came back to sit at the table with him. "Is it a burden, dealing with a super nose?"

He laughed, which was her intention. She didn't want to let the mood dip all the way into gloom and doom.

"I don't think of it that way," he said. "But I'm used to it."

"But you haven't had that ability all your life, right? Because if you had, that would be a clue that someone had been born Were."

He put down his coffee and gazed at her. "Good observation. You're absolutely right. Until young werewolves hit puberty, their senses aren't any more developed than a human's."

"That's too bad, in a way." She dug into her omelet, which wasn't half-bad, if she did say so. "If they showed that tendency earlier, wouldn't that help sort things out?"

"Maybe for the mixed-species couples, but think about it. A baby is enough of a challenge. What if you had to worry about whether your little baby girl would suddenly turn into a wolf cub as you pushed a buggy through Central Park? Then what?"

"I see how that might be a problem. But if the werewolf tendencies showed up slightly sooner than puberty, that would take the mystery out of situations like the Wallace brothers have."

His green gaze sharpened. "You got pretty far into MacDowell's book, I see."

"Couldn't help it, Jake. With an imagination like mine,

how could I resist something as exotic as rich were-wolves? Is it true that Wallace Enterprises owns the Chrysler Building?"

"I believe so. It's through a dummy corporation, but that sounds right. The Wallaces have major holdings in New York. Howard Wallace was elected president of the Were Council last fall in Denver."

"And yet both of his sons have mated with humans. I find that amazing."

Jake sighed. "I find it depressing. Don't Aidan and Roarke understand that they're Wallaces? It's the proud-est werewolf name in North America, and they behave as if they have no sense of tradition or solidarity."

"Apparently they fell in love." The minute she said it, she wished she hadn't. Last night had been all about the love between her and Jake, and that statement might make him think she wanted to use that love as an excuse to defy tradition. "I didn't mean that the way it sounded."

"I know." He pushed away his plate, even though he'd eaten only half of his omelet. "The Wallace brothers are a sore spot for me. I grew up hearing about the mighty Wallace dynasty from my mother. I could hardly wait to meet members of the Wallace pack because I just knew we'd hit it off and share common values. Not so much."

"Jake." She shouldn't say anything, but she couldn't seem to stop herself. "I'm trying not to take offense, but you're sitting at the table with a member of the other species, the one you so object to the Wallace brothers taking up with."

He glanced at her and had the decency to look em-barrassed. "You're right. I apologize."

The mood was permanently ruined now. Maybe that was just as well. Anger at his attitude could keep her from feeling the pain when he left. "It's probably time for me to drive you over to your cabin so you can rendezvous with the Hunters."

"I'll help you with the dishes first."

"Never mind the dishes, Jake. Let's get this over with." That was harsh, but damn it, every word out of his mouth since they'd sat down to breakfast had made her feel like a second-class citizen. She wouldn't tolerate that, not even from the one she loved.

Jake took the hint and left the dishes. The trip over to his cabin was made in silence, a heartbreaking contrast to the closeness they'd felt all through the night. But Rachel felt Jake moving away from her and closer to his new pack. They wouldn't want him to have close ties to a human female. Jake might choose to give up that little mental telepathy trick they'd discovered last night.

The Hunters' SUV was parked in front of Jake's cabin when they arrived, and that irritated Rachel even more. They were too blasted eager, in her estimation. Jake had lived in Polecat for many years, and they seemed ready to pluck him out of there as if he had no roots in the community.

So maybe it was a human community and not one of their precious Were packs. Rachel realized her attitude was deteriorating rapidly, but the sight of that black SUV sitting in front of Jake's cabin got her back up. They had to know she'd be bringing Jake home, and apparently they didn't trust her to deposit him and leave.

When she pulled in beside the SUV, Jake cleared his throat. "You can just drop me off."

"I don't intend to do that, Jake."

"Why not?"

"Because if I drop you off and drive away, it'll look like I turned tail and ran away from those two werewolves. I realize I'm not supposed to know they're werewolves, but I do, and I don't want them to think I was intimidated by them."

"Does it matter what they think?"

She glanced at him. "It does to me. At this point, I represent my fellow humans. I'm an emissary for my species."

"All right, then. Let's go over and say hello." He opened the passenger door, picked up his duffel, and stepped down.

"Fine." She climbed down from the driver's side. She hadn't been expecting to meet the Hunters when she brought Jake back around the lake, so she hadn't taken much time with her appearance.

But as she walked around the front of her truck toward their vehicle, she reminded herself that she was an internationally recognized artist. Collectors from all over the world, including a few werewolves, according to Jake, gladly paid high sums to have her work in their homes and office buildings.

She didn't know what the Hunters had going for them, but she refused to let them treat her like some riffraff that the heir to the Hunter throne had been dallying with. Jake loved her, even if he might not ever admit that to them. Maybe he shouldn't, come to think of it. She was still a little worried about the dungeon and the maggot-infested crusts of bread.

The Hunters, who were apparently gifted with good manners, got out of their SUV to greet Rachel and Jake. They both wore designer sunglasses. Ann smiled at Jake first and Rachel second, but that wasn't so surprising. She knew Jake better. They had history.

Bruce was more reserved. He shook hands with Jake without smiling and nodded in Rachel's direction. Bruce telegraphed brisk efficiency, as if he hoped they could dispense with the pleasantries and get this show on the road.

Rachel wasn't inclined to indulge him in that. "We didn't have much time to chat yesterday," she said, directing her conversation mostly to Ann. "But I'm thrilled that Jake is reconnecting with family again. I'm sure he's missed that."

"His family has missed him, too," Ann said. "Having him back in Idaho will be wonderful."

"I'm sure it will be." Having him leave Polecat would be quite a bit less than wonderful, but that was her problem.

"We should probably get in there and start packing," Bruce said in an ill-disguised attempt to move Rachel along.

Rachel chose to let herself be moved. "Yep, don't want to hold you up." She had no interest in a prolonged visit with these two. "I should be going, anyway. I have an important project to finish, so it's time I got to work." She glanced at Jake and her heart constricted. His jaw was clenched as if anticipating a blow. She understood the feeling.

She stepped closer to him. He'd worn his sunglasses, so she couldn't see his eyes. Might be just as well. "Take care of yourself," she said softly.

His voice was husky. "You, too."

She turned and fled. Hearing the grief in those two words nearly destroyed her. Somehow she got her truck started. By some miracle nobody was on the road, because she backed onto it without looking and peeled out.

She didn't remember the drive back around the lake, but somehow she pulled into the parking spot beside the path leading to her cabin. Leaving her truck, she hurried down the path, fighting tears all the way. She didn't dare break down. Lionel would show up in less than thirty minutes, and she instinctively knew that if she let go, she'd still be crying when he arrived.

I love you, Rachel.

The words brought her to a screeching halt. She looked around, almost expecting to see Jake. But of course he wasn't here. He was at his cabin with Ann and Bruce.

Yet he'd sent her a message with the words he hadn't been able to say before she'd left. Taking a calming breath, she focused all her attention on him and returned the favor. *I love you, Jake.*

Warmth enveloped her, as if he'd mentally wrapped his arms around her. She knew that in his mind, he had.

Then he sent one more word winging over the lake. *Always.*

She concentrated on him with all her might. *Yes, my love. Always.* And that would have to sustain her. Walking toward her cabin, she vowed that it would.

She hadn't locked up because she'd known she was coming right back. As she opened the front door, she thought about the breakfast dishes waiting for her. She might not be able to face them without breaking down.

So she'd leave them. Might as well walk straight out the back door and over to her shop. Work would help. It always did.

She'd taken two steps in that direction when she heard a soft noise behind her. And something didn't smell right, either. Maybe she was developing Were sensitivities.

She started to turn around, but before she could, someone grabbed her from behind. She would have screamed, but a hand holding an acrid-smelling cloth covered her nose and mouth with a grip like iron. She struggled for only a second before everything went black.

Chapter 23

Ann and Bruce had come armed with packing boxes and offered to tackle that job. Jake hadn't moved in years, so he gladly turned the chore over to them. He was about to call a local real estate agent about selling the cabin when he had the strangest feeling, as if his contact with Rachel had been abruptly cut off.

Although she hadn't sent him any more messages after her last one, he'd still sensed a connection humming between them. Now there was nothing, as if the line had gone dead.

Well, maybe that's the way she wanted it. Because her dramatic exit had meant they'd left important words unsaid, he'd sent them to her telepathically. When she'd returned his message, his heartache had eased a little.

Hers might have, too. If so, she'd probably retreated to gather her forces. Maybe she'd gone out to her shop and immersed herself in her work. He could picture her doing that.

If plunging back into normal life helped her, then he didn't want to interfere with that. In fact, he might as well do the same. He made his call to the real estate agent, who arranged to come right out with the necessary papers.

Considering how long Jake had lived in Polecat, he was surprised at how quickly his connection to the community could be severed. A couple of phone calls to the utilities took care of that. Once the real estate agent arrived and he'd signed the listing papers, he'd be cut loose from his former home.

The way Ann and Bruce were working, they'd have him packed up in no time. They'd convinced him to leave everything except his clothes and his food. They'd even talked him out of taking any of his books.

While both of them were busy in the kitchen sorting through the cupboards, he glanced over the books and decided they were right about leaving them. He'd read all the paperbacks and didn't plan to read them again. He wouldn't need Alaskan hiking-trail information anymore.

And now was the time to jettison *Alaskan Artisans of Today*. He should take Rachel's note out, though. He didn't want some stranger to find it and sell it on eBay. But the note wasn't there. He riffled through the pages, thinking he might have tucked it in a different section.

Finally he turned the book upside down and shook it. No note. Okay, that was strange. Or . . . maybe not. He thought of all the snooping Rachel had done prior to his coming home from San Francisco. She'd probably noticed this book. If she'd opened it and found her note, she might have taken it out, planning to ask him about it eventually.

With all they'd had going on, it was no wonder she'd forgotten the note. Come to think of it, she still had his favorite T-shirt, too. He'd noticed it draped over one of her dining chairs this morning and had meant to stuff it in the plastic bag with the other dirty clothes. But their discussion during breakfast had become awkward and she'd been eager to get him out of there. He hadn't remembered to grab the shirt.

"If you're considering taking that book, I would advise against it."

Jake glanced up to discover Bruce gazing at him from the kitchen doorway. "It's an expensive book." Jake hadn't planned to take it, but he didn't care for Bruce's commanding tone. "Besides that, it would be a good souvenir of my life here."

"It has Rachel Miller in it. You'd be better off leaving it here."

That might be a true statement, but something about it bothered Jake. Finally he figured out what it was. "How do you know Rachel's in here?"

Bruce's gaze shifted. Not much, but enough to give him away. "It was a good guess, judging from the title."

"I don't think you were guessing, Bruce."

The older Were shrugged. "Okay, I looked at it."

"When?" Although Jake had been on the phone for the past half hour, he'd been right here in the living room. Until a few minutes ago he'd thought Rachel's note was still in the book. Because of that note, he certainly would have noticed if Bruce had pulled the book off the shelf.

Bruce waved his hand dismissively. "I couldn't tell you exactly, but I looked at it and saw she was in it. If you take it with you, that's waving a red flag. Don't do it. Anyway, Ann wants to throw away all the meat in the freezer. She sent me out to make sure you're okay with that."

"I don't care about the meat in the freezer," Jake said quietly. "But I do care that you and Ann came in and went through my stuff when I wasn't home."

Bruce flushed. "Don't make accusations without proof, Jake. Your parents taught you better than that."

"Oh, but I have proof." Jake hefted the book in both hands. "This book is special to me. If you'd picked it up while I was here, I would have been very aware that you had looked at it." Now Jake wondered if Bruce had taken the note, but it wasn't the main issue.

No, there was something else going on, something that worried him far more than knowing the Hunters had searched his cabin. They would have had multiple opportunities to do that, because once again, he hadn't bothered to lock up. He just wasn't in the habit.

Then again, it might not have mattered if he'd locked the doors or not. If they were determined enough, they would have found a way to get in. Jake had never worried about tight security in this cabin.

He gazed at Bruce. "Maybe you should have a seat. In fact, I think Ann needs to come in here and sit down, too."

The Were's blue eyes narrowed and his tone turned icy. "How dare you give *me* orders?"

"I've been asked to be your alpha, Bruce, and life doesn't go well for those who lie to the alpha."

"I haven't lied to you!"

"Okay, you aren't telling me the whole truth, which is pretty much the same thing. Unless you intend to overpower me and drag me to Idaho, which I can assure you isn't going to happen, I'm staying put until you tell me what's going on."

Bruce turned his head. "Ann! We have a problem. You'd better come on in here so we can straighten it out."

Ann walked out of the kitchen, a paper towel in her hand. "What's the matter?"

"I'd like you and Bruce to sit down." Jake gestured to the sofa. "We need to talk."

"He says we're not telling him everything," Bruce said.

"Oh." Ann walked over to the sofa and settled down with a calm expression on her aristocratic features, but she balled the paper towel into a tight wad the size of a golf ball. "What do you want to know, Jake?"

Jake waited for Bruce to take a seat next to his mate. At last he did, although he frowned at Jake as he did so. Jake moved to the easy chair, sat down, and looked at these two Weres who had been family friends for longer than he'd been alive. Yet he couldn't shake the idea they'd betrayed him.

He took a deep breath. "Let's start with the alpha position. Is there one after all?"

"Yes." Ann tightened her grip on the balled-up paper towel. "Keegan really wants to step down."

"But there must be other candidates who are already living in Idaho. Why come all the way to Alaska to get me?"

"The Hunter pack has been impressed with your efforts with WARM," Bruce said. "We admire the leadership qualities you've displayed. You're intelligent and even tempered. At least, that's what I thought until five minutes ago, when you started acting crazy and throwing accusations around."

Jake sighed. He should have known the setup was too good to be true. "But somebody's mighty worried about my relationship with Rachel Miller, aren't they?"

Ann swallowed. "There have been some . . . concerns. Her signature wolf looks exactly like you, Jake."

"No, it looks exactly like my father, but that's neither here nor there." He decided to make a guess and see how they reacted. "How long has the Hunter pack had me under surveillance?"

"It's not just the Hunter pack," Ann said. Then she gasped and looked at Bruce. "Sorry. I shouldn't have said that."

"No, but he was going to find out, anyway." Bruce looked at Jake. "No matter which wolf Rachel Miller has been carving over and over, you can't deny that you've acted with increasing recklessness when it comes to her."

"No, I can't deny it." Some of Jake's righteous indignation seeped away. "So this is a rescue mission, then?"

Bruce nodded. "We need a pack alpha, and the . . . Consortium thinks you should leave the area. You've made excellent progress with WARM, but you're putting those efforts in jeopardy. We need you in Idaho, and you'd be out of harm's way. It's a nice little two-for-one deal."

It was a long speech, but Jake latched on to one particular word in it. "Consortium?"

"A like-minded group of Weres that keep an eye on potential breaches of security and quietly take care of any we find."

"Breaches?" The word sent icicles of fear into Jake's heart. "What makes you think there's been a security breach?"

Bruce gazed at him. "The Consortium is thorough, Jake. We have documentation."

Shit. Suddenly Rachel's worst-case scenario didn't look so paranoid. "But the Were Council knows about this Consortium, right? You're acting under its direction."

"Well, no, Jake, because they would want to regulate us and tie our hands. We're far more effective operating under the radar."

A chill went down Jake's spine. "Sorry, but I can't go

along with that. I'm no big fan of the Were Council or WOW, but at least they operate out in the open."

Bruce eyed him with irritating smugness. "Doesn't matter whether you approve of us or not. You won't report us to the council or anyone."

"Watch me." Jake stood and pulled his cell phone out of his pocket. He still had Howard Wallace in his list of contacts.

"Jake, that's a really bad idea," Ann said.

"Don't think I care about the Hunter alpha position. I don't give a rip about that anymore. I have bigger fish to fry. This Consortium is dangerous and I intend to see that it's exposed."

"What about your precious WARM?" Bruce's tone was mild, but his eyes glittered with malice. "You not only had a sexual relationship with a human—you created a security breach in the process. If that gets out, WARM will be finished. Duncan MacDowell will dance on its grave."

Jake longed to punch Bruce in the face, but the Were had him by the short hairs. They exchanged malevolent stares. "You're a real bastard," Jake said.

"And you're a real traitor to the cause. Tell me, are you prepared for the entire Were community to know how you've betrayed them with Rachel Miller?"

Jake's stomach churned. Duncan MacDowell *would* dance on WARM's grave if that came out. All that Jake had worked for would be down the drain. Once he was branded a hypocrite, anyone on the fence probably would go over to MacDowell's camp. At least Duncan stuck to his beliefs.

By giving in to his desire for Rachel, Jake had paved the way for others to do the same, assuming Bruce made good on his promise to reveal the relationship. But

Bruce had something to lose, too. "You won't expose me," Jake said. "If I go down, that weakens your campaign to keep Weres and humans apart. We both lose."

"I'm counting on your intelligence and dedication to the cause, Jake. Work with me. Work with the Consortium. WARM will be the public face of the movement and the Consortium will be the private enforcer."

"Sounds like a bargain with the devil, to me."

"Do you have a choice?"

Jake looked into his cold blue eyes. "Oh, yeah, I always have a choice." He couldn't work with Bruce. He knew that, and yet the alternative made him sick. He had to get out of here, away from these toxic Weres. "I'm going for a drive around the lake."

"I'd advise you not to go over to Rachel's," Bruce said.

Jake gazed at him. "Yeah? Well, Bruce, you can take that advice and shove it where the sun don't shine. One more visit to Rachel isn't going to make this any worse than it already is, and she happens to help me think straight. Besides, I need to satisfy myself that she's okay. Because something about your tone of voice makes me wonder." Reaching into his pocket for his truck keys, he walked out the door.

All the way around the lake, he realized he was running to a human to help him solve what was essentially a werewolf problem. That wasn't logical, and yet he trusted Rachel and wanted to make sure she was okay. He no longer trusted Ann and Bruce Hunter to guarantee that. And he definitely didn't trust this *Consortium* they'd hooked up with.

He'd assured Rachel that the Hunters weren't activists, and apparently they weren't in the normal sense. They didn't join organizations like WARM, or HOWL, the one Kate Stillman had founded as an acronym for Honoring Our Werewolf Legacy.

No, the Hunters had decided to go underground and create some shadow group that didn't answer to anyone but itself. The concept made Jake shudder. He shouldn't be surprised that the debate over human and Were inter-action would spawn a fringe group like this. The climate was ripe for it.

And he'd fallen right into their hands. They'd proba-bly been monitoring his movements for at least a year or more, soon after Rachel's carvings became world-famous. Jake had known some Weres had suspicions about his potential involvement with Rachel, but he'd never dreamed that an ultraconservative group was spy-ing on him to gather evidence of a breach.

If so, they had all the ammunition they needed to bring him to his knees. They'd probably recorded his nightly runs over to her cabin. They'd have the bear at-tack on tape, and once he'd entered her house as a wolf, the plan to remove him from Alaska must have begun.

He'd been naive enough to think that the Hunters' request was simple—the pack needed a new alpha and he was a good candidate. He'd been flattered and unwill-ing to look a gift horse in the mouth. But now he could see that hauling his ass all the way from Alaska was an extreme solution to their alpha issue. There had been more to it—much more.

When he pulled into the parking area beside the path to Rachel's cabin, the presence of both Rachel's and Lionel's trucks calmed him. These were sincere, good people. Yes, Lionel had put a bullet in his shoulder, but he'd done it out of loyalty to Rachel. The kid would lay down his life for her, and Jake treasured that, even if it had caused him pain.

Because he expected them both to be working, he headed straight for the workshop. But instead of an atmosphere of creativity and good cheer, he found Lionel sitting alone on a stool, staring into space. Rachel was nowhere around. Maybe she'd gone to the cabin for a cup of coffee.

Lionel looked startled when Jake walked through the door. "What are you doing here?"

"I wanted to talk to Rachel. There's been a . . . problem. I wanted to talk to her about it."

Lionel stared at him as if he'd lost his mind. "She's not with you?"

"No, of course not. We agreed that I'd go to Idaho to be with my . . . extended family, and she'd stay here."

"That's not what her note says."

"What note?"

"This one." Lionel picked it up from the workbench and handed it to Jake. "I've read it about a hundred times, and I still don't believe it. She wouldn't leave without seeing me."

Jake scanned the note.

Dear Lionel,

I've decided to leave with Jake when he heads to Idaho to be with his family. I'm starting a new life there, so I've decided to be wild and crazy and leave everything here instead of going through the hassle of packing.

I know this will shock you, but I want to leave the house, the workshop, and all the tools to you. The sky's the limit! Walk in my footsteps, dear friend.

Warmly,
Rachel

Jake reread the note as he tried to figure out what the hell was going on. "But she's not going to Idaho," he said. "That was never the plan."

"But it's her handwriting," Lionel said. "I've seen it a bunch of times, and she wrote that. I'd swear to it."

"All I can tell you, Lionel, is that she wasn't planning to go to Idaho with me. And it's not like she showed up over at my place and announced she was doing that. She wouldn't have. Not considering everything."

"You know that better than I do, Mr. Hunter. But she's not here."

"So you've been all through the house?" In his desperation, Jake prayed that she was still inside her cabin, maybe in the bathroom. Lionel wouldn't have opened that door to check on her.

"I've searched everywhere," Lionel said. "Even the bathroom."

That killed Jake's hope that she was in there.

"It's like she said." Lionel gestured around the shop. "She left without taking anything." He turned to something lying in a heap on the workbench. "She left dirty dishes in the sink, and this draped over a chair." He held up Jake's wolf T-shirt.

A sense of dread settled in the pit of Jake's stomach. "Something's very wrong about this."

"Well, duh, I know *that*. But what about her note? Why did she write something like that?"

Jake studied the note. After three years of looking at Rachel's thank-you note to him, he knew her handwriting well. At first glance, this looked exactly like it. But there were subtle differences. The loops weren't quite as open, and the pressure on the paper wasn't quite as deliberate. Rachel wrote with an artist's flourish, and this handwriting was more controlled, more tentative.

The longer Jake looked at this note, the more he became certain that someone, probably whoever had swiped her note out of his coffee-table book, had forged her handwriting. His money was on the Hunters, or someone connected to this Consortium they'd hooked up with.

He gazed at Lionel. "This note makes no sense because she didn't write it. The handwriting's slightly different, and besides, she signed it *Rachel*. If she'd written it, she would have signed it *Miss M*."

"You're right!" Lionel sucked in a breath. "Then who did write it?"

"The same creeps who have made her disappear."

"Oh, God. You think she's been kidnapped? Or . . ."

"Kidnapped." Jake wouldn't let himself think of the alternative. Although his heart pounded frantically, he had to keep his mind clear, for Rachel's sake. "Yes, I think she's been kidnapped."

"Then I'm calling the cops." Lionel pulled out his cell phone.

"Wait." Jake had a good idea who had taken her, and calling the human police might do no good whatsoever. He laid a hand on Lionel's arm. "Let me try something else first."

"What?"

"Don't laugh, but Rachel and I have a psychic connection."

"I'm not laughing. I believe in psychic connections, Mr. Hunter. Can you tune her in?"

"I'm going to try." Dear God, please let it work. Then he remembered how the connection between them had seemed to go dead about an hour ago and his blood ran cold. If anything had happened to her, he would have no reason to live. No, that wasn't true. He'd have a reason—finding those who'd harmed her and making them pay.

"If you get a bead on her, we're going after her," Lionel said. "You and me."

"Absolutely, Lionel." Panic clawed at Jake's insides, but he refused to give in to it. She was alive. She had to be. And her fate could well depend on his ability to handle this.

He briefly thought of going back and forcing the Hunters to tell him what they knew. But they might not have details of the plan and he'd only waste valuable time trying to get the information out of them.

Connecting directly to Rachel would be faster. If he couldn't do that, then he'd confront Ann and Bruce. But either way, he would find her. She was everything to him, and he finally knew that.

Chapter 24

Rachel tried to fight free of the dreamlike fog that enveloped her so she could think. She had an urgent need to think, but she wasn't sure why that was, and her brain wasn't working right.

"She's coming out of it."

Rachel didn't recognize the voice. Was she in a hospital? Had she crashed on the road between Jake's cabin and hers? No, she remembered arriving at her place, parking her truck, and walking into the house.

"Should we put her under again?" A different voice, although both were male.

"Nah, that'll just make hauling her around tougher."

"Good point."

Rachel listened to the conversation with growing alarm. These men, whoever they were, didn't have her best interests at heart if they referred to her as a piece of luggage. *Hauling her around.* Good grief. Gradually she figured out she was in the backseat of a vehicle, some sort of SUV.

Her captors, and she was reasonably sure that was the right term for the two men in front, were taking her somewhere, but why? For ransom? She supposed that her parents would pay to get her back, but her net worth was greater than theirs. A smart person would kidnap her parents and make *her* pay up.

Maybe she was in the hands of idiots, never a good thing. Well, it could be a good thing. If she could outsmart them, she could get away.

She went back over the events that had led to this situation to try to make sense of it. She'd left Jake's cabin in quite an emotional state. Then, as she'd walked down the path to her place, she'd felt that psychic connection with him. They'd reaffirmed their love for each other. So far, so good.

On the way into her house, she'd decided to go straight out to the workshop and use her art to soothe her raw emotions. But she hadn't done that because someone—one of these two thugs in the front, no doubt—had grabbed her and knocked her out with a nasty-smelling hankie. While she was unconscious, they'd put her in this vehicle and driven away from her cabin.

Although she wasn't happy with her next conclusion, she admitted this probably had something to do with werewolves who didn't trust her as much as Jake did. Shit. If that was the case, she needed to gather information before they threw her in the grimy dungeon she'd imagined.

Anyone who'd watched movies that featured dungeons knew that once the iron door slammed, you got zero information. Your keepers were sadistic cretins who spoke in monosyllables and enjoyed watching you suffer. Your only friend would be the tiny spider in the corner of your cell.

Sitting up a little straighter in the seat, she noted that

they had not belted her in. She rectified that oversight. Her throat was dry, but she worked up enough spit to talk without sounding like Golem. "Where are you taking me?" That was the classic kidnap victim question from all the B movies, but she really wanted to know.

"It doesn't matter," said the brown-haired, beefy fellow in the passenger seat.

"Because you're going to kill me?" She didn't think so, but it didn't hurt to ask. If they'd wanted to kill her, she'd be dead by now and her body would be in an unmarked grave.

"Oh, no," said the driver, who was equally muscular but had reddish hair. "You've got it made. You're headed for a penthouse in a Vancouver high-rise."

"Vancouver, BC? Are we driving all that way?"

"Yes, ma'am, we are." The driver glanced in the rearview mirror. His shades made him look quite forbidding. "Karl and I will be trading off so we don't have to stop along the way."

"That's insane. It's a really long way."

The driver shrugged. "It's not so bad." He checked the time on his cell phone, tucked in a holder on the dash. "We've already logged in almost an hour. With no complications, we could make it in late tomorrow night or early the next morning."

Rachel wasn't about to spend two days with these goons, who were most certainly werewolves if they were cool with driving straight through to Vancouver. Nobody did that. But they'd have to let her get out of the car to use public restrooms during this marathon trip, and that's when she'd get away.

"Oh, and so you don't waste time dreaming up your escape," the brown-haired one named Karl said, "you'll only be allowed to leave this car for one reason, and we brought a little camping potty along for that purpose. Mitch and I would catch hell if you climbed out a bathroom window and got away."

Damn. So she hadn't been captured by idiots, after all. That would make escape more difficult, but she'd be watching for every opportunity.

In the meantime, she'd pretend that she'd accepted her fate, so they might relax their vigilance. "So what happens once you deliver me to this penthouse?"

"You live in the lap of luxury—that's what," Karl said. "Great view, terrific food, luxurious surroundings."

"What's the catch?"

"The usual thing. You can never leave."

Panic threatened to close her throat and make her choke. She couldn't be confined like that. Maybe someone, a Howard Hughes type, would be thrilled with such a setup. But for her, it would be like being dead.

As a prisoner in a penthouse, she wouldn't be able to work. She'd be cut off from her family and friends. She'd have life, but nothing worth living for. Considering that, she might as well be in a dungeon where she was fed maggot-infested bread.

But she wouldn't end up in this penthouse. By now, Lionel would have come over and found her missing. He'd sound the alarm. Maybe not right away, because he might think she was over at Jake's, but eventually he'd try to find out where she was.

She cleared her throat. "You realize that people will come looking for me. I have friends and family. I have wealthy clients. They'll try to find me." And that wasn't counting Jake. But before she tried to summon him telepathically, she wanted more info. "This isn't going to work the way you think it will."

"Yeah, it will," said Mitch, the driver. "It seems you

left a note saying you were headed off to Idaho and a new life with Jake Hunter. You turned your place and your workshop over to Lionel."

"What note? I didn't write a note!"

"No, but the note is in your handwriting," Karl said.

Mitch glanced at his traveling companion. "I'm not sure you should be telling her all that. Especially after the phone call we got a little while ago regarding you know who."

"Look, the note bought us time. All we needed was a chance to get the hell out of Dodge."

"I guess."

"We have a head start. You and I are the only ones who were told the ultimate destination, so we're golden." Karl turned toward the backseat. "Your future is in Vancouver, sweetheart. Just accept that and move on."

Rachel wasn't accepting a damned thing, but fighting with Karl and Mitch would waste precious energy. She was beginning to get the picture now. The Hunters were more than emissaries who wanted to recruit Jake as their new alpha. That might have been one of their goals, but the other was getting her out of the way.

The sample of her handwriting had probably been her original note to Jake. The Hunters had gotten hold of it somehow. Then she had a horrible thought, the worst one yet.

Had Jake known about this plan? No, surely not. She couldn't believe that he would have agreed to it. If he'd betrayed her so completely, then . . . He wouldn't have. She refused to think he was capable of such treachery.

And if he *hadn't* known about this, then it was time she told him. Naturally the werewolves had taken away her cell phone, but she had a secret weapon, one they wouldn't even know she was using.

* * *

"You might think I've gone off the deep end," Jake said
to Lionel. "But I'm going to—"

"Listen, if you have to take your clothes off for this,
then okay, but I'll have to leave while you do that."

"No, I'm not planning to get naked."

"Good." Lionel pushed his hair off his forehead.
"That's a relief, Mr. Hunter."

"I'm going into the cabin to get that wolf carving off
her mantel."

"Oh, yeah." Lionel followed him out of the workshop.
"You mean the carving you ditched. I thought that was
the craziest move I'd ever heard of. Do you know what
that thing is probably worth?"

"If touching it focuses my thoughts on her and we can
connect easier, then it's priceless."

"You have a point there."

Jake took the steps to her deck two at a time. Ever
since deciding to connect with her, he'd been trying to
get the same sense he'd had earlier this morning, when
they'd sent their thoughts to each other with such perfect clarity. He was relieved that something seemed to be
happening now. When he thought of her, he didn't get
the feeling of dead air between them, thank God. But he
was picking up a lot of static.

Thinking the piece of wood might make a difference
was possibly both corny and wrong, but he felt the urge
to do it, and under the circumstances, he was going with
his gut. The carving had been their first link. Maybe it
would come through for him now and cut through that
static.

Inside the cabin, he made himself ignore all the things
that threatened to get him choked up, like the untidy

kitchen, which he could see by looking through the pocket door. He'd been an ass this morning, raving on about werewolf superiority, but he couldn't let himself be swamped with regret right now.

He had a job to do. Taking the carving from the mantel, he sat down on her sofa and put it in his lap. Instantly he felt closer to her, as he had all those times when he'd stood beside his own mantel and gazed at her work.

"She's a great artist." Lionel settled himself in an easy chair next to the sofa. "Nobody carves wolves the way she does."

"She has a gift, all right." Jake looked over at him. "I don't know how long this will take. You don't have to sit here unless you—"

"I'll sit here." Lionel's dark gaze was troubled. "The minute you figure out where she is, we're leaving."

"That's if I find out."

"You will. You have to."

Jake looked at the kid, whose every muscle was tense with worry. "I know." Taking a deep breath, he closed his eyes and spread his hands over the remembered grooves of the wolf carving. *Rachel, where are you?*

At first he got nothing except a fuzzy transmission that could have been his own thoughts ricocheting around in his brain. He was easily as tense as Lionel. He forced himself to relax and try again. *Rachel, where are you?*

Jake! I'm in an SUV.

He sucked in a breath. *Where?*

Alaskan Highway going south.

The bastards had taken her! He gripped the wood. *How long?*

About fifty minutes.

Color?

Black.

Hang on, Rachel. We're coming. Watch for my truck.

Hurry, Jake.

I damn well will. Opening his eyes, he stood and carefully laid the carving on the sofa. "Let's roll."

"Where is she?"

Jake filled him in as he headed for the front door.

"Should I bring my gun, then?" Lionel followed close behind. "It's in my truck. I have ammunition."

Jake debated for a second. He wasn't a fan of guns, especially the exact rifle that had wounded him a short time ago. He would never shoot any creature. But tires ... that was a different matter. "Yeah," he said. "Bring your gun." He walked out the front door with Lionel right behind him.

"How about my red emergency light?"

"Your *what*?" Jake had no idea what the kid was talking about, so he continued out the door and down the path to the parking area, moving fast.

"Just an old one, the bubblegum kind."

"Why do you have it in the first place?"

"Oh, you know. Something I picked up for fun, to scare my friends." Lionel hurried to keep up. "You can stick it on the top of your vehicle, and when you turn it on, at first glance you look like a cop."

"Isn't that illegal?"

"Well, yeah, but you can get away with stuff like that out here. Not too many cops to catch you doing it. Me and my friends, we play tricks on each other all the time."

"Okay. That might come in handy." They reached the parking area and Jake started toward his truck.

"I have a siren, too."

Jake looked at him and shrugged. "What the hell? Bring everything." He didn't know how this would all shake out, but he'd use whatever tools presented themselves. An emergency light and a siren might be just what he needed as a distraction.

Moments later, they were heading toward the highway, going way over the speed limit.

Lionel glanced over at the speedometer. "See, here's my thought. If we put the bubble light on top, we can fool anybody on the road into thinking we have a right to speed."

"Except a cop."

"Which is why I brought my fuzz buster." Lionel stuck it on the dash. "And my converter plug so we can run everything."

"Good Lord." Jake kept his eyes on the road because he really was going way too fast, but with all of Lionel's paraphernalia, they might get away with racing along like maniacs.

Fortunately, the SUV they were pursuing would be driving at a very sedate pace. Whoever was in the car with Rachel wouldn't want to be pulled over with a kidnap victim on board. But by the time Jake finished with them, they might wish it had been the real cops who pulled them over.

As they raced along, Jake tried not to worry about Lionel hanging out the window while he used his long arms to slap the bubble light on the roof of the cab. "Don't fall out, okay?"

"Hey, this is nothing! You should see me doing it while I'm driving!"

"No, thanks!" That was the moment Jake realized he would have to work hard not to be an overprotective father when the time came. Maybe Rachel could help him with that and remind him that all kids, werewolf and human alike, needed space to grow.

Lionel got the light working, and Jake took full advantage of the fact that cars pulled over to let him by. The emergency light was a brilliant concept. They were making excellent time.

"Want me to crank up the siren, Mr. Hunter?"

Jake glanced over at him and recognized the light of battle in the kid's eyes. "Sure. Let's give 'em all we've got."

"Awesome." Lionel added the siren to the mix, and cars pulled over even quicker.

Jake slammed the pedal down and turned the big V8 loose. The truck screamed down the highway. Apparently luck was smiling on them, because they didn't pass a single cop car as they hurtled along. Jake factored in the speed of the SUV compared with his speed, and when he thought they might be getting close, he told Lionel to keep an eye out for a black SUV.

"We might see more than one, you know," Lionel said.

"I guess." Jake thought about that. "But I have a feeling I'm going to know it when we see it." He couldn't explain the emotion burning in his chest, but the closer he got to Rachel, the hotter the flame. Those bastards had Rachel. He would stop at nothing to get her back.

Chapter 25

From the moment Rachel had made telepathic contact with Jake, she'd had trouble sitting still. She knew he was coming for her. She could feel it.

She almost felt sorry for the two werewolves in the front seat. They had no idea what they were dealing with. Their pursuer had faced down a grizzly to keep her safe. Taking on a couple of thugs like them would be a piece of cake.

When she heard the siren and turned to see the flashing light on the top of Jake's black truck, she had to clap her hand over her mouth to keep from laughing and shouting for joy. Now, *this* was what she called a rescue!

Mitch glanced in his side-view mirror. "What the fuck is that idiot doing?"

He's coming for you, Rachel thought with barely controlled glee. *Be afraid. Be very afraid.*

"Just pull over and let him go by," Karl said. "He's probably drunk."

"Yeah, probably is," Mitch said. "These backcountry types love to tie one on, don't they?" He swung the SUV to the side of the road. "Go around, idiot!"

The black truck didn't go around. Instead it pulled up behind the SUV, its big engine rumbling. The siren stopped screeching and the emergency light switched off.

"Mitch," Karl said in a low voice. "I think you'd be wise to get the hell out of here. I smell a Were in that truck."

"When you're right, you're right." Mitch gunned it, but the SUV didn't get very far. Two shots rang out. Mitch started swearing as the car swerved, its two rear tires blown out.

Mitch pulled the SUV to the shoulder and looked over at Karl. "You ready to fight Jake Hunter?"

"Was that in the contract?"

"Not the one I read."

Rachel unlatched her seat belt and turned to watch Jake and Lionel get out of the truck. Maybe it was her imagination, but they seemed to radiate power as they approached the SUV, like a couple of gunslingers from the Old West.

Karl turned to look, too. "One's human."

"Yeah, and he's carrying a rifle. That's not good."

"You armed, Mitch?"

"Not me. How about you, Karl?"

"You know I hate the things."

Mitch sighed. "Then how about we give them the woman and call a towing service?"

"That's not going to make us very popular."

Mitch glanced in the side-view mirror one more time. "Hey, their plan didn't work! Is that our fault? You know the rap sheet on Hunter. He challenged a grizz not long ago. And won. Personally, I don't care to tangle with him."

"Me, either." Karl unsnapped his seat belt and opened

his door. "Hey, don't shoot! You can have her! We surrender!"

As Rachel scrambled out of the car, she realized two things. All Weres weren't as courageous as Jake, and from this moment on, he'd have to pry her away from his side with a crowbar. Whether he wanted her or not, she was his forever.

"Put your hands over your heads!" Lionel shouted, pointing his rifle alternately at Mitch and Karl. "This gun's loaded, and I wouldn't hesitate to shoot you."

"I can testify to that," Jake said. "Come on over here, Rachel."

She didn't have to be asked twice. Running to him, she accepted the protection of being tucked firmly against his side while he kept his attention on Mitch and Karl. "Thank you," she murmured.

"Don't mention it." He held her so tight, she wondered if he'd cut off the circulation in her arm. And he was trembling. He'd managed to intimidate the two werewolves who'd abducted her, but he was vibrating from the residual fear. For that matter, so was she.

Even so, his voice was steady as he spoke to her captors. "We'll leave with Rachel now. Want us to call a tow truck for you?"

"We'll handle that," Mitch said.

"Up to you." Jake took a deep breath. "You might want to reconsider your choice of friends."

"Trust me," Karl said. "I'm already doing that."

"Good. Come on, Rachel. We're done here."

Lionel kept his rifle at the ready. "You two get in the truck. I'll keep these idiots covered until you beep the horn."

"Thanks, Lionel." Jake gave Rachel a squeeze. "Let's go home."

"Do you mean that?"

He hustled her toward the truck. "I do. In every sense of the word. I'm never leaving you again."

Her heart soared. Maybe getting kidnapped wasn't such a bad thing if it could convince the love of her life that he belonged by her side.

Once they were all in the cab, with Rachel wedged between Lionel and Jake, Lionel was full of questions. "I never did ask why somebody would take Rachel in the first place. I mean, who were those guys? They seemed to know who you were, Jake."

Rachel decided she'd better take the lead on this one. "I got some info while I was in the SUV. They thought if they kidnapped me, eventually I'd cave and empty my bank account to buy my freedom."

Lionel considered that. "I suppose that makes sense, but how did you figure that out, Jake?"

"When I saw the note Rachel had supposedly written, I knew they'd decided to use me as part of the scheme. I'd planned to move back to Idaho to be with my extended family, and the kidnappers made it look like Rachel had gone with me, to throw everybody off until they were ready to make their demands."

"That's what I get for being a little bit too rich and famous," Rachel said. "I'm going to be much more vigilant from now on." She hoped the story would pass muster with Lionel, because he must never find out the truth. She didn't want him to be put under house arrest for the rest of his life.

"So are you going to Idaho, Mr. Hunter?"

"No, not anymore. I realized my life is here, with Rachel." He reached over and laced his fingers through hers.

She adored Lionel and was incredibly touched that he'd come along to help facilitate the rescue. But she had so much to say to Jake that couldn't be said. She'd have to wait until they were alone and hope she didn't explode from frustration in the meantime.

The rest of the trip home was filled with a recap of the exciting chase and the satisfying ending. Lionel had obviously had the time of his life and could hardly wait to share his hero status with his friends and family.

Rachel blessed that urge, because when they pulled into the parking space near her cabin, Lionel was fidgeting in his eagerness to leave.

"I'm really glad you're home safe, Miss M," he said as he stood with his gadgets piled in his arms. Jake held his rifle for him.

"Lionel, I can't ever thank you enough for coming to my rescue."

He beamed at her. "You had to know I would. Jake and I, we knew we'd get you back. It was a given."

"It was." Standing on tiptoe, she kissed Lionel on the cheek. "Now go party. You deserve it."

He blushed. "Thanks."

"Oh, and Lionel . . . do you happen to know any women who might be interested in Ted Haggerty?"

"Mr. Haggerty? He likes being single! He said so a bunch of times."

"Well, he's not quite as happy as he wants us to think."

Lionel nodded. "All right, then. I'll ask around. See you in the morning, okay?"

"You bet." Rachel gazed at him with fondness. "By the way, is your carving in the woodshop?"

"Oh, yeah. I left it there. We can talk about it tomorrow."

"I may pay it a visit before then."

"Aw, you don't have to do that, Miss M. You and Mr. Hunter probably need . . . well, you know."

Jake wrapped an arm around Rachel. "We can take time to look at your art, Lionel."

Rachel didn't think she could love Jake any more, but that comment made her full to the bursting point.

"Well, see you two later." Lionel dumped his gadgets in the passenger seat, took the rifle from Jake, and climbed into his truck. With a wave, he drove away.

Rachel sighed and leaned her head against Jake's shoulder. "Oh, my God."

"Yeah." He leaned down and kissed the top of her head. "Let's go see Lionel's carving. If we don't do it now, we'll forget."

Tears threatened to spill from her eyes. "Okay." No one else had understood the dreams she had for Lionel, but Jake did. After a short walk through the midday sun, they stood in the workshop, arms wrapped around each other as they gazed at the piece of wood that she'd given Lionel to carve.

She'd wondered if Lionel would choose to carve wolves because she did. But no. He'd wisely decided to take a different path. In his carving, a majestic eagle soared over a rugged mountain range. The rush of freedom he'd caught in the eagle's flight took her breath away.

"It's good," Jake said.

"It is." She tightened her hold on him. "Very good. He's going to make it as an artist."

Jake was quiet for a moment. "I'm glad I'll be here to see it happen."

She glanced up at him, so afraid that his choice would be painful for him, at least in the beginning. "Will you become a pariah because of me?"

His gaze was filled with love. "Even if I did, I wouldn't give a damn. But I won't. If there's one thing werewolves understand, it's the importance of finding a soul mate. I'll have to eat some crow when I admit that my soul mate turned out to be you, a human female, and WARM will take a big hit."

"I hate that. It was your baby."

"I know, but thanks to this humbling experience with you, I realize the concept was too limiting. I have to expand my thinking, and there will be those who criticize me for changing my mind, but . . . it's a small price to pay for being able to love you for the rest of my life."

"What about the Hunters?"

A shadow crossed his features. "I'll have to deal with them, no question. They've hooked up with some fringe group called the Consortium, and I'll have to report that to the Were Council."

"They don't want me to live in your world."

"No." His jaw tightened. "But they're renegades. I'll protect you with my life, and so will those who support our nonviolent heritage, which is most of us. Don't be afraid, Rachel. You'll be safe from the likes of them."

"But your life is more complicated because of me."

He laughed in that low, intimate way she loved. "Of course it is. I'll have hell to pay, and MacDowell will be insufferable. But you're worth it." Still holding her, he turned so that they were face-to-face. "I humbly ask you, Rachel Miller, if you will consent to be my mate."

She looked into those green eyes, knowing that they were the eyes of a creature she only partly understood. But she knew his heart, and it belonged to her. She didn't intend to give in quite that easily, however. After all, he had recently rejected her on the basis of her human genes. "It's a thought. I've always wanted a wolf of my own."

"You're going to make me beg, aren't you?"

"Yes." She smiled up at him. "You spurned me before, so now you'll have to work to win me over."

"Rescuing you from the kidnappers wasn't enough?"

She laughed. "It was a start."

"My God, you're issuing a challenge!"

"Are you up to it?"

He gave her a slow, easy smile filled with all the confidence of a sexy werewolf alpha. "Yes, my love, I am."

Everyone in Vegas who'd heard about tonight's poker game said Pierce Dalton was crazy. As he sat across the table from Benedict Cartwright in a staged venue that provided room for two hundred paid spectators, Pierce briefly questioned his own sanity. He'd lured Cartwright to this game by offering to bet the deed to the Silver Crescent Casino against the deed to Cartwright's neighboring bar, Howlin' at the Moon. The casino was worth twenty times more than the bar.

But a lopsided bet in a public game was the only way Pierce could have coaxed Cartwright to the table, and by God, he wanted that bar. Cartwright, whose blond good looks made him a favorite with the ladies, wouldn't sell at any price. But he'd agreed to wager the bar for a chance to win the Silver Crescent and a lot of glory. In fact, he hadn't been able to resist. Pierce had counted on that, and he was itching to settle an old score.

For the past ten years, the Daltons and the Cartwrights had been the Vegas equivalent of the Hatfields and the McCoys. Angus Dalton, Pierce's dad, was no longer alive to celebrate if Pierce won, and Harrison Cartwright, who had been such a thorn in Angus's side, was also six feet under. But the feud was still alive and well in the next generation. Pierce could see the gleam of battle in Benedict Cartwright's eyes.

It hadn't always been this way between the two families. Angus Dalton and Harrison Cartwright had once been friendly competitors who'd enjoyed weekly poker games. Their fortunes had grown and so had the stakes. They'd started betting real estate.

They'd regularly traded Vegas properties and neither had seemed to worry about it much. But then, on a night when the liquor had flowed freely, Cartwright had taken a dare and bet his premier holding, the Silver Crescent. He'd lost.

Harrison Cartwright had loved that casino more than any of his establishments except for the bar next door, Howlin' at the Moon. The bar had been Harrison's first successful business venture, and income from that had allowed him to finance construction of the Silver Crescent.

For the first time in their long history, Harrison had accused Angus of cheating. Enraged by the accusation, Angus had vowed never to play with his old rival again, which meant Harrison couldn't win back his beloved casino.

What followed had become Vegas legend. Harrison had tried every trick in the book to avoid turning over the deed. The legal battle had been long and costly on both sides. In the end, Angus had been awarded the casino and had asked the judge to throw in the bar, too, as compensation for his pain and suffering.

The judge had refused. Pierce thought his dad should have been given the bar, and having a Cartwright property next door to the Silver Crescent had infuriated Angus. He'd resented it until the day he died. Even though he wasn't here to share in the victory and probably wouldn't have approved of his son sitting down to play with a Cartwright, Pierce was determined to right this wrong as a tribute to his dad.

He would have been willing to play Harrison himself for the deed, but the feisty old guy had died suddenly of an aneurism a couple of weeks after Angus and had left his fortune to his twin boys. Vaughn, older by two minutes, had inherited the majority of the Harrison Enterprises properties. But the sentimental favorite, known to locals as simply "the Moon," had gone to Benedict.

Pierce hadn't discovered that inheritance factoid until a month ago, but once he had, he'd begun to set his trap. Benedict suffered from younger-brother syndrome. He was desperate to prove himself so that the Cartwrights, and specifically his brother, Vaughn, would take him seriously.

So Pierce had made him an offer he couldn't refuse. It was a risky move for Pierce. Benedict had a reputation as a natural-born gambler with great instincts. But Pierce figured he was no slouch at the game, either. His dad had taught him everything he knew.

He and Benedict had agreed to play three hands, and whoever had the most chips at the end of that time would be declared the winner. Two games in, Benedict was ahead and looking confident. As the dealer shuffled the cards in preparation for the last hand, Pierce's body hummed with tension, but he relaxed into his leather chair as if he hadn't a care in the world.

He even glanced toward the group of onlookers who supported him, which represented about half the crowd. He smiled at his little sister, Cynthia, recent magna cum laude from Yale, beautiful and far more brilliant than he'd ever be. She didn't smile back. She was mad at him.

If only she'd quit hanging out with Bryce Landry, a high-stakes gambler from 'Frisco, but there they were, arms around each other, looking cozy. Landry struck Pierce as a playboy with too much money and not enough responsibility. But Cynthia, who was scary smart when it came to academics and not so smart when it came to guys and planning her future, thought he was perfect.

Pierce returned his attention to the table as the dealer asked him to cut the cards. This was it. For all the marbles.

Well, not quite *all* the marbles. If he lost the casino, it wouldn't be a complete financial disaster for the Dalton Corporation. He could continue supporting his mother's lifestyle in Provence.

He'd also have enough spare cash to send Cynthia to the grad school of her choice, if only she would go. But no, she wanted to become a showgirl, of all things. She was furious with him for not hiring her and for warning his casino-owning friends not to hire her, either. Damn it, she was supposed to end up in a job where she wore tailored suits and carried a briefcase.

If this last hand went south and Cartwright won the Silver Crescent, Pierce wondered if Cartwright would hire Cynthia just to cause trouble. Probably not. She was a Dalton, which kept her from getting a job at the Cartwright casinos under Vaughn's control. It was about the only good thing about this feud.

But Pierce didn't plan to lose the Silver Crescent. His mother and sister might not have to make any immediate sacrifices if he did, but Pierce couldn't discount the ripple effect. His reputation as a mover and shaker on the Vegas scene would suffer, which might affect future deals.

Assuming he pulled off this hat trick, he'd still be called crazy, but there would be a measure of respect thrown in. People would admire his balls. If he lost, he'd be forever labeled as the crazy SOB who never should have bet a multimillion-dollar casino against a bar. People avoided doing business with anyone they considered stupid.

The room was so quiet that the sound of the cards dropping onto the felt seemed unnaturally loud. Heart thudding, Pierce scooped up his hand and glanced at it. Okay. He had a chance. Being careful to breathe normally, he slid two cards back to the dealer and accepted two replacements. When he looked at those, he kept his expression blank.

And the betting began. Pierce slow-played the hand, reeling Benedict in. Nothing in Pierce's behavior indicated that he had aces over kings. Even better, the cards in his hand denied Cartwright the possibility of a royal flush.

Finally Pierce shoved all his chips to the center of the table. "All in." Benedict Cartwright was going down. Pierce actually felt sorry for the guy.

Benedict's twin brother, Vaughn, wasn't part of the large crowd that had gathered for the match. Pierce had heard through the grapevine that Vaughn had tried to talk Benedict out of accepting this challenge, even though on paper it was a chance worth taking. But Howlin' at the Moon was a Cartwright legacy, and Benedict's rep would suffer greatly if he lost it, especially to a Dalton.

Only a slight twitch in Benedict's right eyelid betrayed his nervousness as he pushed his chips forward. "Call." He laid out three queens and two kings. Not bad. Not enough. Howlin' at the Moon now belonged to Pierce Dalton.

After a collective gasp from the crowd, the mood shifted. Some cheered and others cursed and called for a rematch. Smiling, Pierce shook his head. He had what he wanted.

In the midst of the chaotic scene, he heard something odd—a distinct and very canine snarl. Maybe someone had brought a service dog into the room, but he couldn't see an animal anywhere. Yeah, maybe he was going crazy, after all.

I'm in Paris.

Melanie Shaw stared at the facade of Nôtre-Dame as the deep-throated bells counted down the hour. Ten o'clock in the morning. Instead of mucking out stalls or riding the fence line at her daddy's ranch outside of Dallas, Texas, she was standing in front of frickin' Nôtre-Dame. Amazing.

Her plane had landed two hours ago, and she still couldn't believe she had both feet planted in Paris, France. Only one thing could have made this moment better—if her friends Val and Astrid could be here with her.

They'd become friends in college, and five years later, they were tighter than ever. A few months ago all the planets had been aligned for this trip. They'd found a killer plane fare and spontaneously booked it. Then Val had been unlucky enough to get caught in a mob scene when a fire had broken out during a concert. She'd suffered a broken arm and two broken ribs. Although those had healed, she avoided crowds and wouldn't be traveling anytime soon.

Melanie had adjusted to having Val stay home. Astrid was a great traveling companion and they'd still have fun, even without Val. Then, a couple of weeks ago, one of Astrid's clients developed a problem with a pregnant mare. With the mare's life on the line, Astrid had reluctantly canceled her trip, too.

Melanie had almost given up once her friends had bailed. The hotel they'd booked was way too expensive for her to handle alone, so she'd canceled that reservation. But she'd held on to her airline ticket because she couldn't bear to think of not going. An online search had yielded a cheaper hotel, although it was also far from the main attractions.

Her boyfriend, Jeff, had said she was crazy to consider traveling alone, but he wasn't about to go with her to someplace where he didn't speak the language. His provincial attitude had pounded the nail in the coffin, and she'd ended their relationship. It had been on the skids, anyway.

Now that she was actually here, though, she'd better get busy and take some pictures with her phone. She'd left her suitcase with the hotel desk clerk because she couldn't check in until noon, but she had her backpack with all her sightseeing essentials crammed inside. Shrugging it off, she unzipped a side pocket and reached for her phone.

Without warning, the backpack was ripped from her hands. At the same moment, someone else shoved her from behind, knocking her to the ground with such force that the breath left her lungs.

"Hey!" A deep male voice from behind her issued a challenge.

She raised her head in time to glimpse a dark-haired man in jeans and a brown leather jacket dash after the thieves. Then folks who were obviously worried about her hurried over and blocked her view. An older gentleman helped her to her feet while two women clucked over her in what sounded like German.

She wasn't hurt except for a couple of scrapes on the heels of both hands, but if the guy in the leather jacket didn't catch the thieves, she was in deep shit. Her backpack held almost everything she had with her of value — her phone, both credit cards, and two hundred dollars' worth of euros. Her passport, thank God, was tucked in a pouch under her shirt, but thinking that she might have lost everything else made her sick to her stomach.

Members of the German tour group patted her shoulder as she stood up and dusted off her clothes. They offered words of comfort she couldn't understand but appreciated anyway. She made the effort to smile her thanks as she scanned the crowd for signs of a tall, broadshouldered man wearing a brown leather jacket. He'd looked athletic, so maybe he'd be able to tackle the guys who had taken her backpack.

On the other hand, she didn't want some stranger risking his safety for her. At least two people had been involved in the mugging, which meant the guy was outnumbered even if he should catch them. She crossed the fingers of both hands and waited, heart pounding from a delayed adrenaline rush.

At last she saw him coming toward her. His eyes were hidden by sunglasses, but his angry strides and the tight set of his mouth told her all she needed to know. Her hopes crumbled. The backpack was gone.

Despair engulfed her, but she was determined to thank him properly for trying. She hoped he spoke English. All she'd heard was his shout of *Hey*, which might be one of those universal expressions used by everyone. She hadn't traveled enough to know if it was or not.

When he was about ten feet away, he shook his head. "I'm sorry, ma'am. They got clean away from me."

She gasped at the familiar accent. "Oh, my God! You're from *Texas.*" Hearing a voice from home made her want to hug him. She restrained herself, but the world brightened considerably.

"Yes, ma'am." He drew closer. "Are you all right?" He took off his sunglasses and gazed at her with eyes the color of bluebonnets.

"I'm fine." He must have known taking off his sunglasses would help. Seeing the concern in his gaze, she didn't feel quite so alone. "Thank you for chasing them. That was brave of you."

He shrugged. "Not really. Anyone could see they were yellow-bellied cowards if they'd attack a woman. Speaking of that, they knocked you down. Are you sure you didn't get scraped up?"

"Just a little." She showed him her hands.

"Let's take a look." Tucking his sunglasses inside his jacket, he grasped her wrists and examined the heels of her hands. "Damn it. You should put something on that."

His touch felt nice. His big hands were gentle, and she found that sexy. Although it would be totally inappropriate, she wished he'd kiss her scrapes and make them all better. "I have Neosporin in my suitcase back at the hotel." At least she'd have a place to stay. She'd given them her credit card number. That card was gone, but she hoped to get a replacement before she checked out.

"Are you traveling with someone? I can call them." He reached inside his jacket and pulled out a phone.

She shook her head. "I came by myself."

"Then let's start with the police. Did you get a look at those old boys?"

"Not really."

"Never mind. I did." He punched in a number and spoke in French.

Melanie listened with great admiration. He no longer sounded like a Texan as he carried on a conversation without stumbling. Prior to this trip she'd enrolled in an online course and had learned enough to find a bathroom and order a meal. But this guy was fluent, which was her good luck.

If she was super-lucky, he had an international plan and she'd be able to borrow his phone to call Val, who could help her straighten things out with the credit card companies. Maybe it was cheeky to ask, but she was in desperate circumstances.

Although he was dressed casually, his jacket looked expensive and his watch might even be a real Rolex. Judging from his ease with the language, he could be a businessman who traveled to Paris regularly. If so, he wouldn't mind loaning her his phone for two minutes.

He disconnected the call and tucked the phone inside his jacket. "They're sending someone over, so we need to stay put." He gestured toward a stone bench a few feet away. "Let's sit a spell." He was once again her guy from Texas.

"Sounds good." She wouldn't mind sitting down. She felt a little shaky. "I'm afraid I've ruined your plans for this morning."

"No, ma'am, you certainly haven't." He waited until she sat down before joining her on the bench. "You're the one with ruined plans. When did you get here?"

"This morning."

He swore softly under his breath. "I figured that might be the situation when I saw you eyeballing Nôtre-Dame as if you'd never seen it before."

"I hadn't, except in pictures." Then she realized the

significance of his statement. He'd noticed her before the mugging. "Did I stick out that much?"

He smiled. "Let's just say I pegged you as an American."

"How?" She liked the way he'd managed to smile without appearing to patronize her. And he had a great smile, one that made the corners of his eyes crinkle just enough to add character. As the shock of being mugged wore off, she registered the fact that her rescuer was drop-dead gorgeous.

"White gym shoes, for one thing. Frenchwomen don't usually wear gym shoes unless they're working up a sweat. But the whole getup—the jeans, the hoodie, the backpack—told me you were from the States, probably a new arrival."

She grimaced. "I'll bet the muggers figured that out, too."

"They might have." He held out his hand. "I'm Drew Eldridge, by the way."

Eldridge. She'd heard that name, and she thought it might have been from Astrid, whose family was rich. Did that mean her Texan was wearing a real Rolex? His handshake was warm, firm, and gave her goose bumps. She was really sorry when the handshake was over. "I'm Melanie Shaw."

"Pleased to meet you, Miss Melanie. I wish it had been under different circumstances."

"Me, too." If he was related to the Eldridge family Astrid knew, Melanie wouldn't have been likely to meet him under any circumstances, unless she was with Astrid, who moved in those circles. "Are you from Dallas?"

"Yes, ma'am."

"Then you might know a friend of mine, Astrid Lindberg."

"Astrid Lindberg." He chuckled. "I haven't seen her in a coon's age. We were at the same equestrian camp one summer, although she was with the younger kids. Some old horse tried to run off with her and I was handy. I was worried she'd swear off riding, but she didn't."

"She sure didn't." Melanie noticed that although Drew had come to Astrid's rescue, he'd downplayed his role by saying he was *handy*. "She's a large-animal vet now."

"Is she? That's great."

"So, are you here on business?" Melanie imagined multinational deals involving millions. From what she could recall, the Eldridge family was loaded.

"Some business. Some pleasure."

"Ah." So the multinational deal making was followed by glittering parties and sophisticated Frenchwomen who never wore gym shoes with their regular clothes. Yet he'd interrupted all that to help a stranger from home. "Listen, I really appreciate all you've done. I'm sure I've screwed up your morning and you're too polite to say so."

"Nope. It's a sunny day and I'd decided to—" A soft chime interrupted whatever he'd been about to say. "Excuse me." Taking out his phone, he glanced at the readout. "I should take this." He stood and walked a few feet away.

Hanging out with such a good-looking guy was a heady experience that kept her adrenaline pumping, so she was relieved for a few moments alone to gather her thoughts. If not for her friendship with Astrid, she might have been intimidated by someone like Drew Eldridge. As it was, she was simply grateful. And a little turned-on, which served as a great antidote to worrying about losing her stuff.

Having Drew show up was a stroke of luck. Someone

with his wealth would have an international-calling plan. If she didn't pay him back until she got home, he probably wouldn't care. Once he was off the phone, she would ask to make a call. Val had a key to her apartment and could retrieve her credit card information.

The police arrived right after Drew ended his call, so she didn't have a chance to borrow the phone. Thank God, Drew was there to guide her through the process, though. After the officers left, she glanced up at him. "Do you think they'll recover my backpack?"

"There's always a chance."

"But not a very good one, right?"

"I won't lie to you, Melanie. They may find your backpack, although I figure it's in a Dumpster by now. But the contents . . ." He shrugged. "Not likely."

"Speaking of those contents, could I please borrow your phone to call my friend Valerie back home? She can access my credit card info so I can cancel my cards."

"Yes, ma'am, you sure can. Tell you what. I'll give you a lift back to your hotel so you can doctor those hands. You can call your friend on the way there."

"You have a car?"

"I do."

Silly of her to think he'd be on foot, like she was. "You know, that's a lovely offer but my hotel isn't very far away." That wasn't quite true. She'd walked at least ten blocks to get here. "I'll just borrow your phone for a minute. I've taken up too much of your valuable time already."

"Sorry, but my mama raised me better than that. You've suffered a shock, and I intend to see you safely back to your hotel."

Oh, wow. He not only looked like a god—he knew the

right things to say that would make a girl melt into a puddle. She'd be a fool to resist a display of gentlemanly manners by a heroic figure like Drew, especially when she'd just been mugged by two guys from the shallow end of the gene pool.

"I can't lose her." Fletcher Grayson crouched beside the
bay mare and stroked her sweat-dampened neck as she
lay on her side in the foaling stall, her breath labored.

"We're not going to lose her." Astrid Lindberg was
determined that both mare and foal would survive this
night. Fletch had called her emergency line at ten p.m. It
was a testimony to her lack of a social life that she'd been
home on a Saturday night.

She'd rushed out to the Rocking G, driving through a
summer downpour. It was what locals called a trash
mover of a rain, falling in endless sheets of water. Four
hours later, the rain continued to pound the roof of the
barn, and Janis still hadn't foaled.

Astrid had monitored the pregnant mare for weeks,
ever since the first signs of edema. Because of the swell-
ing, Janis's abdomen was far more distended than it would
be in a normal pregnancy. The condition was worrisome,
and recently Fletch had kept her confined to the barn
and a small paddock to restrict her movements.

Some vets might have performed a C-section by now.
Astrid preferred to see if Janis could deliver naturally,

which would mean a better start for both mother and baby. Luckily Fletch agreed with her.

Fletch tended to agree with her on most things, which made her job as his vet much easier. It also made her life as a woman frustrating as hell. From her first glimpse of the broad-shouldered rancher, she'd been in trouble. Fletch Grayson was hot. And single. And a client. He was definitely off-limits.

"I think she wants to get up." Fletch stood and backed away. Concern shone in his brown eyes. "I wish she'd just have that foal and be done with it."

"Me, too." Astrid rose and edged back as Janis lumbered to her feet. "Let's move out of the stall and give her room to pace if she needs to."

"Sure." He followed her out and they leaned side by side against the front of the stall so they could observe the mare as she walked the perimeter of her enclosure.

Standing close together in this cozy barn and watching Janis as the rain came down outside was the most natural thing in the world for them to be doing. Yet stormy nights always made Astrid long to be held, and it drove her crazy to be within touching distance of the yummy Mr. Grayson. She imagined the feel of all those muscles under his blue denim shirt and barely controlled a shiver.

He'd named his ranch the Rocking G because he had a fondness for classic rock and roll. This horse honored Janis Joplin, and the stable was filled with namesakes of other famous rockers. In Astrid's opinion, Fletch was the one who rocked.

He'd hung his Stetson on a peg outside the stall. When he was nervous, he had a habit of running his fingers through his chocolate brown hair, which only made that wavy hair sexier. No one should look this good at two in the morning. Or smell this good. Fletch's woodsy after-shave was one of the many things about him that made her pulse race.

He possessed a killer combo of square-jawed masculinity and a heart of gold. The same passionate love of animals that had propelled her into the field of veterinary medicine had caused him to sink all his savings into a horse-breeding operation. Although he was finally turning a profit, he did so only by carefully managing his budget.

They'd become so comfortable with each other during the six months she'd tended his horses that he'd shared major decisions, such as when he'd postponed the purchase of a new truck so he could install more efficient heating in the horse barn. She treasured those long conversations, even though they stirred up inappropriate thoughts. Would he be even better at pillow talk?

But she also treasured her professional standing in the Dallas area, so she wouldn't be sharing a pillow with gorgeous Fletch Grayson. It was hard enough for a girl to be taken seriously as a vet in Texas, even harder for someone like Astrid, the daughter of a rich family. Besides, she didn't know if he would welcome that idea. Sometimes she imagined him looking at her with interest, but that might be wishful thinking on her part.

"One thing's for sure," he said. "I won't breed her again. She deserves a rest."

"Yes, she does." Although he didn't know it, Astrid could offer to invest in his ranch and eliminate most of his money problems. She constantly battled the urge to do exactly that. But giving him money would change their relationship forever, and she selfishly wanted to keep that relationship as it was, even if friendship was all she'd ever have.

Read on for a look at the third novel
in the Perfect Man series by Vicki Lewis Thompson,

Safe in His Arms

Available now from InterMix in e-book.

One minute Valerie Wolitzky was drinking margaritas
with her two pals, Astrid Lindberg and Melanie Shaw, in
their favorite Dallas watering hole, the Golden Spurs
and Stetson. The next minute an alarm shrieked, and Val
leaped from her seat, knocking over her chair and her
drink. She had to get out. *Now.*

Panic buzzed in her ears as she charged the front
door. She had to beat the mob of people. If she didn't,
she'd be trapped . . . just like before.

Wham! She hit a solid wall of muscle and staggered
back. A cowboy blocked her way. She shoved him hard.
"Let me out!"

He grabbed her shoulders. "Hold on there, ma'am.
What's the problem?"

Was he an idiot? With adrenaline-fueled strength, she
pushed him aside and barreled through the door, almost
knocking down a second man right behind him. But she
got out the door.

Safe! She was safe! Shaking, she leaned over and
braced her hands on her knees as she gulped for air. The
warm breeze of a summer night touched her wet cheeks.

She swiped at them as she slowly straightened. She needed to sit down, but there was nowhere to—

"Val!" Astrid's shout penetrated the buzzing in her ears, and she turned. Her two friends burst through the door of the bar and rushed toward her.

Relief that they were okay was followed by hot shame. She hadn't thought of them, hadn't even tried to save them. She'd only thought of herself.

"Omigod, Val." Melanie, brown hair flying, reached her first and hugged her. "It's okay. Some smoking oil set off the smoke detector in the kitchen. It's okay. It's okay."

Filled with gratitude for her friend's safety, Val hugged her back without paying much attention to what she was saying.

Astrid joined the huddle and rubbed Val's back. "Easy, girlfriend. Take it easy. Everything's fine."

Gradually Valerie's heartbeat slowed, and the grip of fear eased. She took a quivering breath and wondered why she wasn't hearing sirens. She stepped out of Melanie's embrace and looked around. "Where are the fire trucks?"

"There's no fire." Astrid continued to stroke her back. "Just a little smoke."

"Did they evacuate the building?"

"No, sweetie." Melanie gazed at her with compassion. "They shut off the alarm right away and came out of the kitchen to explain the problem."

Valerie's heart started pounding again. *Dear God.* "I was . . . the only one who ran out?"

Both Melanie and Astrid nodded.

"Well, except us," Melanie added. "We took off after you."

"Oh, no." Val covered her face as embarrassment

flooded through her, scorching her cheeks. She'd over-reacted. Caused a scene. Involved her friends in her craziness. Slowly she lowered her hands and stared at them in misery. "I'm so sorry," she whispered.

"Don't worry about it." Astrid squeezed her arm. "But, Val, it's time to get serious about—"

"Ma'am? Are you all right?" The cowboy Valerie had smacked into when she fled now walked over to her, trailed by the other guy, who wore a business suit. They both looked worried.

Val thought of the old cliché and wished the sidewalk really would open up and swallow her. "Yes, thank you." She wished the words didn't sound so wobbly and uncertain.

"You don't look all right." The cowboy kept coming. He had a purposeful John Wayne stride, and he towered over the other man. "You're shaking like a newborn foal. What happened in there?"

Melanie put a protective arm around Val's shoulder. "Thanks for your concern, but she'll be fine."

He paused and tipped his Stetson back with his thumb. "I'm sure she will. I just . . . Was it the smoke alarm that spooked you? I heard it go off right before I got to the door."

He seemed like a nice guy who only wanted to help. Val couldn't fault him for that after she'd tried to knock him down in her full-out panic mode. He must have seen the terror in her eyes. "I'm afraid I overreacted." She cleared her throat and summoned her lawyer's voice. "I apologize for plowing into you and yelling. That was rude."

"No worries." He glanced at Astrid and Melanie standing on either side of her. "I'm glad your friends are here." He hesitated before bringing his attention back to Val.

His eyes were gray. Not a gloomy, dark sort of gray, but light, almost silver. They shone with kindness. "Listen, I don't know you at all, and I'm probably butting in where I have no business, but I understand a little something about post-traumatic stress." He turned to the man who'd come up behind him. "And my buddy Will wrote the book on it. Literally." He looked at Val again. "If you need—"

"To see someone?" Val managed not to choke on the words. "I appreciate the thought, but I have that covered." She had nothing covered because she was determined to handle the issue herself, despite what her friends thought she should do. But he didn't have to know any of that.

Also available from

Vicki Lewis Thompson

Werewolf in Denver
A Wild About You Novel

When blogger Kate Stillman takes on political bad boy
Duncan MacDowell in a public debate on werewolf
segregation, she is confident she can handle the challenge.
But she soon finds herself attracted to the sexy Scottish
founder of WOOF (Werewolves Optimizing Our
Future)—who happens to prefer dating human women.
Yet what hope do they have when their future together
depends on Kate losing her argument?

**"Devour…Vicki Lewis Thompson's books
immediately." —Fresh Fiction**

vickilewisthompson.com

Available wherever books are sold or at
penguin.com

facebook.com/ProjectParanormalBooks

S0480

Also available from

Vicki Lewis Thompson

Werewolf in Seattle
A Wild About You Novel

The last thing Colin MacDowell wants is to inherit his Aunt Geraldine's mansion in the San Juan islands off the coast of Washington. As the pack leader of the Trevelyans in Scotland, he has little time to travel halfway around the world to take care of his inheritance.

But the trip takes a pleasant turn when he meets Luna Reynaud, the young secretary his aunt hired shortly before she died. He isn't sure which surprises him more—Luna's clever plan for turning the mansion into a resort or the fact that she's drop-dead gorgeous. Both intrigue him—until he learns that Luna is only a half-breed. There's no way a pack leader can mate with a woman who's partly human…or is there?

"Another keeper. This is not just another werewolf romance."
—The Romance Dish

Available wherever books are sold or at
penguin.com

facebook.com/ProjectParanormalBooks

Also available from

Vicki Lewis Thompson

Werewolf in the North Woods
A Wild About You Novel

When Abby Maddox's grandfather swears he saw Bigfoot in the woods behind his Portland, Oregon, home, his neighbors decide to bring in a prominent anthropologist to prove him wrong. Rather than see her grandpa made a laughing stock, Abby sets out to send the professor packing...until she sees how hot he is.

Roark Wallace can't risk having tourists comb the woods for Bigfoot—not with a local pack of werewolves to protect. When Roark meets Abby, sparks fly—but can he pursue this fiery red-head without compromising his pack?

**"I love Ms. Thompson's unique spin on
the werewolf myth."
—The Romance Dish**

Available wherever books are sold or at
penguin.com

facebook.com/ProjectParanormalBooks

Also available from

Vicki Lewis Thompson

**TWO ORIGINAL NOVELLAS AVAILABLE
ONLY AS DOWNLOADABLE PENGUIN SPECIALS**

One Night With a Billionaire
The Perfect Man

Melanie, Astrid, and Valerie may be best friends, but
they have very different ideas of what kind of man is
more fun—one with a pocket full of cash or a guy with
spurs on his boots?

Tempted By a Cowboy
The Perfect Man

The sisters of Gamma Delta Rho just can't agree
whether the perfect man is rich or rugged. But can a
cowboy ever prove he's worth his weight in gold?

Available wherever books are sold or at
penguin.com

facebook.com/LoveAlwaysBooks